THE LOST AND THE BLIND

CURTIS SMITH

RUNNING
Wild
PRESS

The Lost and the Blind
text copyright © remains with author
Edited by Peter Wright

Paperback ISBN: 978-1-955062-61-9
eBook ISBN: 978-1-955062-62-6

Suppose one of you has a hundred sheep and loses one of them. Doesn't he leave the ninety-nine in the open country and go after the lost sheep until he finds it? And when he finds it, he joyfully puts it on his shoulders and goes home. Then he calls his friends and neighbors together and says, "Rejoice with me; I have found my lost sheep."

— LUKE 15.4-6

For Michele and Evan, again

* * *

B y the end of summer—this summer of the farmhouse and Amy and her baby—my mother no longer makes a secret of shooting up. She's never been discrete—I've long known the truth behind closed doors—but since coming here, she's brought her needle and works into the open. That may sound dire, but this is not the case. Indeed, these past few months with Amy are as close as my childhood has gotten to idyllic. I have a bed—not a sofa or a spot on the floor—and a room all my own and a door to shut. There are chickens, a grass-nibbling goat. The farmhouse we share an island, and around us, an ocean of green alfalfa that distances us from the man who threatened to kill my mother and, as an afterthought, me.

I stand eating a turkey leg in the kitchen doorway. My mother and Amy brush past, each carrying what calls them and trailing the scents of cigarettes and rain. They settle onto the couch. They wear their catering outfits, their most recent stopgap gig, black slacks and vests; white, ruffled shirts. "Our penguin suits," my mother joked, but at the moment, no one's laughing. My mother with her spoon and shot glass and candle. "Jesus," she spits. A curse for her tremors, for Amy's bawling baby. A curse for the exit she can't make fast enough. Amy cradles little Grace, and her free hand fumbles with her blouse and bra. I should look away, but I don't. Grace latches on, and the room fills with a soft static. The baby's suckle. The rain in the fields and the sizzle of cooking junk. The man who threatened to kill us died last weekend. This fact brings me peace but not joy, and the knowing his fix could have just as easily ended up in my mother's arm makes him feel both alive and near.

We arrived at Amy's the day after Christmas and one step ahead of our own bad luck. The sun bright, and the snow's pained glare. The car crammed with the things we'd shoved into garbage bags, what we couldn't fit left behind. Halfway down the farmhouse lane, our car got stuck, so we trudged ahead, the drifts up to our knees. Our thighs. My garbage bag ripped, and I struggled but was never quite able to corral the spill. My mother forged on, stumbling, righting herself, never looking back. The sun glinted on the snub-nosed .38 she'd stolen from the man we were escaping. I had no gloves, and my mother had no coat. The distance between us grew. We neared the farmhouse, but it still looked small, swallowed by white and blue and a sun that offered no warmth. A woman stepped onto the porch, and my mother announced our arrival by lifting the .38 to the cloudless sky and squeezing off a round.

My mother eases back the plunger. The needle in soaked cotton. A flicker in the candle's shine, and with it, a glimpse of how pretty she'd once been. I've cleaned her vomit. I've endured her moans as she fucked strange men. I've distracted clerks as she shoplifted our supper. I saw her stab a junkie who'd flicked a cigarette into my face, a steak knife driven deep in the meat of his thigh, his jeans soaked with blood. When she isn't jonesing or adrift, when she's rooted in the moment and puts her arm around me and calls me her "little man," I feel like there's still a chance we can make peace with our lot.

But those moments never last. I wasn't destined for the world of little league practices and doctors' appointments and getting to school on time. My mother too raw, too obsessed with pushing back the flood we both know will one day consume her. So we tread water, struggling, cursing one another, saving one another. Every slight an arrow and every wound met with curses or fists or tears. She often tells me she loves me. She's never said she'd die for me, but I know she would. She hates herself, I'm convinced of this, and I've spent much of my seventeen years trying to ease her heart—jokes, ambushes of kindness—hoping my love might atone for the mother who drank herself to death. The father who broke her jaw. The high school she either dropped out of or was expelled from, her story depending on her mood. Only the needle lifts her from the tide. Each dose a rapture and rescue. Her first waking and last drifting thoughts a calculation of when she'll fix again. Her greatest desire to shut out the voices of the present and past and have a final say-so in a life where she's had none. But this erasing of the world is a sloppy affair, and in the process, she's erased jobs and bank accounts and a man or two who could have been good to us. And when her eyes roll back and the needle slips from her fingers, I understand she's erasing me too.

She knots her tubing. She slaps her arm, and her veins rise, and on them, the scars she hides beneath long sleeves. I no longer flinch when the needle pierces her skin. Her thumb slow on the plunger. She claws at the tubing. A drop of blood on her palm, another on her penguin pants. She sinks into the couch. A weak cough. The junk in her throat, and her hand rises to her neck before flopping onto her lap.

Amy eases her daughter from her chest. "Give me a hand, sweetie."

I take the baby, and again, I consider her breast, its roundness, the wet nipple. She buttons her blouse and smiles. At the base of her throat, a simple silver cross. Amy is ten years younger than my mother. She doesn't know the power ballads my mother sings along with. She lacks the motives and hard stances of my mother's other friends. In her own way, Amy's remained childlike. The ease with which she slips into wonderment. The God she prays to. She loves her parents, even though they're on the outs. She's never spent a night in jail. I can't picture her plunging a knife into a man's leg.

"Did you eat?" I ask.

"At work, yeah." She turns on the end table's lamp. Its turtle-shell shade of stained glass. An antique, she claims, its soft light upon her as she rolls up her sleeve and lassoes her belt around her arm. She mixes powder and water and holds her spoon over the candle's flame. "We might not have a lot, but we eat like rich folks, don't we?"

I think of all the nights I've gone hungry. "Sometimes."

"Just a little taste for me." The cotton soaks up the spoon's liquid. She raises the syringe and taps its side. I walk away. The baby's asleep, but even so, I don't think it's right for her to be in the room while her mother's fixing. "Mark?"

I turn back. Amy's teeth bite the belt. The strain in her neck. "Thanks."

I take the baby to the back porch. The kitchen light spills onto the boards. The rain soft on the overhang, and in the fields, the rhythm of a million drops. A late summer rain that brings no relief, only the promise of a hazy sunrise. I hold the baby close, her head over my shoulder, and pat her back. I listen to the workings of her lungs and to the rain and crickets, and I'm buoyed by the life all around me. Then, in a breath, the sadness of knowing my mother and I won't stay. Our existence operates under a different system of physics. Our reckless velocity. The gravity of poor decisions. Still, on a night like this, when I hold a sleeping baby and feel safe, I can imagine this place as home. Or as much a home as any I've known.

Inside, I lay Grace in her living room playpen and pull up her blanket. Amy blinks as I lift the needle from her fingers. I grind out my mother's cigarette but leave the candle burning. I hold a hand near my mother's nose. I fear her death. Fear losing what little history I own. Fear I'll fade without a set of eyes that understands my heart without me having to speak it. My mother blinks, and in this room of stalled time and flickering light, I wonder if I'm her dream or if, through her haze, she knows I'm near.

I set to work in the kitchen. The leftover containers like little presents, and I open the lids to find green beans. Twice-cooked potatoes. Prime rib. Remnants from the night's serving line. All of it cold but good, and I take a few bites from each before stacking the containers in the fridge. I wash the dishes and wipe the countertop. Sweep the floor. Put away the silver-ware, the drawer's slide weighted by the .38 that heralded our arrival. Last month, my mother taught me how to shoot. A hot day. Beer bottles lined before a hay bale, glittering explosions. The gun heavier than I'd expected, its kick in my bones. She grinned, her mouth twisted around her cigarette. "Not bad, champ." She asked if I'd be afraid to use it if the man we'd escaped came trundling down our lane. I told her no because that's what she wanted to hear, but we both knew it was a lie.

The baby's first cry a simmer. A sluggish awareness. I lean over the playpen and smell the diaper. Grace isn't family, but I treat her as such. When her mother is absent in body or mind, I plant myself close. I read to her. I rub her feet. I hold toys for her to grab. I let her pull my hair. I want to be her witness.

Want to record her coos and whimpers before they fade into the farm's green sea.

I pick her up. The diaper's weight shifts. I retrieve a box of wipes from the bag by Amy's feet. I lay Grace on the carpet and unbutton her onesie. I hum a song my kindergarten teacher used to sing, the words lost, something about birds and pies. Grace stops crying. Her eyes, watery in the candlelight, fix on me.

The shit is soft and brown, and I clasp her ankles, lifting gently, wiping as much as I can with the diaper. I turn Amy's bag upside down. The carpet littered with ointment bottles and receipts. Bobby pins. A broken pencil. A parking ticket. A teething ring Grace clutches and sticks between her lips.

There are no diapers in the kitchen. No diapers in Amy's car. I kick through the clothing tangles surrounding the bed my mother and Amy share. In the living room, a naked Grace crawls toward a coffee table littered with powders and needles. I scoop her up, blow out the candle, and scour for something diaper-like. The paper towels too coarse. The dishtowel smells clean, but I worry about germs. I go to my room and sift through my clothes, picking a T-shirt my mother bought for a quarter at Goodwill. Faded letters across its front—*Superstar!* I lay Grace on my bed, folding and refolding and cooing baby talk, the job not finished until I secure the shirt's loose ends with duct tape.

"What're you doing?"

Amy leans in the doorway. The hall light behind her. Flyaway strands lift from her bun. I pick up Grace. "We're out of diapers."

"Shit." An utterance I infer as part of a larger story. "Shit." The syllable dragged out, her tongue thick, a note that slurs from agitated to teary. She shuffles off, and I follow. She holds a steadying hand on the wall, the doorway, the house listing beneath her. I picture her collapsing beside my mother and crying her way back into her stupor. Instead, she grabs her purse. Her car keys jangle as she reaches out, and I immediately regret handing her the baby. Again, I follow her. Her thigh strikes the kitchen table, and her keys clatter to the floor. The baby flinches. I pick up the keys before she can. "You can't go like this."

"Meant to get them after work." She reaches for the keys, but this time I'm not letting go. Her hand rests on mine. "Was in a rush. I wanted to get home. Wanted to . . . I'm so fucking stupid."

"It'll be OK." I consider giving her a hug, but I fear my clumsiness. And I fear if I held her, she'd melt. Her quivering lip. Her body's drugged sway. "We'll get them in the morn—"

"No!" Her nails dig into my hand. The baby cries. Amy's hand drops, and she staggers, the grasped countertop saving her and Grace from collapsing into my arms. "No," she whispers, righting herself. I'm used to her tears. She cries when she fights with my mother. She cries watching TV movies. She cries some nights after her temp shifts at the nursing home. People are always dying there, and if I listen closely, I can tell which tears come from relief and which are from sadness.

She holds the baby close. Their wet cheeks glide against each other, Amy whispering she's sorry, so goddamn sorry, and me unsure if she's talking to her girl or herself. I rub the spot where her hand held mine. The house quiet and a decision to be made. My fear she'll drive away after I've gone to bed. My fear for Grace and for all of us if the cops bring her home. I listen to the rain, to the shallow breathing of drugged hearts and the thump of my own. I don't want to fight. I just want to end the night with all of us beneath this roof, safe and taken care of. "I'll drive," I say.

Desperate times call for desperate measures. My mother

said that before she took a hammer to a coworker's windshield. She said it as she knotted a bed sheet for our climb from a second-story window the night our apartment burned to the ground, and as I ease down the rutted lane, I understand the saying—and my mother—in a new way. Amy, my mother, me— we're perpetually desperate, our normal always a stumble away from calamity. A blown transmission, a broken arm—these could set us back months. Our hopes built on shifting foundations. Our beams brittle. Our pockets stuffed with kindling and the world aglow in sparks.

Reason tells me to turn around, but reason is a luxury for those with options. The darkness, this narrow road. The turns coiled just beyond the headlights' reach. With me, a sleeping child in a duct-taped diaper and a nodding woman who's already asked twice where we're going. I'm tentative with the gas and heavy on the brake, but in time, the rhythms find me. Amy and the baby quiet, a dreamer's lull. The wipers' rockabye.

Amy's hand fumbles across the dash until she turns on the radio. A news report. Last week's bombing of the American embassy in Caracas, this week's influx of US troops. Rocket attacks at airports and military outposts. Amy pushes another button. "That's good." She closes her eyes and hums along. "Like this song. This was big when I was a kid." She opens her mouth but doesn't say anything else. The music masks the rain. We pass a barn set back from the road. A light burns inside, a shadow-man in the open door. "You don't do that, do you?" Amy asks.

I say nothing. "Drive your mom crazy," she says. She smiles and rubs my neck. "I did." Her hand falls onto my shoulder. A squeeze, and when she pulls away, her finger snags my T-shirt's collar. She wriggles free. "You'll break hearts." She pats my arm. "But not hers. That's why you're a good one."

"Amy?"

We crest a slope, the low plateau the farmlands rest upon. Town's lights come into view. I turn down the radio. She continues to hum, but it doesn't sound like the song that's playing. I wait until the song ends. "Amy?"

"Hmm?"

"Where're we going?" We stop at an intersection. Her car's rough idle, the muffler she'd sweet-talked a mechanic into ignoring at her last inspection. I use the turn signal even though there's no one around.

"Don't you know where the diaper store is?"

"No."

A streetlight's gray ebbs over her. She tussles my hair. "I'm fucking with you, baby. The Kmart. The fucking Kmart."

We pass the playground where I punched a boy for calling my mother a whore. The boy with a bloody nose, but I was the one who left in tears. We stop at a traffic light. The red shines on the windshield's streaks. A police cruiser rolls to a stop across the intersection. Just the two of us, the road empty. The light changes, and we pass each other in the deserted intersection. The cop glances our way, and I try not to acknowledge what scares me most.

I navigate side streets. The way dark but not my memories. The alleys I explored on my bike. The church my aunt whisked me to, the nave empty save the reverend and us, water dripped on my forehead and prayers for my soul and the promise to never tell my mother. We pass the apartments where I've lived —some for a whole school year, others for a week, a day, and I wonder why my mother has never left town. Wonder what hold this place has on her and wonder if it has the same hold on me. We reach the strip mall, and I park beneath a light, a distance staked from the other cars.

I turn off the engine and we sit. Rain falls. The outside

blurred, and the inside, populated by Amy, the baby, and me, comes into focus.

"I'll go," I say.

She climbs out and opens the back door. The dome light reveals a mess I hadn't noticed—wrappers and coffee cups, a crumpled cigarette pack. She fumbles with the seat's buckle and lifts Grace. The baby gasps, the agitation with being woke, with the rain on her face and her mother's clumsiness. Amy slips a nook between the girl's lips. "No one's going to let you use my credit card, hun."

We cross the lot. Rain dampens my hair, yet the drops carry little weight. Amy veers, and I put my arm around her shoulder, a righting, a steering into the light. She's shorter than me, thin, and folks who didn't know better might think she's in good shape. Steam rises from the macadam. Headlights pass over us, a moment's lifting from the dark. School will start in a few weeks, and I imagine running into a teacher shopping for supplies. My teachers had once been full of encouragement, the citing of potential, of decent test scores. Then each school year's inevitable slide, the unexcused absences, the sighs that met my returns, and I can't blame the ones who stopped reaching out. How could I explain living in a house with no clocks or clean clothes. How could I tell them I spent the days I did attend thinking not of my lessons but of home, of the urgency of return and the daily hesitation of opening the door, my mother's name called, and in me, the fear of what I'd find.

Glass doors slide apart, one pair then another. Cool inside, and I squint, this avalanche of light. The black beneath Amy's eyes on display, her tears and the rain. Music plays, and the melodies, faint and tinny, ripple around us. Grace in her circus-animal onesie, her bottom bulging and my T-shirt sticking out of the leg holes. We pass workers in red vests. An obese woman balanced atop a puttering scooter. A skeleton wheeling his oxygen tank, a tethering of plastic tubes. Mothers almost as dazed as Amy, sleepwalkers herding children sunburnt and wild, others dull eyed, their thumbs stuck in their mouths. I keep a hand on Amy's elbow. I expected stares but receive indifference, and this calms me. We pass aisles of baseball bats and fishing rods and radios. Microwaves and toasters and vacuums. All of it new and shiny and full of promise. I think of the perfect commerce in Amy's blood, a consumption that only leads to a greater desire. Amy and my mother aren't criminals—they're the poster children for naked capitalism—their drives as natural as envying those who have more and mistrusting those who have less. Amy wanders into the cosmetic aisle and retrieves a tube of lipstick. I take the baby, a gentle touch, and not wanting to start either of them crying, I'm even more gentle when I remind Amy why we've come.

"Right." She nods, bites her lip. "Right."

We turn two aisles down. Around us, shelves of children's toys. Stuffed animals and bright colors. Grace's fingers clutch, and I hand her a furry bear. "Shit," Amy mumbles. "Next aisle. Hold on."

She disappears. Grace rubs the bear against her lips. I don't follow Amy. I want to give Grace a chance to marvel over a blue-furred bear. I want to keep her here, to indulge her, if only for a moment. Folks love children because they're innocent, and what's more innocent than the not-knowing of the truth. The not-knowing there is darkness and it will someday break you and all those you love. I sniff her hair, and I'm sad in the understanding that she's destined to learn this sooner than most.

Voices from the next aisle—a man's, then Amy's. The words indistinct, the tone unmistakable. I picture a security guard, the lipstick Amy could have just as easily slid into her pocket as back onto the shelf. A call to the police. I hurry around the corner.

Her back to me. A bag of diapers under her right arm, her left hand gripping a shelf. The man shifts his focus from her to me. I know him, not personally, but his type. I know he scrapes by paycheck to paycheck. Know he'd think nothing of punching me in the eye. Know he probably came up little different than me. Know he's the kind of man waiting at the end of my shadow. He wears a sleeveless top, his arms brown and ropy. A black ponytail, weathered cheeks. Paint flecks on his hands and boots. He stares at me, Amy's accusations and pleadings ignored, and I straighten as I feel myself measured in his gaze.

Amy turns, and the man grabs her arm. "Fuck, Chief!" she snaps. Her sleeve bunched, each attempt to free herself met with a yank. Amy staggers, and I step between them. Whiskey on the man's breath. His eyes brown and bloodshot. His lips curled, a lifting of his goatee. A bully's yellow-toothed smile. I hold Grace close and grab his wrist. The blue bear falls. His hand bony and strong, and I imagine it wielding a wrench or balled into a fist. A blue-ink cross tattooed on his middle finger. He stops pulling and stares. "You're Jill's boy." A slight accent. His smile melts. "You're part of this whole fucked-up scene, aren't you? Your mom and Amy and fuck knows what else going on at that farm—"

"Fuck off, Chief." Amy breaks free, a stumble before she rights herself. I let go and cover the back of Grace's head. I follow Amy, picking up the diapers she's dropped and turning at the aisle's end. The man framed between shelves of wipes and blankets and ointments. He kicks the bear, and it slides, silently twisting, until it hits my feet.

In the parking lot, I strap Grace into the back. Amy's head rests against the rain-streaked window. I start the car, and the wiper's first pass reveals Chief, bag in hand, leaving the store.

"Is he the dad?"

She covers her eyes. "No. Christ." She sighs. "He says I owe him money."

I keep the lights off and pull from our space. Chief stands alongside a white pickup. He reaches into one pocket then another, his bag switching from hand to hand. I step on the gas, a hydroplaning of worn tires. I don't look back. The lights from the other stores blur in the puddles and across our windshield. "Do you?" I ask.

"Do I what?"

"Owe him money?"

"I owe him. He owes me." She slides a bobby pin from her bun and shakes out her hair. "We're all in this together. Him, me. Everyone."

We pass through town. Homes with flowerbeds and gardens, and in their driveways, cars no one's threatening to repossess. Houses I've been inside back in the days I was still invited to birthday parties. The porch lights left on until all the children come home. Homes free from Amy's tangle of owing and debt. I keep an eye out for the white pickup and police cruisers, but I see neither. We pass my school. The square's quarry-stone bank. The bar where my mother worked until her drawer came up short one time too many. The structures heavy and solid, yet they all slide past, their edges softened by motion and rain. There are stretches I find myself lost in the hush, abandoned by my histories, and while I dread being alone, I can't say this sensation is unpleasant. Town's lights fade, then the deeper night of fields and pastures. No headlights in the rearview, and in me, an unwinding. The baby asleep and the radio off. The tires' hum and Amy's soft tears. I don't know the right words, so I say nothing. My mother can erase me with a needle, and for a moment, I imagine returning the favor and driving west until the sun catches me, but that's a fairy tale. My truth and destiny are tied to my mother. The more we lose, the more important she becomes, and all we have, no matter how damaged or fucked up, is each other. Amy's a junkie. My mother's a junkie. And I'm a junkie's son. All of us chained to our burdens, to our loves and fates and demons, and none of us are getting out anytime soon. A junkie knows there's dignity in going down with the ship. There's loyalty in not abandoning a lost cause. There's closure in sitting through the final scene, even if that scene is what I fear the most.

The lane's gravel pops. I park and turn the key. Above, the ink clouds, our kitchen light the sole shine against the dark. "I'm not sad," Amy says. Rain dots the windshield. The house blurs, and I imagine my mother inside, lost in another kind of blurring. Amy's hand settles on my shoulder. She's full of such gestures, touches as thoughtless as they are intimate. They come in passing, come as the punctuations of jokes. But then her palm slides up the back of my neck. Her face glistens, her tears, the watery light. Her fingers laze in the hair I've let grow this summer. She wrestles up a smile. "Well, I guess I'm a little sad, but I'm not sorry for myself. People change. We're always changing. Just need to point ourselves in the right direction and let the world spin." She sighs. "Think it's that easy, Mark?"

I clear my throat. "I don't know." I want to say more, but the entirety of my body has migrated to the few square inches where her flesh meets mine.

"Are you happy, Grace?" I don't correct her, afraid she'll blink away the wetness that feels like an ocean waiting to drown me.

"I am," I say. "Mostly."

She leans forward, and I try to meet her the way movie stars do, but my body has turned thick. Her mouth on mine, her lips soft, opened slightly. The taste of her breath in my throat. The lazy weight of her tongue. She pulls back and rests her forehead against mine. "I hope you're happy, sugar. Now and always. I really do."

I follow her inside. I set the diapers on the kitchen table. The window fan rattles, and on its current, the dank of wet earth. Amy hands me the baby. Grace's bottom damp. I take a diaper and follow Amy into the living room. She sits, and I can't tell if my mother's murmur is an expression of greeting or annoyance. Amy lights the coffee table's candle. The glow soft and kind. She rolls up her sleeve. I lay Grace on the carpet and change her. Grace blinks, her eyes on me, and to her, I must loom as big as an oak, a shadow blocking the sky and stars. She anchors a finger in her mouth, spittle on her chin. Amy preps. Water. A cigarette's stripped filter. Powder and flame. She speaks, but her focus remains on the task at hand. "There's formula if she needs it."

"I know."

She manages a smile. "I don't fuck up everything. At least not all the time."

"I know."

I hold the child to my chest. In her, the heaviness of sleep, the struggle to observe, to utter a last sigh. Amy taps the syringe's side. The drop at the needle's tip shimmers in the candlelight. She pulls the belt around her arm and looks at me. Perhaps she's waiting for me to leave, but I don't feel like going. "Sometimes I just need to see the good for what it is, you know?" She clenches the belt in her mouth and speaks through gritted teeth. "I need to let it happen and then let it find my heart."

She slides the needle in. Blood curls in the syringe, a red blossom. I lay Grace in the playpen. Grace shivers, as if feeling a draft I can't, then drifts, and I pull a blanket over her chest. I sit beside Amy. The belt drops from her mouth. Her eyelids sag. I blow out the candle, and Amy whispers from the dark. "There's ways to see things. Different ways."

I lay two fingers at the base of her neck. I think of her pulse and the chemicals it carries. I think of her kiss and wonder how it will compare to the first kiss of a girl my age. I wonder if all the kisses for the rest of my life will be rooted in the feel and taste of her lips. And I think about her belief in a spinning world because I feel it moving now. My steps through a hushed house. The dream that belongs to everyone but me.

I kneel and slide off Amy's shoes. I could go to my room, but I don't want to be alone. A couch pillow beneath my head, I stretch out beside the playpen. I lace a finger through the pen's mesh and touch Grace's arm. Sleep comes, more a plummet than a drift. My solid parts fade, this night of heat and crickets.

When I open my eyes, I'm unsure where I am. Outside, the crunch of gravel. Headlights creep across the walls then rise, illuminating cobwebs, the ceiling's water stains. The engine cuts and the room goes dark. I pull aside a curtain, and in me, a hardening, the air in my lungs replaced by cement. The counter drawer slides open, and I grope among the long knives and ladles. The light from the microwave's clock shines green on the .38's chrome. The gun heavy, and in my body, the memory of its kick and the bang that swallowed the wide summer sky.

I turn the door's deadbolt. Prop a chair beneath the knob and squat by the window. A faint steam rises from the pickup's hood, and behind its windshield, a cigarette's orange glow. Bent double, I pass through the living room, lock the front door, and return to the kitchen to watch Chief exit the pickup.

The porch boards squeak beneath his boots. He raises a pint to his lips, a last swallow before he hurls the bottle into the yard. I crouch, my eyes just above the sill. He takes a drag from his cigarette, and a ribbon of smoke eases into the kitchen. He

THE LOST AND THE BLIND

reaches for the knob, and I speak. "You can't come in." My voice choked by dust and heat.

Chief steps back. He considers the door then the window. "Do I hear you right?"

"Yes, sir."

He twists the knob. The propped chair rattles. He flicks his cigarette and bends forward. His silhouette blacker than the night beyond the porch overhang. "I didn't come all the way here to turn back." An accent I can't place. The tone I've known all my life. "Now show some smarts and open the door."

I think of the living room's stillness, a sleeping baby. I think of my mother rousted from her stupor, think of her temper and how easily she could snatch the gun and pull the trigger. "I can't do that."

"You want me to kick this door in, is that what you're saying, boy?"

"I'm not saying that."

"Because I will. I'll kick my way from one end of this shit shack to the other."

"I'll call the cops."

He snorts. "Bullshit. Not unless you want your mama and everyone else in there to go to jail tonight. Both of us know the cops would find enough shit in there to do that and more." He leans closer, his face inches from the screen. "You ever been in the system, boy? Getting passed from one fucked up family to the next? And that baby, shit. Although maybe it'd be best for the both of you. Ain't no good coming for you either way." He stands. "Now you let me in before I get proper mad."

I listen to the rain, to the purr of a sleeping house. I become a fulcrum, a balance of variables and fates. I cock the .38's hammer. Its cylinder turns and clicks into place.

Chief slaps a palm against the door. The cupboard's dishes

rattle. "That's not clear thinking, boy. And I'm guessing you don't even know how to use that thing."

I swallow. "You're wrong. I do. And I will. If I have to."

He steps back. "This is a small town. I'll be seeing you around. And you know I never forget a face."

"Neither do I."

"Maybe I'll see you alone in town."

"Maybe I'll have this gun."

"I doubt that."

"Maybe my mom will have it. Maybe she'll be looking for you come sunrise. Maybe you'll need to be the one looking over his shoulder."

He steps off the porch, a backwards walk across the lawn. The pickup's engine rattles. A jerking turn and the spit of gravel. The headlights jostle, the lane's ruts, Chief's paint-spattered boot heavy on the gas. Then darkness. The rain and crickets. My hands shake as I ease back the hammer. The chill of sweat on my skin, and beneath, a deeper chill. Adrenaline. The reckoning of fear. I return the gun to the drawer but can't escape its feel. I lay an afghan over my mother. I brush the hair from Amy's face and allow the back of my hand to rest against her cheek. I pull the shades and curtains, knowing how my mother hates the morning sun. I return to the floor near the baby. My heart calms, and with it, a weight greater than my body. The weight not a burden, but a good thing, a weight rooted in the desire to be here come morning. To change Grace's diaper and sing her back to sleep. To fetch my mother and Amy water to soothe their parched throats. To know we have another day.

I drill a guide hole then twist in the last eyelet. The work harder once I reach the stud. Sweat on my brow, and the old man in his straight-back chair. His cane between his knees. Wrinkled hands folded atop the cane's grip. His clouded eyes. His world of grays. He grew up in this farmhouse, and when he came home from the Navy, he built the bungalow at the end of the lane. A sanctuary for him and his new bride. His parents gone now. His brothers. His wife. His fields plowed by his nephews and their sons. His world narrowed. This house. These rooms. The stairs he's afraid to climb.

"Appreciate this." He raps his cane's tip against the floor-boards. "It's a lot of work."

The living room's center bare save a green couch. The chairs and footstools pushed against the walls. The couch an island in a blind man's sea. The curtains taken down and an exposure of dirty glass. The window to my right offers a view of rolling alfalfa. The window to my left looks upon the barn, its red paint long weathered—and then down the gravel lane to the honeymoon house the old man built in another life. Amy says the old man isn't long for this world, and once he's gone, she worries what's next for us. The rent locked thirty years in the past and rarely paid on time. "Rather drink poison than go back to town," Amy says.

I brush plaster from my jeans and retrieve the twine. The old man turns as I pass, and I think of the nights I've watched him from our porch. The lights he never turns off. The silhouette that drifts from window to window.

"You want my TV?" The TV unplugged and pushed into a corner. "Took going blind to see how stupid it was. Did you ever just listen to it? It could kill you." He taps his head. "Up here."

I lace the twine from eyelet to eyelet, following the old man's plans. In the kitchen, I snip the twine and secure a double knot. Next I string the other circuits. Kitchen to living room. Living room to bathroom. Bathroom to the bedroom he's moved to the downstairs study. I secure the last knot then stand too quick. My empty stomach and the rush of blood, and I need a breath to push back the sparks. In the kitchen, I set the twine and scissors on the counter beside his wallet. The wallet opened, a billfold of tens and twenties. The old man stands and taps his way to the wall.

"A little to your left," I say. "You've got the height right."

He fingers the eyelet. His thumb and index finger circle the twine, and as he walks, I imagine the twine's warm rub. The line lifted, the hint of slack he told me to leave. He makes his way to the living room. "Nice work," he says.

"Thanks."

He reaches the circuit's last eyelet then taps his way back to his chair. "Do you know the story of Theseus?"

I say the name in my head. "Don't think."

"Theseus and the Minotaur?"

"Not either of them, I think."

"Greek. The myths. Guess there's lots of new things they have to teach you these days. Computers and what not."

"I know some myths." I see a book. I'm five. A crash house where the wind pulsed in the plastic we'd duct taped over a busted window. The bedroom with its stained shag and our shared floor-mattress, and piled in a corner, three forgotten books, one a collection of myths. The book a fascination. The pages studied during my mother's absent hours. Stories I couldn't read. Inked drawings that tunneled into my dreams. The book in my hands, plain as day. A young man in a cave. A ball of string. A horned beast.

"Hold on," I say. "The half-man, half-monster thing."

"Hope is not lost." A grin lifts his gray whiskers. "Theseus was barely older than you." He refolds his hands atop the cane's handle. "Know what the lesson of that story is? A body's got to act, but just as important, a body's got to think."

"So everything turned out OK for Theseus?"

"No. Not really. At least not like he planned." He sucks in his lip, stares his blank stare. "I'm pretty hungry. How about you?"

I try to let a moment pass before I answer. "Yeah. Some."

"You up for handling the duties?"

I've cooked for the old man before. Nothing fancy. I like his kitchen. Everything clean and in its place. The refrigerator more full than not. His daughter's weekly visits, the food she brings, the old milks and moldy cheeses thrown out. Today I make us bacon and scrambled eggs, butter and toast. The smells build, and I push back my empty-bellied swoon. I set out our plates and place a fork in his hand. I've learned the evolution of hunger. The yearning that leads to fogged thoughts. The fogged thoughts that lead to desperation. Then pain—but after that, a kind of ecstasy, a landscape of static and peculiar light and cotton-muffled voices. With my first bite, the air seeps from that shimmering mirage and I spiral back, my want so deep I barely remember chewing as I stare at my crumb-littered plate.

A fleck of egg dots the old man's chin. "Get yourself some more, son."

* * *

I sit on the porch and squint back the sun. The heat different out here. No macadam. No brick. No rowhomes where rooms bake like plaster ovens. Here, I have the haze of pollen and dust. The shadeless acres and clear-air ripples. The alfalfa swaying on a liar's breeze, a wind that brings no relief, only more heat.

A car turns down the lane. Glare on the windshield. Andy's a friend of sorts. Our overlapping orbits of misfits and underachievers. His sister at the wheel, a girl as focused as he is un. Her full load at community and twenty-hour weeks at the Amazon warehouse. Her pre-dawn commutes and library weekends. I've only talked with her a few times, but there's no mistaking her smolder to one day put a thousand miles between herself and this place.

The car stops. Sunlight snares in its veil of kicked-up dust. "Markus!" Andy calls. The car door slams, and through the

23

settling haze, his sister's stare. My history no secret. My mother and her scenes. My father. Always my father.

"I'll be back at five." She shifts into reverse. Andy and I bump fists. His hands full, a tackle box and a pair of fishing rods. "You hear me, Andrew?"

Andy's back to her. His face made spastic. Tongue out, eyes rolled. "Five o'clock."

She backs up. More dust. "It's a long walk home, dickhead."

Once she passes the farmhouse, Andy pulls a joint from his shirt pocket. He sparks a lighter then pauses. "We cool?"

"We're cool."

He puffs, his face lost behind the smoke. His is the luck unique to good-natured white boys. A *yes, sir* or *no, ma'am* often all he needs to sidestep trouble. He's walked away from a rolled pickup. Had a switchblade pulled on him in the Patch. On the weekends, he serves breakfast and lunch in a retirement home. He chats it up, pushes their wheelchairs across the grounds, and in return, the old folks slide him tens and twenties. They tell him he's a good kid. They tell him he should meet their granddaughters. They confess their wishes to be his age again.

Andy's stepfather says Andy should learn a trade. A plumber perhaps, and he reminds Andy again how much he paid to have their bathroom redone. His mother thinks he should become a teacher, perhaps work with handicapped kids. When Andy told me this, he held out one hand then another, a weighing of the world's offerings. "I can't decide which I'd suck more at."

He hands me the joint. Smoke escapes the corners of his mouth. "Dig it."

I've only smoked a handful of times. Each time with Andy, our shared shop class, the wing's unsupervised lav. Our snickering return drowned by lathes and drills. My next class on the third floor. A window seat and a daydreamer's view. The football field. A gym class's lazy laps. The streamy blue sky and stepping-stone clouds, and on a clear day, the Appalachian ridge. Miles and miles of nothing, and I melted into the blur.

I take a hit. The heat in my lungs. I cough, but by the third toke, the swell and sparkle settle behind my eyes. Andy punches my arm. "Fucking A, am I right?"

He asks what I've been up to. I think of kissing Amy in this very spot. Think of a gun trembling in my hands and how Chief's silhouette cut a space darker than the night. "Not much." I exhale. "Doing some odds and ends for the guy who owns this place." Over the field, turkey vultures circle the blue. "I'm kind of looking forward to school. Weird, I know, but just for a change, you know?"

Andy snuffs the joint and slides it back into his pocket. "Fucking seniors, man."

"Fucking seniors."

He pedals my bike across the parched grass. The breeze lifts his blond hair. A hand on the handlebar, the other held high. "Ride 'em cowboy!" He circles wider, and as he disappears behind the stacked haybales, I worry about the bottles I shot as my mother looked on. I almost tell him to watch out for broken glass, but then I know what that would lead to, and the last thing I want is a stoned Andy handling a gun. He picks up Chief's empty pint bottle. "Looks like I missed the party." He sets the bottle atop a hay bale, pedals back, and returns my bike to the porch.

With our rods slung over our shoulders, we set down the tractor road that leads to the creek. Grasshoppers pluck our shins. Cicadas hum. The turkey vultures above, their shadows joining ours. The scent of sun-rotted flesh with us for a moment then not. Andy grins. "This is some real Huck Finn shit you got going here, brother."

"You're the one who brought the fishing gear."

"I'm just making the picture complete." He waves his rod like a paintbrush. "Putting on the finishing touches."

We reach the tree line, and in its shade, the creek. The water low. The creek clean, a last gasp before it meets the river's sludge. We sit in a sycamore's shade. June bugs in the shallows. Dragonflies.

Andy relights the joint. His voice pinches as he holds the smoke. "I'm not big on fishing to be honest." He exhales. "When I was younger, yeah, but now I just like the being here part." He hands me the joint. "The water going by and everything slowed down and shit."

I take a hit. Sunlight on the water. Squirrels in the branches above us. I'm about to tell Andy I know what he means but instead I start laughing.

"What?" he asks.

"Nothing, man. Just feeling good." I bring the joint to my lips and think of the emptiness in my mother's eyes when the junk hits her brain. I look to the sky then shut my eyes and listen to the water's murmur. The clock slows, and I sink into the all-and-everything of a warm summer day.

* * *

The late-day sun flickers across the corn's tassels. Amy at the wheel, a drive into town to pick up my mother, and in the car, the swirl and rush Amy once said reminded her of a seashell. "You're kidding," she said when I told her I didn't know the story of seashells and the ocean. When I told her I'd never seen the ocean either, she didn't say anything else.

She fiddles with the radio. News of protests and counter-protests in Miami and Washington and New York. The Chairmen of the Joint Chiefs announcing raids on outposts deep in the jungle and the prediction all resistance would be squashed in a few weeks. We take a bump too fast. The car lifts, a roller-coaster drop in my gut. Grace's eyes wide, and to keep her from crying, I offer her jellied teething ring. Even on our shortest trips, I sit in the back with Grace. Maybe I'll feel different when she gets in her front-facing booster. For now, I don't like to think of her cut off from the faces she knows, alone with the car's drift and the back-window's view of passing sky, with the radio songs and seashell breezes that tatter her mother's voice.

Our wheels veer onto the shoulder, a slip into a weedy ditch before Amy hits the gas and spins us into a U-turn. "Did you see that?"

She straightens the car, and within fifty yards, we turn onto a farmer's lane. A hand-painted sign flashes outside my window —FREE KITTENS. The car jostles, Amy's impatience, the lane rougher than ours. The drool-wet ring firm between Grace's lips. Ahead, a barn and farmhouse, clothes on the line. Amy gets out, calls "Hello," then reaches back in to honk the horn. Behind her, a divided horizon. Green corn and blue sky, colors from a child's crayon box. Her hair pulled up in a pink scrunchie. Her overalls too large, and her thumb jerks up the strap that's slipped again from her shoulder. I unbuckle Grace. A man, his face hidden by a straw hat's shadow, appears on the porch. "The kittens?" Amy asks. He waves, and she follows him to the barn.

I climb out. I hold Grace facing forward, pointing and talking, giving her names for all she sees until the words feel stupid on my tongue. "Chickens," I say, pointing. "Chickens. Chickens. Barn. Your mom. Your mommy."

Amy lifts a cardboard box. A wide smile. A victor's pose. She sets the box on the hood. She holds the kitten, and a strip of shredded newspaper falls from its paw. The kitten black and white, more fur than flesh. Grace drops her teething ring. Her fingers buried in her mouth, a chorus of drooling nonsense.

The cat in the front seat for the ride into town. Its *mew, mew, mew* a new thread in the seashell hum. Our first stop a supermarket. I push the cart. Grace strapped in its seat. The kitten's muffled cries rise from Amy's shoulder bag. Amy fills our cart with the burgers and rolls and watermelon we've come for. Then the pet aisle. Litter and a plastic box. Amy reads labels on tin cans. "Organic turkey dinner. Grain-free Atlantic salmon. Shredded boneless chicken in sauce." She stacks them in the cart. "This little girl is going to eat better than us." A final pause to toss in a catnip mouse. "Think we have milk at home?"

"Probably not." I take Grace out, holding her to my shoulder and pushing the cart with one hand. On her, the smell of fresh pee. "We have diapers?"

Amy takes the cart, and I hustle to keep pace. She tells me about Cocoa, the cat she had as a little girl. How she loved to watch it lap milk. Its focus, the blur of its pink tongue. I imagine the cat—then Amy, a girl half my age. I imagine parents who believed in Jesus. Orderly rooms. Bedtime prayers. A kitchen without a revolver in the silverware drawer. A refrigerator that always had milk. A door the cops hadn't kicked in. A hundred notes then a hundred more that make it easier to imagine myself standing in front of the ocean than growing up like her.

We get milk, and in the baking aisle, Amy's overcome by the urge to make us a cherry pie. She scrolls for ingredients on her cracked phone and throws crust mix and canned cherries into our cart, and it's then I realize she's speeding. The restless hands. The kitten-and-pie impulses. Her pupils' deep black. My mother used to tweak, the year we shacked up with Double D, a cooker now doing ten-to-twenty. I fetched Double D's beers and lit his cigs, and he called me Mr. Trouble, and was, outside his doping, a decent guy. But the house's amped currents found their way into me, and in time, I, too, became restless. My sleep fitful. My distrust of the door and the phone and the noises outside my window. How many times had I woken on the couch, the sun etching a halo around the blackout curtains, only to blink Double D into focus as he returned from a morning beer run or perhaps my mother, her knuckles bloodied from her bathroom scrubbings. All night they'd rage, mostly just the two of them, but sometimes, when his prison friends crashed with us and the whole place was flying high, I'd eavesdrop on their overlapping conversations. The schemes that rose like rickety spires. The words that circled up into an atmosphere where vertigo and lack of oxygen only fueled a tweaker's logic. To a meth-addled brain, happiness shines, close but always just out of reach. A kitten. A cherry pie. A scam to run. A dealer to jack. A new town where life was bound to be better. But their plans always crumbled. They were too dumb. Too stoned. Too distracted by the need to take another hit, and the few dreamed-for salvations they attained never amounted to anything more than dust in their hands. So they said *Fuck it* and snorted another rail and set off toward the horizon's next glittering promise . . .

People stare. A teenage boy carrying a baby. A flash-talking woman whose overall strap keeps sliding off, exposing her bare shoulder and sunshine-yellow halter. A Chinese symbol she says stands for serenity tattooed on the back of her neck, a butterfly on her ankle. More stares, narratives spun, who belongs to whom. Each with their judgments. Our clothes. Our stink of poverty. And I stare back. Not angry. Not seeing them as anything but brothers and sisters. The only difference being that the clouds we drag in our wake are easier to see. Their shade deeper. The sun's warmth less familiar on our skin.

Ten minutes later we're parked on a narrow street. Rowhome shadows. Concrete stoops. Glass in the gutter. On the corner, shirtless men pass a paper bag. I unbuckle Grace and hand her to the front, and in return, Amy gives me the kitten. Each with their smells. Each with their sounds. The kitten's fang-bearing mews. Grace's suckle, frantic at first, then softer. On the corner, a man raises his arms, threats exchanged with a passing car. I've spent most of my life here in the Patch. Fifteen square blocks. Three wide thoroughfares crisscrossed by side streets and alleys and abrupt dead ends where no stranger wants to find himself after dark. There're no supermarkets or movie theaters here. There's a park where someone's stabbed or shot every few months. And there are pawn shops and bail bondsmen and check-cashing joints. The Patch bordered on the north by the rail tracks that fed the old mill and on the east by the polluted river prone to leaving its banks. When I was little, I often passed The Pirate on his perch atop a wooden crate outside the liquor store. "Arrgh," the meaner kids would say, a mocking of his eyepatch, but I never bothered him. One afternoon, he lifted the patch and invited me to take a look. He smiled, teeth yellow or missing. "People call it the Patch because they don't want to see what's beneath." Truth was, there wasn't anyone who knew why they called it the Patch, and the Pirate's explanation made as much sense as any. What most agreed upon was the truth of the neighborhood's oldest joke—that when the mill closed, the Patch died, only it was too stupid to know it.

The kitten kneads my jeans then settles into my lap. Its purr a tiny engine, a sound louder than the body I can cup in my hands. We once lived on this street. A couple chaotic months, a rainy spring. A crane of my neck, and I study the dirty windows of the second and third floors, the bedrooms and attics. I can't pick out our old place, but I have no trouble seeing the boy I was. Hungry, often afraid. The lies I told teachers and counselors. The escapes I made from the corner boys. The fights I could and could not talk my way out of. I see a face in a window, and while I might not know the house, I know a dozen like it. The burst pipes and brown tap water, the thin walls and the rawness of so much hard luck herded into such a small space.

My mother turns the corner. Her name called, a raised middle finger for the corner's shirtless drinkers. Amy honks. I know why we're here, but I don't ask. I keep an eye out for the cops. The kitten lifts its head and mews. Up front, Grace has finished her suckle. Amy holds her and pats her back. Grace facing me, a white drop on her lips. Her eyelids flutter. A lulling daze in a night destined to be full of dazes.

My mother climbs in. On her, a bar's stink. Beer, cigarettes. She cradles Amy's face between her palms and kisses her flush on the lips. She reaches back and squeezes my hand.

She's wearing sunglasses and my reflection bends across the lenses. "Hey, kiddo." Her smile freezes. "What do I hear?"

"I got us a kitten," Amy says, and I hold up the proof. The kitten's claws dig, but not enough to hurt. "From that farm. The sign we saw before."

My mother lowers her sunglasses. "You're lit, aren't you? Where'd you get that shit?" She reaches back, and I give her the kitten. She considers the kitten and rubs its nose with hers. "He's ours now, huh?"

"She." Amy strokes the kitten's back. "At least I think so."

My mother lifts the tail. "She it is." She turns to me. "You're in on this, too?"

"I guess."

Amy starts the car. I imagine the flyweight powders in my mother's purse and the jailtime they could earn. My pulse thick and the fizz behind my eyes. The burden of worrying about those too blind to worry about themselves, my breathing easier only after we buck over the mill's tracks and leave the Patch.

My mother turns to me. "What're we naming her?"

"Don't think she's mine to name."

Amy eyes me in the rearview. "You go ahead, Markie. Think of something good." She stops at a strip mall's light. "We need anything for the weekend?"

My mother rubs Amy's neck. "Fuck no. We're fucking gold, pony boy."

. . .

I take the first bite from my burger. Haze from the grill, and above, a bright half-moon. Around the moon, the spark of the constellations I taught myself long ago. Lyra. Aquila. Sagittarius. My mother bounces Grace on her knee, and Amy's head rests on her shoulder. The cherry pie unmade. We eat, and I allow myself to be happy in the moment. The fields' good smells and the beautiful sky. The taste of meat. This hand-to-mouth life where untroubled moments shine brighter than any summer star.

Grace falls asleep, and I take her from my mother's arms. She is all weight and no will. I cradle her head. Her breath warm against my neck. Inside, I change her diaper and lay her in the crib. The nightlight's soft shine, and in this room of stillness and shadows, I see her life. A million unimaginable details —the singular foundation of being born into a need that runs deeper than love.

In the living room, my mother and Amy slump into each other. On them, the stained-glass shine of Amy's lamp. My mother reaches out, a clumsy stroke of my cheek. Another still room. Another kind of sleep. I stub out their cigarettes. The kitten performs a tightrope walk across the couch's top before it arches its back and settles into the hushed tide.

* * *

I set a kitchen chair in the yard. I'm bare-chested, showered, my hair wet, and once I'm seated, I drape my towel over my shoulders. The shower's coolness evaporating beneath a heat that makes moving a labor. The kitten in the grass, chasing crickets, pinning one beneath her paw then letting it go.

Amy steps onto the porch. The screen door eased shut, Grace's afternoon nap. "Found them," she says, and in her raised hand, a pair of scissors whose silver flashes in the sun. She stands before me. Head tilted, hands on her hips. Lining up, judging. "Not too much, right?"

"Not too much, but not this shaggy."

"It looks good." She slides the comb and scissors into the bib pocket of her overalls and pulls up her hair in a scrunchie. "Like a surfer."

"I'm no surfer."

"Bet you could be. If the circumstances were different."

She steps forward, circling me, combing out my hair. She moves with a junkie's harmony of heavy and light. Her hip grazes my shoulder, and a slur whittles the ends of her sentences. She stands in front of me, knees bent. A peek of cleavage. A smile, and I smile back.

"How're those girls going to keep themselves away?"

"They've done a pretty good job so far."

She combs my hair over my eyes. "That'll change."

She starts in the back, a nudge to lower my head. I study my bare feet in the grass. I listen. The scissors' snip. The goat's grazing shuffle. The crickets and cicadas. The electric wire's low hum. My hair begins to curl in the heat. A tug on my scalp as she straightens and clips. Snippets fall, soft as whispers, as she speaks.

"I learned when I was about your age by cutting my first boyfriend's hair. He had hair like yours." The drift in her voice easier to detect without looking at her, the pull of memory, and although I've never met him, I think of him and the other men she's told me about. The one who maxed out her credit cards. The one who fucked her best friend. The one who beat her with a belt when she told him she was pregnant.

She stands in front of me. The tracks on her arms pale against her tan. She pushes my head down again. "It's nice," she says. "How you and your mom are close. I've been a disappointment to my parents, I see that now. They've tried. They've tried harder than I have. But they love Grace. I can see that, too. And seeing that has helped me see how they loved me. They just wanted things for me, and when I didn't want the same things, they worried. I understand that now." She sniffs, and I wonder if it's allergies or tears. "But we're going to work it all out soon. You and me and your mom and my parents. All of us, together. It'll be better."

She pockets the comb and scissors and fluffs my hair. She steps back and I lift my gaze. The clash of red eyes and a wide smile. She brushes her cheek. "Look at you," she says. "Ready to take on the world."

* * *

D usk comes but it can't break the heat. On TV, video of an Army helicopter crash, a plume of smoke, and when the camera pulls out, the plume thins until it's lost in the jungle. I've made dinner with the scraps at hand. Diced potatoes and onions, a green pepper. The meat from a half-eaten burger brought home in a caterer's box. The cupboards bare but the flies thick, and the yellow strips that hang from the ceiling sway with their latest catches. My mother doesn't eat, though I wish she would. The knobs of her elbows and knees. Her neck's strained chords as she pulls on her cigarette. Her gauntness a kind of hardening, a reduction to sinew and a simmering agitation. She swats a fly and lights another cigarette.

"She didn't say anything?" She taps her phone, checks the time. She blows smoke from the corner of her mouth. "Nothing out of the ordinary?"

I finish my plate, and she slides hers across the table. "You should—"

She shuts me up with a smoke-trailing wave. "So nothing?"

"Nothing. Just 'I'm dropping Grace off and I'll be home after my shift.'"

She grinds out one cigarette and lights another. An hour passes, then another, and my mother's worry becomes my own. From outside, the call of crickets, louder now than the cicadas. School less than a week away. My mother scratches her neck. A ring, and she checks the number twice before answering. "Yeah?"

She jumps up. Her chair toppled and the kitten spooked. Her purse and keys clutched, the phone pressed to her ear. "Don't cry. Don't cry and don't say a word. Nothing. Not a goddamn word. We're leaving now. Sit tight and shut the fuck up." Her feet a blur down the porch steps. "Just sit tight, damn it. Don't talk. Don't goddamn cry. Don't do a fucking thing until I get there."

I take the passenger seat. I'm neither invited nor un. The moment hazy but my mother's fury on full display, and I need to be near, to say the right words when she's lost in the storm. The gravel lane, and our headlights jostle, pointing up into the starless night then down. We reach the road. My mother's face lit in the dash's underwater hues. A tight turn, and our backend fishtails.

"Jail," she snaps. We veer over the double yellow. "Fucking jail."

"Are we posting?" I think of the bondsman we use in the Patch. **LISA** tattooed across his knuckles. A scar that runs from eye to jaw.

"She got a DAT." I grab the dash. Our speed, the road's bends. "Just paraphernalia."

"So we're good?" I may not have known the seashell-ocean story, but I know a DAT means Amy's coming home with us.

"For now, yeah, we're good." She slows. "But she's a fucking wreck."

Last night, Amy got teary-eyed over a commercial for a children's charity hospital. Then later, over another about abused dogs. My mother lights a cigarette, and her face lifts from the dark. "Fucking pigs."

I've seen my mother handcuffed. Pepper sprayed. Hogtied. Spat upon. Seen her brought up on bullshit resisting charges and doubled over by a nightstick to the gut. I've seen cops pocket her dope, seen others grab her tits for a laugh. I don't hate any cop who hasn't given me reason to hate them. But I'm old enough to know serve and protect means serve and protect the rich, and every time I catch my reflection in a cop's sunglasses, I know I'm only a breath away from staring down the barrel of a gun. In their voices, the slam of a thousand cell doors. In their hands, a history of broken bodies that stretches back to the pharaohs.

We park in the station's lot, and I go in alone. A walk beneath teardrop security cameras and moth-swarmed floodlights. My mother's fear of outstanding warrants. My fear of her zero-to-sixty rage. The station bathed in queasy halogen. My hand on the door. I feel small, lost. Questions from a man behind bulletproof glass. A metal detector's blinking light. A buzz and click, and a door swings back, ghost-like, and as I step through, I think of the minotaur. Think of my father, forever lost in the sunless labyrinth.

I'm buzzed in. A waiting room of bolted chairs and milky fluorescents, a scene that takes its place among the emergency rooms and bus depots and all the way stations of my drift. The door at the room's other end opens, and when she spots me, Amy crosses the room in swift steps.

My hand snatched, a grip that makes me wince. The cop behind the glass shakes his head. Amy's momentum spins me around, and I hurry to keep pace as she pushes her way outside. The parking lot's harsh lights. Her face in shadows. She holds her scrub top, the nursing home gig she's probably now lost. We reach the car without a word. I climb in the back and sit in the middle. My mother turns the key. Amy in the passenger seat, the door slammed.

Amy accepts my mother's half-smoked cigarette. Her other hand over her eyes, and I remember a long-ago movie, a soldier before a firing squad.

"You got the DAT, babe." My mother turns onto the boulevard. A long spine of streetlamps and traffic lights. Stores either abandoned or shuttered for the night. The Patch's sidewalk dramas. "We'll do some community service. Maybe a few meeting—"

Amy's hand remains over her eyes. "My fucking parents will know. They'll read the police report. Or one of their friends will. Someone in the fucking choir or the fucking golf club." She hands the cigarette to my mother. The smoke curls back to me. "They'll know, and then there'll be trouble."

My mother hits the gas, a light just turning red. "First things first. Where's your car?"

"I can't. Not now. I need to go to my parents'." She squeezes her temples. Her eyes still hidden, her lips quivering. "I need to get Gracie."

"Sure. Sure, babe. I'm dim on the directions."

"Take Forester. Then McKay."

Forester. McKay. Tycoons in their day. Mining and lumber, fortunes made on a thousand broken backs, and nothing ever changes. A pair of turns. The Patch's desperation fades, the suburb's balanced equation of less people and more money. Amy points out the turns, and soon, I'm lost. I roll down my window. Scents of mulch. Chlorine from backyard pools. Winding streets. Wooden mailboxes and house numbers painted on the curbs. The sweep of dark lawns and their firefly dances. We park. A cul-de-sac. Two-car garages. Windows lit by electric candles. Amy a shadow beneath a porch light. She rings the bell, hugs herself despite the heat. The door opens, and she goes inside. I get out and claim the passenger seat. "Think they'll find out?"

My mother tries to light a cigarette, but she's got the shakes. I take the lighter and flick the wheel. "They will." She inhales. A deep drag. A pause. The flame dies and she exhales. She considers the house through our gnat-speckled windshield. "They will."

Amy's voice. Her repeated apology strains over Grace's sobs. Her crazy day at work. A lie upon a lie. She pauses on the porch. Her shadow stretches over a lawn just beginning to dew. Grace's wails rip into me. Their persistence. Their need. A language I hadn't understood last Christmas as I trudged through the farm lane's drifts—a note that now swims in my teeth. Amy turns once on the walkway—*goodnight, goodnight*— then a flash of the dome light as she climbs in the back. "Drive. Just drive." She fumbles with her blouse's buttons. Grace sobs. Our car's muffler-rattle, these hushed streets. Grace's cries fizzle into a hard suckle. The silence washes over us. We reach the road that returns us to the country. In the quiet, I glance back. The dimmest of lights. The feeding done. Amy holds Grace close. Gentle pats on her back. Kisses for her forehead. Whispers of love.

* * *

The first day of school, and I wait at the end of the lane. The sun low. A pickup passes. Amishmen, carpenters headed to town. Then nothing. After last year's Christmas break, I walked the ice-slick quarter mile to the trailer that belonged to the old man's niece. Her daughter waited inside, the curtain pulled back. The old man had told me I could catch the bus there, and while I'd never talked to the girl before, she knew of me. My mother—although there were plenty like her. More so, my father. The name I carry. The snuck glances I've grown accustomed to. The stares I've given myself in a hundred mirrors. The wanting to see what lies beneath.

When the bus came, the girl joined me. A slam of the trailer door. A seat claimed far from mine. Her veil of black hair and a coat that stank of cigarettes and kerosene. By spring, she could no longer hide her belly's curve, and when she stopped coming to school, the bus driver began picking me up at the end of my lane.

But this morning, as the sun crests the creekbank trees, I realize the bus isn't coming. A new driver perhaps. My mother not the kind for paperwork or making things official, our residence, as far as the authorities know, still back in the third-floor apartment in the Patch where a NASCAR flag doubled as a curtain. Where the man who'd threatened to kill my mother and me bloated to twice his size before the neighbors complained about the stench.

I'm mad at myself for not thinking things through. Mad about missing the school's breakfast and our pantry's empty shelves. I hurl a rock into the alfalfa and, by chance, flush a pair of mourning doves. Their wings' startled heartbeat, a joined flight until the birds perch atop a sagging powerline. With each step, our house grows larger. My mother and Amy still asleep, and I can't endure another day of Amy's tears. Can't witness the bedraggled ritual of their morning fix. No one calls my name as my bike's tires bounce down the porch steps. The mourning doves coo as I wobble past. Then the road, the smooth pedaling, and I pick up speed.

I discovered the ten-speed last spring in the barn's cobwebbed scrapheap. With the old man's blessing and help from YouTube, I spent the next few months disassembling and degreasing, sanding and priming and painting. I ordered parts and borrowed tools from the bike shop in town, and after watching me count out my pocketfuls of singles and change, the owner started hooking me up with his workroom's scraps. An unbent wheel. A proper seat. Come July, I took my first ride. My mother and Amy nodding off. The old man lost in his shadows. And as I made the turn away from town at the lane's end, I felt not free so much as unclaimed, forgotten—and it felt good. Every day after that, often twice, I rode. The stretching horizons, an unbothered sun, the ache of so much blue and green. Alone, the miles between me and the farmhouse building, I felt the pull of other destinies. Of a hundred thousand towns where no one knew my name.

But this morning at the lane's end, I turn the other way. Five miles to town, and I figure there's worse things than being late the first day. The assemblies and locker assignments. The schedule mix-ups. Mrs. Pike, the attendance lady, will buzz me in, and as she writes my tardy slip, I'll ask about her summer. About her nurse daughter and her son on an aircraft carrier and the black lab she rescued last year. Mrs. Pike's let me slide more than my fair share, and I'm not so naïve as to take such kindnesses for granted.

I roll past the farm where Amy claimed our still unnamed kitten. The bike's chain lock slung over my shoulder. A tap against my chest. A tractor in the field, this rich land. Trucks and cars pass, and I grip my handlebars against their pulse. The farmlands' low plateau, and as I hit the road's crest, the valley comes into view. The ride easier here. The momentum of this mile-long slope. The wind in my face, a speed I haven't reached on my other rides. In time, the road flattens, and with it, the first strip malls and gas stations. The houses that bunch closer and closer. Before I reach the square, I turn down Delmont. The street wide. Maple trees and sunlit shafts. Wrap-around porches and flower gardens. Homes once passed from generation to generation. The road all mine. The breeze of motion upon me. The birds' songs from the maples. I think of my father and wonder if he can still remember such moments.

I notice the hair first. The black ponytail. The white pickup's lowered gate. The bed filled with tarps and cans. The bike's speed, the shade and speckled light, my faraway thoughts —they dull me, and I don't fully recognize him until I'm close enough to smell the cigarette clenched in his mouth. He turns, sensing perhaps. His paint-splattered boots. The cigarette's ashy ribbon. We exchange stares. I can't turn around without giving him the invitation to react, and all that's left is to pick up speed, my ass lifted from the seat and legs pumping. As I pass— a moment of shared awareness. The memory of rain on the porch roof. A knock on the door. A gun in my trembling hand.

I look back once. The front tire shimmies. Chief with a paint can in each hand, a framing of hundred-year maples and the curbside cars that cost more than he makes in five years. He doesn't yell, doesn't drop the cans and charge me. He just stands, watching, perhaps hearing my voice in the moonless, rainy dark. Perhaps not remembering at all.

I cut down a side street then an alley. Garages blur, trash cans. A barking dog. I fight the handlebars' buck. The cracked macadam, my reckless speed, and my heart's clamor eases only after I lock my bike into the rack and climb the entrance's wide steps.

Before she packed up for Florida with her new husband, my father's mother told me stories about the school when it was new. The gym's pine floors and bellbottom dances, the basement's air raid shelter. I think of her here—and my mother and father—and sometimes, when the talk of Shakespeare and finding X fades into the radiator's hum, I feel like an echo. An exhale of a breath drawn long, long ago.

I press a red button, state my name. My reflection in the door glass, and behind me, the morning sun. A buzz, and I open the door, and there's Mrs. Pike, smiling, knowing my face. A hello that makes me feel, for this passing moment, like more than an echo.

* * *

I stop at a busy intersection. The light red, and someone shouts my name from a passing school bus. Left will take me home, the long ride into the country. The light turns, and with my first wobbly pedals, I glance right. Above the signs for gas stations and used car lots, the Lutheran church's steeple, and before I reach the other side, I turn. A haphazard detour. My drift undercut by an angry horn.

The shadows of the cemetery's iron fence flicker over me. Behind the fence, acres of green. Nearest the church, stones as white as chalk. Some with the lean of crooked teeth. Names and dates faded by a hundred years of snow and sun and rain. I pass beneath the arched gate. The lane's gentle twists and radiating arms. Here and there, a tree, and beneath, foraging squirrels. Some stones staked with flowers or flags, souls still remembered. My way navigated by the markers unlike the others. The vaults. The statues and obelisks. The money of this world and the equality of the grave. I'm alone save a man in the

46

distance. His blue hat and khaki shirt. The thinned whir of the weed eater he runs along the base of the stones. The man who, two summers ago, led me to his groundskeeper's garage and pulled out a ledger. His finger skimming over entries of fading ink until he stopped upon the lot occupied by my twin's grave.

I lay my bike in the grass. A cat steps from behind a stone. It looks at me, tail twitching, then bounds off, silent, gone. I question my way. Then the designs I remember, carvings of angels and praying hands, a child's game of *colder . . . warmer . . . burning up* until my shadow falls over my brother's flat stone.

I crouch, picking grass from the stone's edges. *Jason Hayes.* I came first, and I wonder if, imprinted in a place beyond language or reason, I can still hear my mother's bloody screams before giving birth to a child with a defective heart. A child who'd begin to die the moment the doctor cut his cord. It's true he passed that day and that I've never laid eyes on him, yet I sometimes think of him in the lonely gray between consciousness and sleep. Think of him when I sign something official, *Mark Jason Hayes*, a secret I carry tucked in the middle of my name.

In the system, I saw my share of counselors. The young ones, so full of optimism. The older ones who knew better but still came to work and offered love to strays like me. The one I liked best with a sunny office, a room full of toys, and my favorite, one I was free to play with outside the judgement of others, a large dollhouse. I'm seven, maybe eight, and I kneel before the house that splits in two upon its hinges. The dolls and miniature furniture wait for my hand. I hear the therapist's voice behind me, the explanation of how children like me often follow distinct paths (or perhaps I'm confusing memories— perhaps this talk came later, a different therapist, a different office—but I remember it here, in this sunny room as I sit before a tiny house, its rooms bared like chambers of a dissected heart).

Some, she says, adopt our parents' habits. We observe and imitate; this is only natural. Others lash out, wild-eyed, their fists balled, their desire not to hurt but to protect what had been hurt so often. And then there are children like me. Her voice softens. The ones who soothe rough edges. Who shuttle between feuding parties, offering olive branches and compromises. Who rise early to clean up the mess from the night before.

An oak tree nearby, not close enough for shade, yet I hear its cicadas' dying hum. Sometimes I catch myself staring in a mirror, lost, and in these moments, I'm with my brother. The reflection mine yet not. And with me, another life, one that's a mystery and a responsibility.

I stand and brush off my jeans. My bike mounted and my first lazy pedals. Perhaps I'll come again, but it'll have to be before winter. My last visit on a snow day, but of course I couldn't find his stone, and in me, an unease. The thought of him lost and cold. His name erased beneath the white.

* * *

I sit by the quarry's ledge. The rocks I toss fall so far I can't hear their splash, and I think of the jumpers who've braved these cliffs. Daredevils. Drunks. Think of an Army helicopter dropped from the clouds and those final moments of terrible knowledge. Birds circle the pit's hollowed center. Black flecks against white stone. The day still and hot, and I imagine my breath drifting over the quarry's emptiness. The clouds above and the birds below, and me, nestled in the belly of the sky.

I stand and wipe off my shorts. Toss a final rock. The narrow footpath angles down. The shade of hackberries and mimosas. A rusted fence surrounds the pit. The chain link cut, a snare on my sleeve. I lift my bike, and its impression remains in the tall grass. Crickets pluck my shins. The thrum of katydids.

I reach the road and mount my bike. Heat rises from the macadam. The school year's second Saturday. My teachers—for the most part—chill. The understanding that the Common

App and AP scores mean nothing to my crew. We don't want to read Beowulf, don't care about the Compromise of 1850. We're done with all of it. Years ago, I learned to keep my head down and fly beneath the flack of troublemakers and hotheads. I'll do enough to get by. Another year, but then a hitch. Thoughts of June, a graduation gown. And then what? And then what.

There have been teachers who've taken a shine to me. The calm ones. The ones immune to the mayhem and grind. Mrs. Santo, who brought me the jeans and sweatshirts her son had outgrown. Mr. Wainright, who talked the guidance counselor into letting me sit in on his honors trig class, but that experiment fizzled before Halloween. Mine wasn't a home made for homework, and whatever knack I had for numbers faded beneath the hard math waiting for me after the last bell.

Sweat breaks across my back. Heat crackles over the fields. The horizon's shimmer. The road a black taper, and with a crest, the farmhouse comes into view. I think of the day we arrived. The deep white, my sneakered feet numb. I think of what this winter will bring. Then the next. And then what?

I'm a hundred yards away when a black sedan and a sheriff's cruiser turn down our lane. I pedal faster. The macadam then the lane's rough gravel. Past the farmhouse and I dismount, the bike left to roll a few wobbly yards before collapsing to the dirt, its front wheel ghost-spinning, and before I can open the screen door, their voices reach out. My mother's curses. Threats. Tears. My entry a blip, my face registered before the fray is rejoined. Amy, Grace in her arms, framed in the living room entrance. Both crying, the child clutched to her chest. In front of her, my mother, red-eyed and wild. The veins in her neck straining, fists clenched. On the kitchen's other side, a bald man with a reverend's collar, and a man and woman dressed like schoolteachers.

Before now, I've only glimpsed Amy's parents from a

distance. Her mother's beauty-salon hair. Her father's round belly. The thick-shouldered sheriff just inside the door grabs my arm, but I shake him off. The reverend steps forward, hands outstretched, an offering of peace. My mother picks a dirty frying pan from the stove and dares him to take another step.

I stake a place in front of my mother and face the reverend. The two of us intermediaries. Our allegiances with warring camps. In my voice, the spike of my mother's venom as I warn the reverend to back the fuck up.

Amy's father steps forward. "You need to come home with us, honey."

Amy red-faced, eyes slitted and wet. "I'm not going anywhere."

Her mother: "We can help you. We can help—"

"She's not going anywhere, she says!" My mother points the frying pan at Amy's father. "Now get your uninvited ass out of here!"

The reverend raises a hand. "Please—"

My mother: "Shut the fuck up, preacher-man."

"We've got a spot waiting for you in a good rehab," Amy's father says. "We can—"

"Fuck you!" my mother says.

He turns to her. "The sheriff might like to take a look around."

My mother surges forward, and I catch her, an arm around her waist. The frying pan waves. "FUCK you!"

Amy's mother turns pale. Her father shakes his head. "It's not us who'll be fucked if I ask the sheriff to intervene."

"He needs a warrant," I say.

The sheriff breaks his silence. "You've been watching too many TV shows, son."

My mother hurls the frying pan. Amy's father ducks. The sheriff slides the baton from his belt, but Amy's father stops

him with a raised hand. "Out!" my mother cries. "All you motherfuckers!"

"I cosigned the lease," Amy's father says. "I have the right
to bring in anyone I want. And I bet he won't need to snoop
around long before he finds something." He looks at me, then
my mother. "Then all of you will be out on the street. Or
worse." His tone softens. "Amy, honey, come with us. You need
help. And if you can't, then let us help Gracie. She deserves
better."

Amy speaks through her tears. "Who do you think you
are?" She clutches Grace tighter. Grace's little body shakes.
"Better than her mother?"

"Better than the mother she has now."

My mother grabs a dish, and in a single, huffing motion,
sends it flying. The dish cracks against the refrigerator. Shards
spin across the linoleum. The sheriff steps forward. "Get out!"
my mother snaps.

The sheriff grabs my wrist. A twitch in his wide jaw. A gaze
that reduces me from human to obstacle. His meaty grip. The
pressure that lets me know he could snap a bone if he wanted.
A yank, and I stumble forward, the path cleared to my mother.
She slaps him twice before he pins her arms behind her back
and duckwalks her to the door. Grace's snivels blossom into a
room-filling wail.

"Wait!" Amy says. Then softer. "Wait." A curtain of hair.
Her tears hidden. Grace's shrill cry, and in me, the bone-deep
pain of not being able to comfort her. Amy's mother steps
forward and slides her hands beneath Grace. Amy shakes her
head but eases her grip, and for a moment, the baby belongs to
neither. They exchange whispers. Amy shakes her head. *No.
Yes. No. No. No.* Her father joins them. A huddle that could be
mistaken for prayer. More words drowned by Grace's sobs.
Amy's hands go limp, and her mother clutches Grace to her

chest and hurries outside. The reverend and Amy's father on her heels.

"Fucker! Let me go, fucker!" My mother jerks against the sheriff's grip. She slams her heel against his boot. Her feet bare and dirty. "That's fucking kidnapping! Do your fucking job!"

"And that's resisting, sister. And assault." With a shove, he sends her stumbling, and I catch her before she falls. "You're lucky I don't have time for your shit today. Unless you want to press the issue."

He stares us down then clomps onto the porch. My mother and I follow. Amy's father at the wheel of the black SUV. The reverend up front, her mother the only one who looks back. A tight turn. The sheriff behind them, and up the lane, the old man on his porch. A hand clutching a post, his vacant gaze. The cars pass, and he turns to us.

Inside, a new quiet. The baby, of course, yet more. The harsh truths we're forced once again to swallow. The knowing that notions of fairness don't apply to our kind. That the cops and the preachers want us to either bow before them or live in the shadows or rot in their cells. That justice is a fool's belief, and the strong don't think about those beneath their boots, and the folks who live in Amy's parents' neighborhood only care about the Patch when its mess spills into their clean streets. Amy still in the same spot, and when she lifts her chin, I see her open mouth, an expression beyond tears. Her sobs frozen in her throat. Her body as solid as stone. We hold her, my mother on one side and me on the other, and I feel like I did on the quarry's edge. Like I'm standing beside an emptiness as wide as the sky.

* * *

I talk with Mr. Ford after English. Last period, and outside his door, the hallway's shouts. Slammed lockers. Mr. Ford has a.m. bus duty, and as the rest of the class files out, he asks about the bike he sees me riding every morning. He's into riding, and back in the day, he rode a bike like mine. He shoulders his workout bag, his cross-country team waiting for him by the track. He's ex-Army, but you wouldn't know it outside his haircut. His temper saved for the instigators and bullies. A girl in my study hall showed me his freshman picture in an old yearbook. His hair long, his face thinner. His eyes the same. The others at our table laughed, and I paged ahead to the junior homerooms. My mom in her homeroom's first row. Jeans and a sweatshirt. Teased hair. Pretty. Stoned, no doubt, but not yet hollowed. In the hallways and classrooms, this is the ghost I see.

"That must be five, six miles," Mr. Ford says when I tell him where I live.

THE LOST AND THE BLIND

"About that."

He turns off the lights and locks the door. "And you do that every day."

"So far. Winter will be a different story."

"How come you don't grab the bus?"

"Don't think they know where to stop for me." I hesitate. This life of secrets, of us and them. "Don't think we're officially living there, if you know what I mean. Not yet anyhow."

He slides a thumb under the bag's strap and lifts it from his shoulder. "Why don't you come out and run with us?"

I can't help but smile. "You guys go crazy far."

"Folks would say the same thing about you and your bike." He opens a side door. Sunlight streams over him. "Never know. Might surprise yourself."

I pedal out of the lot. The chain link blurs the cross-country team's held stretches. I avoid the neighborhood where I saw Chief, and for a block or two, my route skirts the Patch. Its stoops. Its broken-glass gutters. I think of a place where we once crashed, a breezeway window, and below, the stink of beer and piss. The slurred threats. The moans and grunts. Voices without bodies, and if Amy's seashell could tell the ocean's story, the echoes in that room told the Patch's. A glance down the main drag. Four lanes that dead end onto Front Street and then the dirty river. The sight familiar, yet this afternoon, it shines harsher. Everyone on edge. The knowing there's scant dope. Last week's overdoses. The weekend's busts. Amy with the shakes. My mother downright evil, a sickness I imagine multiplied by a hundred. By a thousand.

Home, and I hear my mother before I hop off my bike. I step inside, and her curses pause for a breath before she turns back to Amy. Amy slumped in a kitchen chair, her head in her hands. Answers of *yes* and *no*, anything longer drowned beneath a new tirade. I piece together their back-and-forth.

The morning's rumors from the Patch. Shipments and reups, a product clean and strong. Amy's afternoon spent on a barstool. Her and my mother's last dollars in her pocket. The leers and come-ons of drunks and perverts. Her eyes lifted for every arrival, sun-bathed silhouettes, men she blinked into focus, none her angel. Then the appearance of a man who knew her connection. He said he'd been running for him all day, and sure, he was beat, but for Amy, he'd make a last hookup. Her money taken with the promise to return before she finished her drink.

My mother shakes her head. "Since when has Johnny ever worked with a runner old enough to sit in a fucking bar?"

"I don't know."

"Fucking think, girl! Jesus fucking Christ. Now we need to find this motherfucker, whoever the fuck he is—"

"Chino," Amy says. She doesn't lift her head. "His name is Chino."

"Chino? Fucking great. Fucking Chino. Fucking mother-fucking Chino."

"He seemed—"

"He seemed? He seemed what? Like a trustworthy guy who just happened to stumble into that scumhole? Like he had a fucking halo over him so you felt cool trusting him with our money?"

"I don't care."

My mother draws back. "Fucking what?"

"I don't care. I don't fucking care. It's the least of my worries right—"

My mother's hand a blur. A smack against the back of Amy's head. Amy cradles her face. Everything still, and I, having witnessed my share of beatings, understand my mother's pause is an invitation—a demanding—that Amy rise up. That she lift her fists. That she shake off the darkness of these last days, the dead-eyed shuffling that has nothing to do with dope. Grace gone, and I can't imagine the weight of absence in Amy's gut. A boulder. A mountain. The world.

But instead of standing, Amy melts. A creep of bone and will that slides her off the chair and onto the dull linoleum. Her hands over her face. A senseless muttering. The only recognizable beats I discern are *no, no, no.*

A fistful of snatched hair lifts Amy from the ground. Her tear-bloated face, a grimace across the lips that have begun to bleed from her picking. I grab my mother's wrist, and again, I am a child, a poser of dolls, a dreamer of peace in a tiny house. My mother's eyes lock on mine before she shoves me with a hand over my face. I grab her other wrist, and on my fingers, her raging pulse.

I let go then turn my back. A hand beneath each arm, I lift Amy. Her feet useless. Her face over my shoulder. The two of us like dancers, our embrace, our backwards steps. Distance, this is my only thought as I guide her to the living room, but our retreat stalls when Amy latches onto the doorjamb and screams.

I turn. The gun shakes in my mother's hands. A doll's house in flames. She blinks. The gun's muzzle an eclipse, and on the other side, my mother—and in her, all that is light and all that is dark. "Mama," I whisper.

Mama, a word I only say in reflex. The utterance of a child afraid of what the next moment might bring. The barrel twitches before she screams, yanks her hand high, and pulls the trigger.

The report swallows us. A plaster snow, flecks in my mother's dark hair. I see the old man frozen in mid-step, his fingers paused upon the guiding twine.

I shove Amy onto the porch, and we stagger into the sun. Halfway across the weed and gravel yard, I look back. My mother hazed by the door's screen. Her white shirt. The black hair that drags her to the shadows. Amy's hand in mine, her half-falling steps and me keeping her upright. Urging. Pleading. *Come on. Come on.*

The path's dirt stains the soles of Amy's feet. The crickets' daytime hum. We sit beneath the creek-side sycamores, this shady patch where I blazed with Andy and thought about the emptiness all around me. An hour passes. More. The two of us silent until Amy says, "Let's go back."

Our walk slower. Our long shadows and a hint of cool. From a distance, I realize my mother's car is gone. Then inside. The kitchen, the ceiling's hole. And in the bedroom my mother and Amy share, the mess of upturned drawers and looted closets. Another frantic escape, the kind I've known all my life.

* * *

The Patch after dark. The wash of streetlights. A scan of sidewalks and alleys. I wait as Amy returns to the bar where she handed over her money, but she exits, shaking her head.

Inside our car, another kind of longing. Amy wrenches her shoulders, scratches her neck. Her dopesick simmer. "You hungry?"

"I am."

"Let's grab something then take another look." She pulls from the curb without checking her mirrors. She hands me her wallet. "How much do we have?"

I count the bills, then the change in the shifter console. "Nineteen. Nineteen eighty-five."

"That's enough, right? Get us a little something."

"Sure you want to spend it like this?"

"You mean not on junk?"

"Yeah."

59

"Yeah." Her voice like water. We pull into a diner lot. "This is as good as anywhere, I guess."

A kitchen radio plays country songs. A man at the counter huddles over his coffee. Two waitresses, one old, one young. The old one tells us to sit anywhere. The young one, a spider tattooed across her wrist's veins, hands us menus. The music swells with the kitchen doors' sway. I wonder if we're the night's last customers. I sift through the menu, adding and subtracting, and settle on meatloaf and potatoes, which aren't bad. Amy orders a cheeseburger but, after a bite, hands it to me. Her knuckles rap the booth's window. Outside, a traffic light. The drift of cars and shadows.

"I'm thinking about doing it." She picks her lip. Wetness in her eyes. "You think I can?"

I take the last bite of burger. "What're we talking about?"

"Kicking. Now. Like right now." She looks outside. Her reflection in the glass. "Not like some bullshit maybe-soon thing. But now. Tonight. I did it before. When I was pregnant." A sigh. "I can do it again."

"That would be great."

"Your mom and I have talked about it, you know."

"That doesn't sound like her."

She manages a weary grin. "I know, right? One night, not long ago." She rubs her neck. "We were trying to imagine it. I was talking about how it could be cool, as long as we were all together, and your mom was into it. She laughed and said it was like trying to imagine China or some other shit she'd seen on TV."

"You going to your parents?" I imagine the kind of rehab they could afford.

Her face, already pained, sours. "No. No fucking way." She plucks a napkin from the dispenser and dabs her eyes. "When I come to get Grace, I'm going in with my head high, not owing them a thing." Her fingernails, which she's taken to chewing this past week, tap the tabletop. "I'll be right back."

She leaves and settles into a corner booth. From the kitchen, a guitar's strum, a woman singing about home. Amy holds her phone to her ear. She nods, wipes tears from her cheeks. The clatter of dishes and silverware. The waitresses at the counter, their gaze lifted every so often to consider Amy then me. Amy, crying now, disappears into the bathroom. The young waitress takes our plates. The older one brings a slice of cherry pie. I think of our $19.85 and say there must be a mistake. The waitress smiles. "No mistake, kid."

Amy returns, lays our money on the table. On the way out, I thank the older waitress. "God speed," she says.

A drive-through ATM, and Amy fishes a card from her purse. "My emergency stash. A secret. Don't tell your mom." She takes out three hundred, two of which she hands to me. The twenties crisp.

"You sure?" I ask.

We pull into the street. "You're going to need something."

Later, as Amy packs, she tells the story of the woman who first shot her up. A coworker. A warehouse, the finches that nested in the girders. An icebox in winter. The woman's tightrope days, the straight world and the life, then her fall. Jail. Her kids taken. A woman now three years clean. Who just this summer reached out and told Amy she'd be there if she ever wanted to quit. Amy zips her bag, pauses, and asks again, "I can do this, right?"

"You've done it before," I say.

"Yeah, but I was stronger then. I had a reason."

"You have a reason now."

She picks up a onesie. "It's hard." The room hot, but she still shivers. "I know it'll be hard."

On the porch, she hugs me. Her face wet against mine. Her

breath's curl in my ear. An embrace like she's afraid she's going to fall. "You make that money last, OK? I'll be back as soon as I can."

She drives off, and in me, a drowning I hadn't expected. Open fields beneath an open sky. My house of empty rooms.

* * *

I check my phone on the way up the lane. My steps slow. Images from a mountain village. Burned houses. Bodies in a ditch, old men and women and children. The government blaming the enemy, but then a different story. A shaky video taken from a cell phone. US troops, Marines in woodland camouflage. The blur of chaos and savagery. Images uploaded even as the person recording is approached by soldiers, their rifles aimed. The camera falls, a picture of the sky and trees, of men who loom like giants. Then darkness.

I knock on the old man's door, but when he invites me in, I say no, figuring it's not right stepping into a man's house when I've come for a favor. I speak, walking the line between the truth and not betraying my people. I tell him Amy's been gone these past three days, my mom too, although not together. I tell him each is navigating their own troubles. Tell him I'm holding things in place until they get themselves together.

A breeze, and on it, the scent of turned soil. The sky blue, the clouds like leaves in a lazy stream. "You have enough to eat?"

"I do. Thanks."

"You mixed up in what they're mixed up in?"

"No. Not in a first-hand way at least."

The door still open, his hand on the knob. "Do you know how I went blind?"

"No, sir."

"Wasn't some explosion or accident. I went blind the way most people go crazy. A little at a time. At first I cursed it. Then I set about taking everything in one last time, and I didn't have time to be angry." He rests a hand over his chest. "I stood out here a lot. I still see it."

"Sorry that happened. Your eyes and everything."

"Yep." He nods. "Yep." He turns toward our house. "That girl wouldn't have landed out here if she wasn't having her troubles."

I'm guessing he thinks the same thing about me, but he doesn't say it. "She's a good person though."

"Yep. I believe she is. Sometimes our compasses fail us. Sometimes the monsters win."

I think on this. "I guess they do. Yes, sir."

"We'll work out the rent after things settle."

"Thank you." A crow perched atop the barn caws. Another answers. "I'm willing to do work. Anything you need."

"You've done work before this without asking for anything." He reaches out. I step forward so his hand can rest on my shoulder. He gives a squeeze. His palm callused, a lifetime of labor. "You're a good man."

"Thank you."

"How about you read to me? A little bit a couple times a week?"

"I can do that."

"The Gospels. You know what the Gospels are?"

"The Bible, I guess. Right?" I hope this isn't a stupid answer.

"Not the whole thing. Wouldn't ask you to do that."

"OK." I imagine the Bible language I've heard. The thou shalls and shants and whatnot. "I'm not the church-going type, though."

"Me neither. Not anymore at least." The crow atop the barn swoops into the yard and pecks the grass, and I wonder if the old man paused because he heard the flap of its wings. He smiles. "But I'm thinking I owe it another listen."

* * *

Amy returns ten days later. Sunken cheeks. A pale silence. A Wednesday night arrival, and I don't go to school Thursday or Friday, and with the weekend, I have four days to bring her tea and toast, to drive her along country roads, the windows down, the rush of air taking the place of conversation. By Sunday, her hands tremble less. The color comes back to her face. Her silences remain.

I return to school on Monday. Amy still sleeping when I ease the door shut. The nights I spend listening to her pacing, to the push of water through thin pipes as she fills the tub she'll soak in for hours. I listen for the tears that once came so easily, but I hear none.

I pedal down quiet roads. A sunlit fog burns from the fields. An autumn haze, the nights cooler, evening's swift fade. I pick up speed. A cinched sack over my shoulders, my gym clothes. A class I may or may not have today, another kind of haze, my inability to recall where I am on the school's six-day cycle. Tall weeds in the ditches, and along the roadside, run-over ground-hogs, some more foul than others. A shadow falls over me. A low-gliding hawk, our paths, for a moment, shared before the bird disappears into the sun.

I reach school. A wave from Mr. Ford at his bus-duty post, his silver coffee cup and ID lanyard. A near collision with a car of red-eyed stoners. Around the flagpole, a hand-holding circle, heads bowed in prayer. A stop at my locker to scribble an excuse, a forging I've been perfecting since middle school. A lie to begin the day, and after that, an absorption into the flow. Homeroom, and after the pledge, the piped-in cable TV feed, teen reporters and product placement, and on most days, no one watches, but today it's quiet. More news about the massacre. The faces blurred but not the blood-soaked clothing, not the ditch's tangle of arms and legs. The rebels chased through the jungle. Villages raided across the Columbian border. Protests in Houston and Los Angeles. The resurrection of the peace sign, crowds dispersed with tear gas and rubber bullets.

The day unfolds. Science. Government. Shop. Each with their dramas and laughs and boredoms. Between periods, I consider the passing faces, and I think of a thousand front doors in the Patch and along maple-lined streets. Farmhouses and trailers. Here, in the gathering of its children, waits this town's truest mirror. Each of us an echo of an echo of an echo. The world pressing down in a hundred ways, and inside, a pushback just as strong. Desire, confusion, dreams. Sometimes, when the hallways are choked and loud and buzzing, it feels like a miracle that the whole place doesn't explode into matchwood.

Last period, and Mr. Ford wins a small victory when he gets my class's knuckleheads to concede all poetry doesn't suck. There's the Monday vibe. The weekend already distant. The weariness of the days ahead. Sally Jessup pecks away at the phone cradled in her lap. Billy Phillips's cigarette stink after he returns from the lav. Mr. Ford's markers squeak across the whiteboard, multicolor diagrams of stressed syllables. His lecture punctuated by repeated wakings of Sammy Gallagher, his invitations to Lucas Smith to get out a pencil and paper and at least pretend to be a contributing member of the class. I raise my hand when no one else will or when Mr. Ford stares at us, an expression like he's wishing he hadn't left the Army. And when I feel the call, I gaze out the window. The football and soccer fields. The smokestacks that haven't smoked for a generation. The wide sky. The spine of distant hills.

Class ends. The day's final bell, the hallway commotion. Mr. Ford asks me to stay for a moment. We talk about my bike, the new tape I've applied to the handlebars. He asks if I want to come from study hall tomorrow to make up my missed work. A poem to analyze, a paragraph to write. We both know I'm coasting, my work absent of the red slashes I see on other papers, the year early, but we've already forged this understanding. Another understanding—Mr. Ford came up hard. He's never said as much, but I can see it in the way he lets the mean-nothing words of angry boys go, in the way he doesn't flinch when he steps between hallway fist-fighters. He points to my bag. "Your gym stuff?"

"Thought I might have had PE today. Lost track of the cycle."

He zips up his workout bag. "Put them on and do our warmup jog with us. I'll call us even for the work you've missed."

I've run—but never more than I had to. Run from cops and store clerks. Run from men blinded by rage and dope. I wonder how different running is than riding a bike. The mechanics, of course. But perhaps they're related in ways I haven't considered. Each with their moments of removal. The sensation of being both still yet in motion. The macadam a passing river.

I'm about to say no thanks when there's a knock at the door. Kate Evans peeks inside. In elementary school, we sometimes found ourselves sitting near each other, the patterns of aisles and alphabetical order. In fifth grade we were even an item for a week. Exchanged notes. A playground peck on the cheek. Our interactions less now. Her college-prep schedule. My absences. Still, we always exchange hallway hellos, hers always with a smile that makes me feel a little less invisible. She's wearing shorts, a tank top. Her long hair pulled back. She smiles. "Hey, Mark."

"Hey, Kate."

"Coach, Aubrey's talking to Mr. Dietz about making up a lab. She said she'll meet us after warm ups."

"Thanks, Kate."

A wave on her way out the door. "See you, Mark."

I wave back, and when she's gone, I turn to Mr. Ford. "Exactly how far is a warm-up run?"

Outside, and alongside the track, I stake a place at the team's periphery. The others stretch, standing, sitting. A nod from Mr. Ford. I mimic the team's moves and fight the pull of staring at Kate's shorts.

The football team marches by. Jostling pads. The scrape of cleats. Soccer on another field. The field hockey team's smack of wood and hard rubber. My experiences with organized sports limited to one disastrous season of Little League. An old glove borrowed from one of my coaches. Practices my mother was too high to get me to, my uniform always dirty. My season cut short on a June morning when Double D got into a shoving match with an umpire. The police called and the game delayed.

Double D wired, days removed from sleep, his shirt ripped off, shouts of "You want to go? You want to go?" His threats snuffed by a taser to a chest choked with cheap tattoos. I snuck off as the cops wrangled him into their cruiser. A long walk back to the Patch and my borrowed glove left on the bench. Kate holds a hamstring stretch, and in me, an imposter's anxiety and the wishing I was on my bike far from here. This intrusion into the school day's second act.

Mr. Ford calls everyone in. He speaks, and I keep my distance. When the huddle breaks, the greyhound boys break away. The others follow, Kate and a few friends in the pack's middle.

"Ready?" Mr. Ford asks.

"I think."

"Let me know if you need to take a break." I know he's taking a chance. My lack of a sports physical, the possibility of a heart attack or car accident or busted ankle. We set off, a slow pace. Ahead, the pack's tail, the undersized freshmen, the seniors more interested in padding their college resumes than making varsity.

We jog in the streets, on the sidewalks. The nicer neighborhoods. The shade of old trees. Around us, the first falling leaves and Halloween decorations. Mr. Ford talks about his kids' costumes and the cafeteria's surprisingly good tacos. About the Farmer's Almanac and caterpillar rings and how much snow we'll get this winter. He asks about the recruiters he's seen me talking to at lunch, then tells me about his own Army stint. The places he's seen. The times he was scared. The things he learned about the world and himself. He smiles, a confession he needed a kick in the ass to get his teenage head straight. I ask about the current troubles, and his smile fades. "I don't know what to think," he says.

I lose track of our turns. Neighborhoods familiar in a

dreamy way. Every so often, I'm granted enough of a straight-away to spot Kate's swaying ponytail. I pull up the rear with Mr. Ford—or perhaps he's just slowing for me. His stride's rhythmic hitch, age perhaps, an injury. His brow glistens, and on hills, he talks less. We turn a corner, and the school comes into sight. Whatever discomfort I feel is set off by the push of blood. The swell of my lungs.

We reach the track. Kate pauses in her stretching and offers a golfer's clap as I pass. The greyhounds stay limber by the start line, ready for what's next.

We stop, and Mr. Ford clasps his hands behind his neck. "Nicely done."

"So I'm good for those assignments?"

"What's a man without his word?"

Our shadows fall over the track's painted lines. "That was a long mile."

"That's because it was two. Two and a half." He walks backwards toward the start line where Kate has joined the others. "Now you've got what, another five or so to bike home?"

"About that."

"Safe travels then. Anytime you want to join us." He gestures, a sweep of his hand, like I was a prince or a king. He turns, jogs to the others. "All right, everyone. First five on the line."

* * *

I'm sore Tuesday, and Kate mimics my gimp on our after-lunch walk to the science wing. On Wednesday the Marine recruiter buys me a milkshake and tells me about the bone-rattle of a .50 cal. On Thursday Tommy Dooley nods out in driver's ed, and his little brother does the same in Spanish, both of them taken to the ER and arrested upon release. On Friday morning, Amy steps onto the porch as I pump up my front tire. Sweatpants, her hair mussed. Steam from her coffee mug on this almost-cool morning. She looks like she's been chewed up and spit from a clanking machine. And she also looks like—herself. Just a little, but more than I've seen in weeks. I slow at the old man's house then turn back.

"Forget something?"

"Nope." I rest the bike against the porch.

"Tire OK?"

"I think, yeah."

72

"I can drive you if you'd like. I need to go into town anyway."

"I'll go with you. Into town. But I don't think I'll do school today."

"You sure?"

"I've put in a good week. I'll call it while I'm ahead."

She blows into her cup. "School wasn't my thing, either." She sips. "But you're a smart kid."

"You've said that."

"Well now that I'm straight, I'm saying it again."

"What do you need in town?"

The sun lifts higher, haze and shadows and golden light. "Pretty, isn't it. Sometimes I don't notice."

I ask again what she needs in town.

"Nothing I need to get so much as say. An apology. At least if I want to be honest about everything."

The kitten climbs the door's screen. The kitten mews, its paws stubborn on the mesh. Amy pulls it off and rubs her nose against its black fur. Baby talk and a chainsaw purr. "What're we ever going to call you?"

Two hours later, I'm pushing a cart, and Amy smiles when I remind her this is the kitten's second supermarket trip. Earlier, I sat in the car for twenty minutes. Amy in an old friend's house, apologies for the things she'd done. Hugs on the porch. Eyes red from crying. The supermarket aisles quiet this morning. Shelf stockers. Piped-in music, songs I've heard on my mother's radio station. The seniors who block our way as they check expiration dates. An old lady stacks her cart with cans of chicken noodle soup, and I think back to Amy's slur as the rain patted in the fields. Her desire to believe in something. To rise above this world's hand-to-mouth.

Back home, and I unpack our haul. Amy sets down a saucer of milk. A stroke for the kitten's back, the red piston of its tongue. She sits on the floor, her knees hugged to her chest, and I think of the day ahead. Her weariness. This kitchen and its memories.

"How about I show you something?"

She wipes her eyes. "Somewhere far from here?"

"Not too far."

She stands, hands me her keys, says she doesn't feel like driving. We roll down the windows, and the hair that's escaped her bun lifts on the breeze. "Is there a girl?" she asks.

"I'm not taking you to see a girl."

"At school, I mean. One you like."

I think of Kate. How I'm careful to walk slow when I'm by her side, the feeling of carving our own space as the crowd rushes past. How there's not much I like better than hearing her laugh. "Maybe."

"You'll make a nice boyfriend. I've had enough bad ones to know."

I pull off and park along the tall grass. Ahead, a patch of scrub trees and a vine-woven fence. I lead the way up the over-grown path. The breeze stirs the grass. I pull back the fence's cut chain link. Amy goes ahead, crouching, and before I follow, a glance back. Our car half-lost in the wavering sea, and not another soul in sight.

Inside the fence, I lead the way. Ferns rub our legs, and I wave a stick to knock down the spider webs. The trees end, and the shade yields to the afternoon's hazed blue. The solid earth switched for the quarry's yawning mouth.

"I've heard of this place but never seen it." She approaches the edge, clutches my arm, then backs up. "How did you find it?"

"Was biking one day and saw the fence." I sit and Amy does the same. "Did a little exploring and found a way inside."

"I feel like I should sit at the edge and dangle my legs over, but I don't think I could."

"I wouldn't want to either."

"Hey!" she calls, and her echo calls back. I think of my mother and how her voice could fill this empty space, and I wonder if Amy is thinking the same. We sit long enough for our shadows to shift around us, for the clouds to parade across the blue. We say little, and I wonder if her thoughts are any different than mine. The questions of who we are and how we got here and what tomorrow might bring.

                                    * * *

I'm unlocking my bike when Andy pulls his sister's car to
the curb. Around us, the after-school exodus. The hotrod-
ders. The cashiers and dishwashers and broom-pushers
rushing to punch the clock. The car's passenger-side window
rolls down, a stereo's blare. "Hey, man," Andy says, "up for a
spin?"

   Derrick Waller considers me from the passenger seat.
Derrick and I aren't quite friends, but we breathe the same air.
Underachievers. The sons of troubled parents. But while I melt
into the background, Derrick carries his anger in his scowl and
scarred knuckles. He used to play linebacker, but he quit last
year. His benchings for late hits and cheap shots. A shoving
match with an assistant coach. Derrick outweighs me by a good
forty pounds. His body made thick by his hours in his garage
gym and, I suspect, by a muscle-head's juice.

   I think of my ride. The return to quiet rooms. Amy working
late, a second chance at one of her old jobs. "Sure."

                                    76

I slip the chain through the bike's frame. Derrick's voice at my back. "No one's stealing that piece of shit."

I secure the lock. "You getting me a new one if this one's jacked?"

He slides his seat forward as I climb in. "Could drive five minutes and steal you a dozen better bikes."

We pull from the curb. A nod for my backseat companion. Jason Tate, a hanger-on. A scarecrow as annoying as he is lost. A boy keen to chime in, to be noticed. A huffer's rash around his nose and mouth. I can envision futures for Andy and Derrick—but not Jason. For him, all I see is static, shifting winds. The fade of watercolors.

Andy merges into the lot's exiting flow. A horn honks, and Derrick sticks out his arm and offers his middle finger. Andy cranks the stereo. We gain speed, the wind rushing, and I think of Amy's seashells, and I wonder how different standing in front of the ocean would be than standing in the middle of the old man's alfalfa, the hypnotizing of a single color that stretches to the horizon. Derrick flicks a lighter, a new scent on the breeze, and when he passes the joint, it rains sparks and ash. Jason leans forward, desperate to engage Derrick or Andy, but, after getting little reaction, he settles back and drums his palms against his thighs. I take a hit then another. The smoke rises into my chest, then my head. The joint circulates until it's a glowing nub. Our ever-more intricate handoffs, the burn on my fingers and lips. I discover a wilted synchronicity. The mesh of music and motion, of scenery and unspoken thoughts. All of it flowing into a kind of movie, and I smile, thinking of a movie of my life and wondering how my days would look through a new pair of eyes.

The cantilever bridge. The river view, the old mill. Flickering shadows. The hum of metal plates. A crossing made for no good reason and soon we're crossing back. Andy talks about some killer skunk he's going to cop, and Jason beams and says, "Dig it! Dig it!" Trees and lawns give way to the Patch's concrete. We park outside a corner store, and Derrick goes in. Caged windows. A beer sign's sputtering neon. Andy keeps the car running. Looks from the opposite corner, the slingers and the hangers-on, a sizing up. Dangling sneakers on the telephone line. "Don't stare," I say to Jason.

Derrick returns empty handed. The car door slammed. "Fuck," he says. The clerk who serves him not working today, a woman demanding his ID in broken English. "Fucking foreigners," he says. He lights another joint, huffing until the smoke roils. I think about my bike ride home, and I'm happy he didn't get served. The heaviness of one high twisting into another. I close my eyes, enjoying the car's motion, and laugh over Jason's off-key mangling of a song's chorus. "Stop, stop," Derrick says, and I open my eyes.

Derrick gets out and steps between a barricade of sawhorses. A car parked along the curb, its bumper lined with peace stickers. On the sidewalk, remnants of a rowhome's demolished porch. Derrick picks up a brick and raises his hand. The brick clay-red, a color lost for a moment against the house's wall of brick before he smashes it into the parked car's back window.

"Holy shit, man! Holy shit!" Jason slaps Derrick's shoulder as we speed off. "What the fuck!" Another slap, a moment's squeeze. "That was fucking badass!"

"Damn, brother," Andy says. "What the fuck?"

Derrick relights the joint. "That's what Jason said."

"I know, right?" Jason shakes his head. "I mean what the actual fuck."

Andy checks his rearview. "You can't go around just looking for trouble, man."

"Fucking hippies, man." Derrick passes the joint back to Jason. "And fuck trouble."

I say nothing. I've seen enough trouble not to invite it into my life or to speak of it with disrespect. My fear of its voodoo. Its long, cold shadow. Andy calms, and by the time we've crossed the river, he's laughing too. The incident retold and relived. The smash of glass. The shock on our faces. The angry shouts as we sped away. Jason slaps Derrick's shoulder until Derrick tells him to cut it the fuck out.

I lean my forehead against the window. Town slides by, a parade of houses and stores and cars. I close my eyes. The movie of my life would suck. An empty wallet. An empty belly. The string of dumps I've called home. The callings of a hundred shitty fates.

"Mark?" Andy says.

I open my eyes. The car slows, stops. The school parking lot. My bike the last one chained to the rack. I get out. "Thanks, man." I stoop and look inside the car. "Later, all."

"Hey, man." Derrick flicks the lighter. The flame studied before he snuffs it. "I heard your old man and mine used to run together back in the day."

I imagine a car ride like this one. Echoes. Ghosts. "Small world, I guess."

Derrick nods. "Small fucking world."

The radio fades as Andy pulls away. I trade the car's motion for the bike's and feel better for it. I pass through the school's shadows, and as my reflection ripples across the windows, I feel the hushed heartbeat inside. The detention-sitters. The student-council do-gooders. The regrouping of frazzled teachers. The tide I'll rejoin tomorrow. The tide that will continue next year without me.

A gunshot. My front tire wavers, an unbalanced moment. I

coast, then stop and straddle my bike. A pack of girls round the track. Half in our school's red and white, half in royal blue. At the turn near me, the lead girls veer off the track. I hear their breathing, the clack of their spikes, and the thinning line makes its way toward the flags that mark the perimeter of the playing fields.

Kate in the pack's middle. The bounce of her ponytail. The focus that makes me doubt she hears me as I cheer her on.

* * *

Amy stuffs Grace's favorite things into her diaper bag. A fuzzy bear. A sand-filled rattle. A jellied teething ring pulled from the freezer. Amy shoos Kitten—for that, at least for now, is her name—from the bag then slings it over her shoulder. A sigh. A rub of her nose. "Ready?"

I'm coming because she's asked me. I'm coming to save her from silence. I'm coming to tell her not to cry. Or to tell her it's OK to cry. I'm coming because her attempt to do the right thing deserves a witness. On the ride, I listen again to the pep talk she's been giving herself these past three days. The accepting that Grace won't be coming home with us. Her desire to make amends, if only for her daughter's sake. The child's history already half-dark. The father she'll never know. The mother who's lived so long in the shadows.

"It was good, my coming up." A pasture outside my window. Cows behind an electric fence. "Not great sometimes. I was sensitive. They expected more. I could have given more, I

81

admit." She shrugs. "I was afraid a lot. Afraid of failing. Afraid of having to explain myself. But I kept it together. At least until I turned sixteen or so." Town comes into view, this stretch I love to bike. "You've got a good head on your shoulders, don't you?"

"Think you've said that before."

"And you've said *that* before."

I nod. "True."

We turn onto a side street. A man mows a lawn. In a long driveway, a girl on rollerblades, a purple helmet and purple kneepads. "Sometimes I wonder if I know what being happy really is."

"You always seemed happy. For the most part."

"Happiness can be an act, too. It's easier getting by if everyone thinks you're happy."

"That makes sense."

"I didn't think about it much before, the acting part. But things are clearer now. Not easier but clearer. At least a bit."

"That makes sense too."

She manages a smile. "Look at me, making all this sense."

We park in the playground lot. Kids on swings. Chases across tanbark. Amy's parents set off from the others. A picnic bench in an oak tree's shade. I offer to wait in the car, to take a walk, but Amy says no. Grace will be happy to see me, she says, and we cross the field together. The grass short and brown, and I try to think of the last time it rained, and I'm sure I'm wrong, but the only rainy night that comes to mind is the night I kissed Amy, and if that's only remembered by one of us, then it's no more real than a dream.

The hugs Amy exchanges with her parents are brief and polite. Her father acknowledges me with a nod, her mother not at all, and I wonder if they see my mother's face in mine. I claim the table's far end. On a nearby field, a soccer game, kids so small their jerseys hang to their knees. The shouts of parents. A kicking swarm. Amy sits across from her mother, snuggling Grace, their cheeks pressed together. Amy's all smiles, and the reunion-tears I'd expected from her make their way into my eyes. Amy pulls back, cooing, and Grace grabs her mother's nose. A breeze, and the oak's branches sway. On our faces, tides of shadow and light. Amy clutches Grace to her chest, her eyes closed, this stone-sober ecstasy. Her parents with their store-manager stares that let me know we're touching the wrong things and the police are only a phone call away.

Grace sits on her mother's lap and digs into the diaper bag, and in my thoughts, all the times I've seen Amy reach into the same bag for her works. Amy holds Grace's hand, her little fingers splayed as she assures her parents that she's OK. That she's getting stronger day by day. Her hushed resolve. The acknowledgment of her failings. The acceptance that her road will be hard. The belief in this chance to turn things around, a gift she won't take for granted. Before, she says, there was a darkness at the center of her life (and in me, the wondering if I am part of that darkness) but now there's a light. She kisses Grace's forehead. A bright, beautiful light.

She asks how Grace is sleeping. Asks what kind of formula they're using. She talks about work and how, in a few months, she'll be in line for a raise and better hours, maybe even a promotion. She says she's thinking about moving back into town and then it'll be easier for her and Grace to visit. Maybe she'll even go back to school. "I want her to be closer to you both." Amy brushes her hair behind her ear. "I want her to have that. To have you both in her life." A kiss for Grace's forehead. "And I want you to have it, too. I want us all to have it." Hidden in the oak, a chirping bird, its song upon the fragmented sunlight. "And I was hoping to bring her home with me. Just for the night."

Her mother glances to her husband, and I understand bad news is coming, that there are secrets and greater forces aligned against us. Amy still smiling, blind to the headlights bearing down upon her. Her mother opens her mouth, but it's her father who speaks.

"We took her to a doctor. There were drugs in her system." His voice quivers. "Drugs, Amy. From you." He closes his eyes, composes himself. "Goddamn drugs. In a sweet, innocent baby."

Amy's smile wilts, and in her body, a greater wilt that allows her mother to stand and lift the baby from her lap. "We went to a judge and got temporary custody."

The bird chirps, the play of shadows. Amy's voice all but lost. "What does that mean?"

"It means she'll be with your mother and me until you're better."

"I am better." Her lips tremble. "I'm getting better."

Her mother: "You abandoned her. You left town without—"

"You took her," I say. In me, the rise of my mother's blood. "She didn't abandon her."

Her father's eyes narrow, and he dismisses me as he would a buzzing fly. "I don't even know what you're doing here. And what matters is—" he turns to Amy "—what matters is that you disappeared. Not a word. Not a trace. You could have been dead for all we knew. We were out of our minds. It took three days to find out you were holed up in some trailer in the middle of nowh—"

"How did you know that?" Amy looks at me then back to him. Grace chomps her teething ring. "How could you know that?"

"We hired someone to—"

"To fucking spy on me?"

"To protect our granddaughter."

84

"I went to get clean. I'm clean now. I haven't—"

Her father stands. "Your baby wasn't clean when she came to us." He closes his eyes, takes a breath. "You're always welcome back with us. All of us together until you're well. And first we'll get you through a real program. One with doctors and counselors, not some trailer-park midwife."

"You can't just come and . . ." Amy sputters, a search for words I know will mean nothing, " . . . dictate all this bullshit about my life." She jabs a finger into her chest. "My fucking life."

Her mother, Grace on her hip, gathers her things. "A scene isn't going to make things better." She shoulders her bag. "We're happy you're on the right path. We just want to help you move forward in the best way. We'll make a regular schedule for your visits. We want to help you, baby. We really do."

I feel a pull in them, the wanting to go to their daughter, to hold her as they once did. To kiss where it hurts and make everything right. But growing up steals that kind of healing, a truth written in Amy's ashen face as her parents turn their backs and walk from the oak's shade and into the field's bright sun.

* * *

A section of twine I strung in the old man's house snaps. He sits, his cane between his knees. His daughter by earlier, the dropping off of groceries, and on the table, the newspaper she read to him. Headlines from the war. An investigation into the village massacre. A picture of a captured US soldier, beaten and bruised, a gun to his head as he read his captors' statement.

"I hear better. Without the eyes." His cane taps, the rubber-on-wood a period to his sentence. "Guess that's not true, but I hear different. Hear the person beneath the words. I can tell when someone's speaking from the gut." He smiles, a blind, crooked smile. "Or out of their ass."

The wind whistles beneath the eaves. Green ripples across the field. I secure the twine, a double knot on top of a double knot. I ask the old man if he ever gets lonely out here—I'm about to ask something else, but I catch myself, thinking of what he said about voices, how he can hear the truth beneath.

86

"Sometimes." He stands. The cane taps ahead of his steps. He stops in the threshold between the living room and kitchen. "But the dark has a way of preserving things." His back to me, he reaches toward the kitchen. "I can see them, my wife and son. Her canning jars. His muddy shoes. And I can see my girl at the table with all her school books spread out." He turns back to the living room. "And I can see myself right here, holding her, no bigger than a bag of sugar."

His wife. His son and daughter. This house of shadows. I wonder how I'll remember the old man, how I'll remember this time and place. I tie my last knot, and the old man takes a lap, his callused fingers on the twine. He nods, says thank you. We shake and say goodbye. He doesn't ask about the rent, only if I have what I need.

I kick a stone down the lane. The wind sounds different here than in town. The open-throated push, the empty miles. Above, the churning clouds, a restlessness mirrored in my gut. Amy's car gone, her return not due until long after dark. A closing shift. The minimum-wage gig she clutches like a raft in a raging sea.

I pause on our porch. The wind, a swirl of dirt and leaves. The old man passes before a window. What I'd started to ask him wasn't if he ever got lonely but if he was ever afraid. Afraid of the openness of it all. The locomotive wind. Winter's drifts. The nights deeper than any I'd imagined in town. Afraid of a beautiful day's spreading sky and the feeling like all this emptiness might consume him.

Inside, and I gather the scraps I'll call dinner. Oatmeal. An egg. The cheese I eat only after trimming off the mold. A gust and the windows rattle. I think of my mother, and in the soft moment where others might pray, I imagine her unharmed, alive—the simplest of miracles. And in the house's silence, I smile as I hear the only bit of repeated advice she's ever offered—that this life is unfair only when it's not busy being cruel.

Night comes. I eat and wait. I'm beat, but I keep myself awake. I want to be here for Amy when she gets home. Want to hear her voice, even if she's bone-tired. I want to make her a cup of tea, the promise of her smile and *thank you* all I need to keep myself from being swallowed by the wind and dark.

The hallway's shuffle, the after-lunch lull. The day's frayed vibe. Kate by my side. The things I say to coax her smile. Our shoulders sometimes touching. We talk about her season, yesterday's meet, her place in the pack. A ping and she checks her phone.

"Anything important?"

"Coach. Says we should all go home and run on our own." She pockets her phone. "Says he has to take his kids to the doctor." She adjusts her backpack. "I'll bet he's a good dad."

"Yeah." Around us, the slam of lockers. The muffled blare of headphones. "So you'll run later?"

"Think I'll go after school. Just a short one. Sometimes I need to clear my head after a day in here, you know?"

"I can understand that."

She smiles. "You saying you want to join me?"

. . .

CURTIS SMITH

Later, I wait by the track. My back to the football team as they count out jumping jacks. Kate emerges from the gym doors, a wave, a slow jog as she ties her hair into a ponytail. I hope my gym clothes don't smell. Hope I can survive a few miles without embarrassing myself. Hope I won't be struck dumb by our release from the familiar, this greater world where I fear our commonalities will fade.

She grabs her foot, stretches one quad then another. "The course yesterday was hilly." She crosses her right foot over the left, her legs together. When she bends forward, her hair hangs down, and on her neck, the raised buttons of her spine. She rights herself, a moment's flush on her cheeks. "I was thinking about the little engine that could. I kept saying to myself 'I think I can, I think I can.'"

"I'll remember that for when I get winded."

She punches my arm. "I know you can. I know you can."

We set off. A steady pace, the kind I jogged alongside Mr. Ford. Then quicker. She possesses a grace I do not. A lightness on her feet. I plod by her side, trying to soften my sneakers' thump. We talk about nursing. The schools she's looking at. The kinds of nurses, so many I'd never considered.

"How about you? What's next after all this?"

"The Army, I guess. Maybe the Marines." We pass the park, and I think of Amy and our silent ride home, the open diaper bag between my sneakers. "Sometimes I'm not sure. I can't totally picture it, you know? Not enough at least to see myself clearly."

"What can you see?"

I time my words between inhales. "I can see myself staying here in town."

"Then why don't you stay?"

I grin. "Didn't say it was a good picture." We turn. This street I ride every day. The tall trees. A tunnel of green. The

90

shadows below and the feeling of being a fish in a gray stream. A sprinkler on a wide lawn. Flags hanging from porches. The Patch might as well be a thousand miles away. "How long have you been running?"

"Ninth grade. I was last in every race."

"That's hard to believe."

"Believe it. It's taken a lot of work to rise from terrible to mediocre."

"You didn't mind that? Finishing last?"

"Hated it. That's why I kept going."

"And you never wanted to stop?"

"I did. But I can be stubborn. And I didn't know what I'd do in its place. And truth was I liked being out. It was good for me. My head and everything."

I imagine the ninth-grade her. A girl I passed in crowded hallways. Each of us with our secrets. Our struggling mothers. The mythologies of our fathers. My heart drums. Our shadows across the macadam, and I try again to imagine myself into a world different than the only one I've known.

* * *

F riday afternoon. Thick clouds and a spitting mist. The school day's drag. Short tempers and bad blood. A fight at lunch, another at the bus corral. My exit made past siren-wailing cruisers.

I pedal past town's last homes. The mist builds into a drizzle. The macadam slick, and the water lifts the oil, swirls of blue, dull rainbows. A pickup barrels by, and I squint against its spray. I think about Kate and how it would feel to kiss her, but I can't put a frame around my daydream. My lack of a car and the miles to town. The feelings I struggle to put into words. Still, I think of it, and if the background is blurry, I can still imagine it in the most important of ways.

On the long incline, I rise from my seat and churn the pedals. A haze over the just-cut fields. The upturned dirt and the cold months ahead. Today's ride harder. The week's weariness. The slick road and the slip of my wheels. I reach the crest and return to my seat. The horizon opens. The stretching fields.

The hills vague and distant. A smothering sky. I think of my mother somewhere beneath the same sky, lost in the mist and rain, and I can't tell whether this thought makes her feel near or far.

I turn onto our lane. My hair matted. My T-shirt a second skin and the chill in my bones. I stand on my pedals and coast. The gravel's vibrations in my arms. I pass the farmhouse. The old man at the kitchen sink, a lift of his sightless gaze. The rain beads on Amy's car. I'm glad she's not working until later. Glad not to return to silence, to have a voice that will call my name. I carry my bike up the porch steps and set it out of the rain. Nine months I've been here. This place as much a home as any I've known. I think of Kate and our stretching shadows and our talk of future lives.

The lights off inside, dishes in the sink. I'm quiet, the knowing that Amy likes to nap before her shift. I peel off my wet shirt. A moment of blindness before I pause at the living room's threshold.

A single candle burns atop the cluttered coffee table, a flame barely alive. She's on the couch. Slumped forward, her head between her knees. Her pale hand dangles beside her foot, and in her curled fingers, her belt. Kitten leaps from the couch's top onto her back. Its claws kneading Amy's shoulders as it accuses me with its hungry mews.

* * *

The road to town. The sky heavy. The barometer's push in my ears. A charge on my skin, this world of invisible forces, and I pedal faster. The road still dry, but once the rain comes, the creeks and lowlands will flood. Ahead, a dead groundhog, and as I pass, the stir of flies. I wear my only button-down shirt. A gift from my aunt. A pinch in the shoulder. The cuffs that no longer reach my wrists. The shirt worn, its tags uncut, to my secret baptism. Then on school picture day. And again today. My first return to a church since the day a preacher dropped his water onto my head, and I brace myself to stand again before God.

The streets made familiar on school mornings different today. The Saturday cough of lawn mowers hurrying to beat the rain. An old woman tends to a flowerbed's last blooms. A straw hat, a trowel and gloves and dirt-caked knees. A long roll of thunder, and she turns her face to the sky. My ride's last block. The church ahead. A sloping lawn. A drive flanked by

94

lollipop trees. Red brick and a steeple that glows against the gray.

Tall columns support the entrance's overhang. At the entrance's steps, a black hearse. The viewing earlier this morning, but it wasn't my place to attend. I prop my bike beneath a stained-glass window. The panes at the window's bottom opened, and from them, an organ's somber notes. Part of me wants to hop on my bike, and if I pedal as hard as I can, I could return home before the first drops fall. But that's not the person I'm trying to be. I know my presence means nothing, but I want to be seen. Want to be counted. I want my face to attest that Amy's life, no matter how lost and sad, mattered.

Inside, a man in a black suit nods a greeting. The organ clearer in the vestibule, and in the thick air, the scent of flowers. I tuck in my shirt and wish again I owned something beyond jeans. The man in the black suit hands me what I at first believe is a bookmark. Amy's name and a set of dates on one side. On the other, a prayer. *Don't grieve for me, for now I'm free.* I pause on the threshold, and no one turns as I step down the side aisle and slide into an empty row. The Reverend rises into the pulpit. A black robe, sleeves that bunch around his clasped hands, and before I can sit, he lifts his arms, and the congregation stands. A prayer, the words, it seems, known by all but me. I lower my head and join the others with my *amen.*

We sit. To my right, another scene in stained glass. Shepherds and their flock, an angel among the stars. The Reverend speaks. I listen then don't. His voice a creek's purr, and only a few words rise above the flow. *Lost. Love. Pain. Love. Forever.* Then the cooing, a murmur of disjointed syllables, and I inch to my left, a new line of sight in this forest of black, until I see Grace. She's in her grandmother's arms. The only face looking away from the preacher and the polished wood box. I imagine what she sees. This place with its music and echoes. The faces that search hers for the same reason I do. The wonderment of her innocence, and the knowing of the heartbreak that waits. All of us thinking both of her and our own pain. All of us reflected in her eyes.

My drift crumbles when I spot him. The other side of the center aisle. A pew as empty as mine. The two of us outcasts among the righteous. He wears a flea-market sportscoat and the same paint-spattered boots that were ready to kick in my door. A gust, a whistle through the opened windows, and the altar candles shudder. Chief leans forward, elbows on his knees. His hands clasped. His ponytail snakes down his back. He closes his eyes, and his hands shake. I inch closer to the aisle, trying to remember if the vestibule has a side door. The angel and shepherds look down upon me. All of us frozen, but unlike them, I'm offered no good news, no deliverance. Chief sits back then looks my way. He stares, the fog pushed back then recognition. His mouth draws tight, then a nod, and there's something conspiratorial in the gesture. The two of us in this together.

Up front, the Reverend competes with the wind's shush and Grace's lilting babble. I picture her new life. More clothes. More attention. A house with a stocked refrigerator and clean floors. A yard and a fence. Also hers—an emptiness deeper than any quarry. I fold my hands, and even though I'm not the praying kind, I pray for her to be raised on the kindness of lies. To long for her mother but never know her truth. The Reverend's hands lift, an imploring of heaven, his robe's black wings. The organ stirs and the choir joins and then the congregation. Some mimic the preacher, their hands raised, beseeching God to rescue them from these raging waters. I step into the aisle and back away. My desire to see Grace less powerful than the shame of encountering her grandparents. Their church manners holding their tongues. The gaze that's bound to shackle me to the sin of my history and birth. Chief's eyes close again. I look back as I make my exit. The voices soar. A call to a life beyond this one.

The first drops fall. The drops weighty, a sting on my neck. The singing stops but the organ sighs on. I'm pulling out my bike when Chief appears. He's also making an early exit, our kind's awkwardness in the straight world, the shaking of hands and wearing of ties and knowing the right things to say. He pauses on the sidewalk. "Hey."

I stand behind the bike. A barrier. An object I could throw in his path if I need to run. And if he catches me, I'll scream until the black suits come rushing out. This place different than the Patch where nobody blinks unless there's blood and some-times not even then. But there's no grabbing, no raised voice. Just a staked distance Chief seems as keen to observe as me.

"I heard you found her."

I say nothing.

He sucks in his lip, nods. "She was a good kid."

I remember that night in the diaper aisle. How he snatched her arm then mine. My handlebar grip tightens. The wind blows, and I brush the hair from my eyes.

"Thought your mother might be here."

He's not accusing or threatening so much as observing. In his eyes, a clarity I didn't see beneath Kmart's queasy fluores-cents. "What do you want?"

Bells ring, and when I look up, I have to blink back the rain. The steeple's slender white. The swirl of wind-blown leaves. The bells toll another song I don't know, and the notes resonate in the hollow spaces of my gut. The others begin to leave. Some hurry-stepping. Others huddled under shared umbrellas.

"Give you a ride if you want," Chief says.

"Last time you came to my house you said you were going to kick the shit out of me."

"Yeah. Well, I'm sorry about that. That was fucked up, but

that's not where my head is at today." He looks over my shoulder. "Anyway, you said you were going to shoot me."

"I did."

"Thanks for not doing that." The drive's maples bow in the wind. One of the mourners drops their umbrella, and it tumbles across the lawn. "I've got to get back to work, but I can give you a lift. It'll be a long ride in the rain."

He walks off, and I follow, my bike pushed. We stop at his pickup. He takes the bike and lifts it into the bed. He climbs into the cab, and after a moment, I join him.

I pick up a thermos from the floor, and as I hold it, I imagine how I could smash it into his skull if the need arose. There's the stink of cigarettes, but outside the thermos, gone is the clutter of my mother's and Amy's cars. He turns the key, and on the chain, a small, silver skull with red-stone eyes. Just a click at first. The second time a grind, his boot pumping the gas before the engine catches. We pull out, but Chief pauses. The engine's rough idle and the blur of rain-streaked glass—and beyond, at the church's entrance, the slow descent of pallbearers and the casket that will take Amy into the ground.

We drive off, saying nothing. I breathe easier with each block, the distancing of myself from the church and the coffin and a baby left behind. A stop light, and without motion, the truck's rattle deepens. The wipers slap. The cab's echo of rain.

To our left, a supermarket. A woman holding her purse over her head. "You need anything in town?" Chief asks.

"No." The light changes. "Thanks."

Our tires spin then catch. The rain comes harder. "How's school?"

"It's OK."

"What year you in?"

We pass the town's last homes. The wind hits us. "Senior."

"Didn't make it through my senior year. Big mistake." He

nods, bites his lip. "I'm sorry about that night." He regrips the wheel. His knuckles, for a moment, pale. "I woke up the next morning in a field out here. Had to get some farm kid to tow me out. Fucking embarrassing, man. Could just as easily wrapped myself around a tree." Another grip of the wheel. A sigh. "Haven't had a drop since."

I think of Amy. Her shakes. The eyes focused on nothing. The smile that reminded me of the cracks in our plates. "That's good, I guess."

We turn onto the farmhouse lane. The wipers can't keep up, the illusion of a melting world. He parks by the porch. He tells me to make a run for the overhang. He wrangles the bike, his hair soaked by the time he carries it onto the porch. The barn's weather vane twists and creaks. The rain in wind-pushed sheets. The gutters overflow, and from the fields, the drum of puddling water.

"Shit," he says.

I lean the bike against the house. I think of myself on the door's other side, gun in hand, and this life's thin margins.

He nods to the car beside his truck. "That your mother's?"

"Amy's. I'm guessing her people will come get it when they're ready."

"I'm sure." He wipes the wetness from his face. "So your mother's not around?"

"She will be. Later. Soon. She's working."

"OK then." He nods, looks me up and down. "Listen, you up for making a little money? Just took on a new job, starts the Monday after next. Could use some help."

"What kind of job?"

"Stripping wallpaper. Painting. Know anything about that?"

"Not much."

"Ain't like it's hard. At least if you're willing to work. Pay you ten an hour. Under the table. I'll make it twelve in a couple weeks if things turn out right."

"I don't have a car."

"I'll pick you up after school. We'll work until seven or so. I'll give you a ride back."

I think about the kitchen's bare shelves and the few dollars I have left. "OK."

"Monday after next then. I'll pick you up outside school. The main entrance." He opens his wallet and hands me a wrinkled twenty. "To hold you over until then."

"You don't need to—"

"Call it a retainer. Or whatever."

I take it. "Thanks."

His boots clomp down the stairs. A dash to the truck. The door slammed. The engine's cough. The sky full of rain and thunder.

*　*　*

I wash my hands at the old man's sink. The old man at the kitchen table. His familiar pose. The cane between his legs. Hands folded atop the curved grip. I rub my palms against my jeans, a final bit of drying, then open the Bible waiting on the table. We started with Matthew, which I read from beginning to end. Then Mark. Since, we've bounced around. The Psalms. Paul's letters. Other passages he's pulled from the well of years. Romans 3:23. Philippians 4:13. Requests that remind me of a Bingo caller. The Bible's cover of worn leather. The first page an inked list. Names and dates. Births and deaths. The old man's name too. *Earl* 1934—. The entries end in 1973, the year, the old man says, of his mother's death. I think of Amy and the set of dates on her prayer card. I think of breaking the news to the old man after the ambulance and police left. First him crying, then me.

He once asked me to read the penned names, and after each, he nodded, and I wondered if the ones without a second date were dead or alive. He said it was too late to go back now because the years have meshed into one another. He said the last time he opened the Bible on his own, he could work sunup to sundown, and perhaps his body's strength had fooled him into not keeping up with the word and the Lord. He didn't sin, but now he wonders if not cupping the light is its own kind of sin. And he says while years have passed without prayer, he's never stopped hearing his mother's voice. This spot, every night. This book, the only one he ever saw her read. The long-ago stories that were her rock.

I open to a random spot and let the pages fan. The edges worn soft, and perhaps somewhere in the shush, his mother's voice. When I'm done, I'll make us burgers. These past two days without meat, but the gnawing dims as I flip the pages. Here and there, passages I've already read. Words like stars in a dark sky. I've surprised myself by enjoying this task. My reading choppy sometimes. The names I can't pronounce. The lists of who begat whom. But beneath all that, a man—or whatever he is—I know in a new way. A questioner. A trouble maker. A man who stood up to the rich and powerful. Who looked the devil in the eye and walked through the valley of death.

He asks for Luke 14:3, and when I find it, I clear my throat. His grip tightens on the cane, and I think of Chief's pale knuckles on the pickup's wheel. Opposite the page, one of the book's black-and-white etchings. A bearded man, sandals and a robe, and carried upon his shoulders, a sheep, its hooves clutched as if he were adjusting a scarf. A caption beneath, **THE LOST SHEEP**.

I read: "And when he comes home, he calls together his friends and neighbors, saying to them 'Rejoice with me, for I have found my sheep that was lost.' Just so, I tell you, there will be more joy in heaven over one sinner who repents than over ninety-nine righteous men who need no repentance."

The old man reaches out, his fingers waving. "There's a picture, isn't there?"

"Yes, sir."

A smile. "I see it."

I consider the lamb's face, and like the old man, I too see what my eyes can not. The black and white lines rearranging into the Minotaur, and I drift back. A cold room and the fear lurking outside my door. A book I can't decipher and images that twist into my heart.

"That's enough for us to think on for today." The old man's cane taps the floor. "How about we eat?"

* * *

I rise from the kitchen table to watch the black car drive down the lane. The old man's house passed, and when the middle-aged woman in a blazer and black slacks gets out, I consider the usual suspects. A school counselor. A parole officer. A social worker. A cop.

I step onto the porch—my mother's rule of never letting anyone in without a warrant, and how many standoffs have I witnessed on stoops, in grimy hallways. The door cracked, slivered views, my mother's curses. The woman sees me and stops at the bottom of the steps. "Mark? Is that right?"

A breeze today, and on it, the smell of the fields. "It is."

"Is your mother home?"

"Who's asking?"

"My name is Darla. My father owns this place."

I've only seen her from a distance. Her hand upon his elbow, his cane tapping, the car door shut after he settles in. She takes him to his appointments, doctors and their sad drum-

104

beat. He's told me enough about her that I can see her as both a child and as the woman who stands before me. A bank manager. The vice president of the local business league. And he's told me about her urgings for him to come live with her and her family. Her worry about him living on his own.

My tone changes. "Sorry. I didn't realize who you were."

"Your mother?"

"She's not here right now."

She looks me over, and I peg her for the kind of woman too polite to call me a liar even though I know she's thinking it. "The woman who died here—you found her?"

"I did."

She nods. "I'm sorry about that." A pause. "I can't have any of that around my father. Drugs. The people they bring. I can't be worrying about that. I worry enough about him as is."

"I agree." I step aside and open the screen door. "Come and have a look. There's none of that here now."

She hesitates, then climbs the steps. I hold the door until she passes, and I'm glad I've just washed the dishes and wiped the counters. She circles the kitchen, and I tell her to open whatever she likes, which she does, cabinets and drawers, my breath held as she passes the drawer with the .38. Her tour continues, and I follow her through the living room, to the bedroom, which she looks into but doesn't enter. She's an envoy from the straight world, and in me, my mother's hard wiring, the instinct to retreat, to throw up the nearest barricade, but I know Darla's only here for her father, and I want to put her mind at ease.

In the kitchen, she grabs the back of a chair, her finger tapping. "My aunt lived here when I was a girl. Then a cousin. Always someone from the family. Coming. Going. Picking up the pieces." She looks up, and I hope she doesn't spot the cracked plaster, the bullet hole I've patched as best I can. "I used to daydream about this being my place, like a life-sized dollhouse."

I follow her to the porch, and she pauses. "I appreciate what you've done for my father. He talks about you." I hear him in her voice, his calm, his reason. "He says you've been reading him the Bible."

"I have."

She nods. "The sheriff's a friend. I've asked him to stop and check in when he's out this way."

"I understand."

She walks to her car. I stop at the porch's last step. "What's the Bible passage you've liked best?"

"Can't say, to be honest. They all make me think some."

"Mine is Matthew 7:15. The one about knowing a tree by the fruit it bears. Do you know that one?"

"Yes."

She opens her door. "If you care for him, you'll keep him safe."

"I do. I will."

She smiles. "Please do."

* * *

S moke escapes Andy's grin. A wisp, then a torrent when he coughs. He hands me the black pen, and I take another hit. A rise in my chest, and in my head, a gathering fog. I hand back the pen then tilt my bottle. The beer's last, warm swallows. Andy's stopped by to catch a buzz before his afternoon shift at the nursing home. He asks about Amy, how I found her, what the cops did. He stares at the couch's end, respectful, silent, and in the hush, I see her, too.

The living room a mess, but not a mess like my mother's. My piles strategic. A box for Amy's things, another for Grace. The closets cleaned out, the dresser drawers, all their loose ends gathered and brought here. "What's this?" Andy's sneakered toe nudges a box.

"Nothing." Andy's OK, but I worry about him getting too comfortable. I don't tell him about my mother—my fear if he learned the truth, he'd be out all the time. My fear of the people he'd bring, the ease with which things could get out of hand. I go to the kitchen. "Another beer?"

"Yep, yep." He joins me. The cap twisted and flicked into the trash. I sit on the counter while he circles the kitchen, talking all the while. The car he'd like to buy. The old lady at the nursing home who thinks he's her son. The girl in his math class he can't stop looking at. His hands fidget, a testing of knobs and handles, and I'm too lost in my haze to stop him before he opens the drawer with the .38.

"Fucking whoa, brother." He holds the revolver, the barrel pointed toward the living room.

"Whoa yourself, brother. It's loaded."

"As it should be. Never know what's going to go down out here in the wilderness." He sets it on the counter. "That's bad ass. Thing's got stopping power. You ever fired it?"

"Some." I think of midday's short shadows and a blazing sun. A cigarette dangling from my mother's mouth. "Not much though."

He pulls the ammo box from the drawer, gives it a shake. "How about it, cowboy?"

"One." I take the gun, check the cylinder then slap it back into place. "One each."

I set the pint bottle Chief tossed the night he threatened to kick in our door atop a cinder block. Behind the bottle, a stack of the old man's hay bales. Glass flecks in the dirt, my mother in the shards' dull reflections. The breeze in her hair. The gun steady in her two-handed grip. Andy lines up his shot. His finger on the trigger and the barrel's waver. Then the crack, and the recoil knocks him back a step. Kitten scurries beneath the porch. A dusty plume from the hay and the bottle untouched. "Damn, man." He smiles. "Fucking all right."

I take the gun. My mother's voice in the stillness. I rest the sight on the target and calm my breathing.

I squeeze and the bottle shatters. I imagine the bang radiating, a ripple across the fields. The mourning doves flap away then roost atop the farmhouse. Andy slaps my shoulder. "Fucking deadeye, man."

He leaves. A handshake, a promise to do it again when the planets align. Inside, I wash the dishes, put fresh water in Kitten's bowl. Andy's forgotten his pen and his six's last two beers, and I imagine him as stoned as me, schmoozing with the old folks who think he's someone else. I stretch out on Amy's bed. I've been cleaning for days, but the blankets still smell of her and my mother. Their smoke and sweat. This bed. This house. My inheritance of a hundred silences.

Dark by the time I wake. 8:04 on the oven clock, but it might as well be midnight. My day's only plan—to bike to the supermarket and spend Chief's twenty—undone by foolishness. In my head, misfiring gears. My gut both empty and heavy with want. I lift Amy's keys from their hook. I think of my mother's saying about desperate times. I think of Amy, slurring and single minded and Grace in a homemade diaper, and when have I ever not lived in desperate times?

The road less familiar beneath the stars. Its turns and rhythms. I crack the window. The country smells with me then not. The street and store lights like a carnival after the farm's dark. A return not to my route's first supermarket but the one where my mother's never been busted for passing a bad check or stuffing a sirloin under her jacket.

Doors slide open. This place always a shock. The brightness and music. The glimmer of scrubbed floors. The aisles' plenty a hall of mirrors, my hunger both a mirage and reflected a hundred-fold. The produce section's flood of color, and in my thoughts, the subtractions that take me from twenty to zero. I stick to generic brands. Hunt for sales. I force myself to think of sustenance, not taste. Oatmeal. Peanut butter. Bread. Eggs.

Potatoes. A ham hock and beans and an onion, a soup Double D made when we were down to singles and change.

I wander into the cookie aisle. Sweets and their phantom taste, and on the speakers, a tune I need a moment to recognize. A chorus Amy goaded me into singing. That day's warmth and sunshine gone. Amy gone too. Grace. My mother. And here I am, another subtraction problem's remainder, left to breathe and eat and tap my toe when the chorus rolls back around. The song a reflex on my lips. *I'm so dizzy, my head is spinning.* In me, the schism between two truths. Her absence in the moment and all that will follow. And balancing that, her presence, indelible, her memory not fading so much as contracting to its essence, a portrait rendered in pen and ink. One minute, she's slumped and cold, the needle still in her hand. The next, she's with me. Her laugh. Her thoughtless touches. Her belief in God and the goodness of others.

My items shimmy on the register's conveyor. I check my math against the display, and I'm happy to walk away with two bags and fifty-eight cents. In town, I come to full stops and keep to the speed limit. My lack of a license and insurance. The questions that would lead to a dozen more. My fear of reuniting with children and youth. The netherworld of foster care, the places I've stayed for a night or two after my world came crashing down. The longer stints, weeks, sometimes months. The Christians who ran their homes on prayer and intricate chore schedules posted on the refrigerator. The money-grabbers who treated their charges like farm animals, our names learned only to yell, their houses' cruel undercurrents ignored. I escaped each of these, most quietly, some wrapped in my Mother's fury, a court order in hand and the promise to burn down their motherfucking house if I'd been wronged. I drive on. The lights and houses fade. The road narrows. Above the fields, a half moon, and I can't remember if last week it was full or new.

Back home, I eat a peanut butter sandwich then another. I bring the beans to a boil and cut the celery and onion. I've been chopping wood for the old man, and in the coming days, I'll fire up the stove. In one of the living room boxes, a camcorder and a single cassette. I wire the camcorder to the TV. My mother said my father showed up one day after work with the camera. An impulse, a luxury they couldn't afford. I like to think he bought the camera, that it wasn't hot or bartered for, that it came home intact in a box, a receipt in his pocket and the hope that a push of a button might make time stand still. I take a long hit from Andy's pen. Stir the soup beans and crack another beer. The cassette clicks into place and I hit play.

There's my mother, waddling, her watermelon belly. In her eyes, a gleam that makes it easier to believe she really did go sober for the duration. The camera handed off, and there's my father. A wave and an exhale of cigarette smoke. An eyeblink, and I appear. A swaddled newborn. A face swollen and shut-eyed that could have belonged to any other baby born that day. Another blink and my father coaxes a bottle's nipple between my lips. I suck, and he turns to the camera, smiling.

I exhale, the tape's last moments watched through the smoke. My father jailed before my first birthday. A bungled robbery, a cop shot, and it didn't matter that my father was just the lookout. Histories interrupted, just like the dates in the old man's bible. Histories interrupted, just like Amy's, a dose that gave her that final distance between her and her regrets and all those who wanted a piece of her. A history interrupted, just like my mother's. Her disintegration into another state of matter, lost and scattered beneath winter's fast-approaching stars.

* * *

I hear Chief's pickup before I see it. The horn's double honk. The engine's rattle. Between us, the after-school rush. I pass the twins who sit behind me in homeroom. The vice-principal and his walkie-talkie. The pickup's passenger window rolled down, and from it, a cigarette's drift. "There's room for your bike in the back."

I wedge my bike between the bed's buckets and tarps and claim the passenger seat. The rattle heavier today or perhaps just easier to hear without the rain. Chief raises his voice. "Everything cool?"

"Yep."

He pulls from the curb. The rattle thins then returns at the first stop sign. The thermos between us, but this afternoon, I don't imagine smashing it into his head. "This place is on Delmont." He takes a final drag and grinds his cigarette into a crowded ashtray. I think of seeing him on Delmont the first morning of school. The street's tall trees, a tunnel of shade. "It's

112

one of those old houses. This doctor's fixing it up. Two doctors, really. Husband and wife. Just bought it."

He shakes a cigarette from his pack. "Can't smoke inside." A hand on the lighter, the other on the wheel. An exhale through a rolled-down window. "You don't smoke, do you?"

"No."

"That's good. I'm not the advice type, but you shouldn't."

"I don't."

"Good. Good."

We park beneath one of the maples. Chief opens the truck's gate. He hands me a gallon jug of vinegar then slings a drop cloth over my shoulder. "Think it's safe leaving my bike here?" I ask.

"This neighborhood, sure." He holds the cigarette between his lips and lifts the bike from the bed. "But we'll put it on the porch, just in case."

In school's first weeks, I saw the lawn's FOR SALE sign, but I never stopped to check out the house. My morning lateness and the bike's speed. The trees' flickering camouflage. Only as I carry my load up the walkway do I notice the slate roof. The wraparound porch. The rounded room on the third floor that looks like it belongs in a castle. Five of my houses could fit inside the gray-stone walls.

Chief sets my bike on the porch. A key shook from his jangling chain. A heavy door and an ornate brass knocker. Inside, an emptiness that reminds me of the old man's house, high ceilings and naked windows. All of the walls papered. Flowers in the living room. Stripes in the dining room. Other rooms I don't know what to call until Chief names them. The parlor. The study. I follow Chief up a staircase wide enough for us to walk side-by-side, and on the second floor, he points out the bedrooms and bathrooms. The room that will be the nursery for the doctors' first child, a baby due in early spring.

The master bedroom at the hall's end, and outside its door, a narrow staircase. Music from the staircase's darkness, violins, a piano. The song clearer as we climb. At the top, a small hallway, and I follow Chief into the front room. A tarp on the floor. A paint-spotted radio, its antenna bent. "I usually listen to classical." He takes the tarp, beckons for the gallon jug. "Don't know much about it, but I like not hearing words sometimes."

I stand in the room's center. This space without corners and windows all around. Outside, the maples' high branches, the sidewalk far below, and I think of the dollhouse I once played with and the lives I imagined inside.

"This here's a turret room. Did you know that? I didn't know that when I was your age."

"No, I didn't."

Chief hands me a wide-bladed scraper. "Who's got time to know shit like that?"

"It's nice." Between the branches, I spy on a boy and girl. His arm around her. Her head on his shoulder. Their shuffling feet. "The whole house is nice."

"Glad you like it because we've got ourselves enough work here until New Year's. You ever stripped wallpaper?"

"No."

"Sometimes it's easy. Sometimes it takes some doing. What's important is doing it right. This is my second gig in this hood. Word of mouth with the doctor crowd could help business."

He teaches, and I pay attention in a way I rarely do in school. The putty knife run along a seam. The scorer's even circles, the just-right touch that cuts the wallpaper but not the plaster. He mixes water and vinegar in a pressure sprayer, and after he wets a panel, we score again. We climb stepladders, and ducking beneath the ceiling, we pinch a panel's corner.

Our pulling slow, a hiss and whisper and an exposure of white. Then a stubborn spot, and the paper tears.

"Not bad." He balls the paper into a trash bag. "If we're living right, we can take it to the baseboard." He sprays the paper below the tear. "We'll wait a minute and score and try again."

A voice from downstairs. "Hola? Estás aqui?"

Chief goes to the door. "Sí, sí." He turns to me. "Score that then get it started with the knife. Gentle, OK? I'll be right back."

I scrape. My touch light, tentative. The voices echo up the stairwell. I limped through Spanish in tenth grade, picked up my share of curses in the Patch, but I only understand a little of what I hear.

Chief returns. "Looks good." He takes an edge, and in centimeter sighs of old glue, we coax down the panel.

He gives the paper a final tug and tosses it in the bag. "If only the rest would be so easy."

"Is that guy you were talking to going to be working with us?"

"No." He guides his putty knife along the next seam. "That's another job. We're doing some evenings for the next couple weeks."

"Must make for a long day."

"They're longer if you got no work to do. Idle hands and all that."

"Didn't know you knew Spanish so good."

He looks at me the way teachers do when they've stirred me from a daydream. "You think they call me Chief because I'm Indian, don't you?"

"Yeah." I shrug. "I mean I guess."

He shakes his head and hands me the scorer. "Sometimes you white folks crack me the fuck up."

* * *

The alarm rings. A dream of Amy, so vivid then gone. The blankets heavy but a chill on my face. I hesitate, wondering if a dream can be rejoined, desiring only to linger in this bed where my mother and Amy slept, their arms around each other, their fears the other might slip away. I could stay, miss another day of school, and the fact that so few would care strikes me as both reassuring and sad. I gather myself and fling back the covers. The icy floor. A tepid shower. My blood-pumping ride into town. The cafeteria's salvation. Andy and Kate and Mr. Ford and Chief. This plunge into another day and nothing ever gets easier.

A blue-sky morning. Frost on the window. The trees just past peak, and ahead, winter's fade. The months of gray and white. The long nights. Two weeks now I've been working with Chief. The wallpaper stripped on the third and second floors. Our quiet afternoons. The chill vibe of the classical station's DJ. Our dances around and with each other, the knowing of my place. Chief works his other project on the weekends and evenings. The friend who sometimes stops by, their conversations in Spanish. The friend smiles at me. "Keep an eye on our boss here."

I've got my own labors today. The wood dropped off by one of the old man's nephews and me with an ax. The logs balanced one at a time on a weathered stump. Some of my swings true. A few missing altogether. Most somewhere in between. The goat nibbles, watching it all.

I set up another log. Last night, as I rode with Chief after work, we passed the high school stadium. The lit field. The pulse of tubas and drums. The crowd's lifted cry. I thought of Kate on the bleachers with her cross-country friends. Thought of their warm gloves and college sweatshirts. Thought of her sitting with a boy who lived a life where sipping hot chocolate at a Friday night football game didn't feel like a scene stolen from a stranger's home movies. Who never had to make excuses for his people or lie about the path he's walked. I swing, hard and clear-eyed. The splits tumble, one to the left, the other to the right.

Inside, and I fill a glass at the sink. The ax's vibrations stubborn in my hands. The faucet drips, slow and steady, and beneath, ripples in a soaking pan. I nudge the handle and the drip stops. Then the silence that I've learned isn't silence but a hundred woven frequencies. The sigh of branches that can no longer hold their leaves. The crickets' dying twitches. There are nights I lie awake thinking of this silence not as the nothingness I'd once imagined but as a forest, deep and dark and wide. And I think of Amy's seashell story, and I see the shell's twisting chambers as our house's rooms. The dead air in each. The hum of lost worlds.

The goat watches as I hop on my bike. Its jaw's disjointed chew. Its impassive eyes. I turn right at the lane's end, away from town and into the country. I pick up speed. The breeze blows back my hoodie. The road a black river, and around me, a sweep of bleeding colors. The illusion of motion—but I know it's just me adrift in the stillness.

I reach the quarry. The cool on my skin. The warm pushback from my heart. I prop my bike against the fence and duck inside. Leaves twist around me. The path a collage of color. Then the clearing, and I sit near the cliff's ledge. Cold lifts from the pit, and I think of Amy and my twin in the ground. Think of stopped clocks and frozen lakes. I inch toward the ledge, and in me, the vertigo of emptiness. The pull of everything and nothing.

The ride home. I pedal, coast, think. Afternoon, but the sun already low, and I imagine the months ahead, the drifts that will close our lane. I hear a car and veer to the road's edge. The car passes, but as I near the creek's narrow bridge, the car's brakes flash. A jerking turn. The car yellow, red pinstripes, ghost flames around the front wheel wells. I stop and the car pulls up. Its engine's fine-tuned purr, the glint of silver rims. My reflection stares back from tinted glass. The driver's window rolls down, and with it, the pump of the stereo's trap-beat and a reefer-smoke cloud. The driver takes off his sunglasses. A pencil-thin beard and mustache. The ace of spades tattooed on his neck. "You're crazy Jill's kid, aren't you?"

I say nothing.

A click, and before the door opens, I'm off. The car slams through a three-point turn. A squeal of rubber, and I'm thrust into a science class word problem. My bike versus this hot rod. The distance between us, our mismatched velocities, the unknown variable of violence he intends, and with the under-standing that my only hope is introducing a variable of my own, I cross the creek bridge, the road abandoned as I turn onto a fisherman's footpath.

The path with its ruts and rocks. My bike's thin tires and lack of tread. I lift my ass from the seat. Wrestle the handlebars. A veil of starlings light from the creek-side trees. The jarring in my elbows and shoulders, the bony clack of my teeth. I'm half blinded, the sun, the vibrations' blur, and I don't see the gnarled root that rises from the path until I'm upon it.

I fly over the handlebars, and my panic dissolves into an odd clarity—the abandonment of bike and Earth—and as I sail, I return to my word problem, the voice of my old teacher, a lecture about bodies in motion. The moment rejoined with my thud into the grass. The wind knocked from my lungs, and behind my eyes, a flash of black.

I gather myself, the impact revisited with each straightened limb. As I raced down the path, I'd imagined him behind me, wild-eyed, his breath on my neck, but this is not the case. He stands on the shoulder in front of his yellow car. We're separated by thirty, maybe forty yards, and his voice carries across the field.

"You tell your mama Dale's looking for her, punk. You tell her I haven't forgotten what she's done. You tell her this shit's going to get worse before it gets better if she don't make things right. You make sure you give her that message, boy."

He returns to the car. A slammed door, the engine's rev, and in the quiet that follows his exit, the starlings return. The flap of wings. An echoed call. I wipe myself off, and when I lift my bike, I notice the bent front rim. I walk the bike to the road. A hitch in my stride. A damaged boy and a damaged bike. A mile's walk. My shadow stretches across the macadam, and the chill rises from the lowlands. Me glancing back then ahead. Looking for the yellow car. Ready to run if I have to.

* * *

I stack an armful of wood beside the old man's stove. I open the grate and feed another log. The warmth radiates, and I wince, the heat on my face. The old man with his fingers upon the twine. His touch a whisper, and when he reaches a line's end, he gropes for the next eyelet. I ask if he'd like to hear the radio, but he says that can wait.

"Been listening most the day already," he says.

"What do you think the President means—a 'regional action'?"

"Think it means we're not abiding by borders anymore."

"I don't understand it much. The why of it."

"The whys you get on the news don't mean much. The only real whys are the same ones you'll read about in the Bible." His cane taps out the words. "Greed. Fear. Power."

"A guy I know signed up today."

"A young man should serve his country. But it's the men with skin in the game who should do the dying."

121

I cut us slices of cheese and ham and layer them on bread. Another Saturday, this one colder than the last. Another week of school. My teachers. The lunchtime recruiters. The words I share with Kate, and later, all the things I wish I'd said. My bike un-ridable. My plans to buy a new wheel soon. A forged note handed to Mrs. Pike, and I now begin my mornings waiting for the bus at the lane's end. My afternoons with Chief, the echo of our footsteps and voices and the classical music I no longer mind. The wallpaper finally stripped, and now we're patching plaster. Our tasks full of gentle touches and attention to detail. The mistakes I try not to make twice. On Friday, Chief hands me cash in a white envelope, and we knock off an hour early so he can drive me to the supermarket. My nights spent alone, the drift between loneliness and boredom and the fear of Dale and his threats. The door locked and a chair propped beneath the knob. Glasses balanced atop the windows' sashes. The gun never far.

I've saved enough to cover my back rent, but the old man says I've earned my keep in chopped wood and made meals and in the conversations that have saved him from talking to himself any more than he already does. Bible in hand, I join him at the table. He requests Psalms 25:16. The pages rustle, but he speaks before I can open my mouth.

"Turn to me and be gracious to me, for I am lonely and afflicted. Relieve the troubles of my heart and free me from my anguish." He rubs his stubbled cheek and gazes over my shoulder. "It's a pretty thought, isn't it?"

* * *

Moonlight on the gun's chrome, a moment's shine before I stash it beneath the porch steps. My fears of Dale and returning to an ambush. Headlights approach, the thump of Andy's system a wrong note in the farm's quiet. We spark a bowl on the way to town. The night clear, the stars crisp then dulled by the glow of gas stations and strip malls. We park along Main then walk a block. My hands in my pockets and my shoulders hunched, and I think about winter and how I might be able to land a warmer jacket. We pass darkened storefronts, signs that declare clearances and vacancies. The pizza shop's lights spill onto the sidewalk, and inside, Derrick and Jason huddle over a pinball machine.

The pot's bloodshot strain in my eyes. The oven's heat. A wall-mounted TV, and on it, the news. Soldiers arrested for their role in the village massacre, handcuffs on boys hardly older than me. Then scenes of street clashes. Anti- and pro-war protesters, tear gas and the police with their riot gear. I turn away. The pinball machine with its whirs and buzzes, the slap of Derrick's fingers. The pulsing strobe on Jason's huffer's rash. "Yeah, man, yeah," Jason says. Derrick leans over the glass, a thrust from his hips, a grasp and a shake. The display goes black, a tilt's dying whir. "Fucker," he spits, a final shove. A cool look from the man behind the counter.

Derrick returns his stare. "How's our pie coming, Hector?"

"Name's not Hector, son."

"Whatever. Don't be skimpy on the pepperoni again."

We claim a table by the window. Fog on the glass. Our faces reddened by neon. Derrick with a thick sweatshirt under his denim. Jason with a skullcap and fingerless gloves. He taps the tabletop. "What this place needs is a jukebox. Some tunes, yo."

Derrick slides a salt shaker from one hand to the other. "What this place needs is some trim to walk in. Brighten up this lame-ass night."

"For real," Jason says.

"What do you know about that kind of action, cuz?" Derrick slides the shaker my way, but it falls off the table before I can catch it. "So what're we looking at here, men?"

"I've got a couple bowls. You score those sixes?" Andy asks.

"Ready and waiting at our spot."

Jason pats his pocket. "I lifted a couple of my mom's Xanax."

Derrick nods toward me. "What're you chipping in, sport? This shit don't come free. Well, Jason's did, but we don't expect much from him."

Jason frowns. "It ain't free, not if you think about it—"

"Shut up, man." Derrick looks at me. "Well?"

"I can get the pizza."

"So you're buying dinner?" Derrick leans back and shouts. "Hey Hector—add an order of fries to that."

The man behind the counter folds a clump of dough. "Said my name's not Hector."

"Whatever. And some onion rings, too, amigo." He smiles. "Knew Andy brought your sorry ass for a reason."

Our order is called, and when I pay, I say thanks—once and again—and after we eat, I return our trays and plates and slide a dollar into the tip jar. "Sorry," I say. The man behind the counter nods but doesn't smile.

We walk the six blocks to the railroad tracks. Main Street's lights and the cruising prowl of kids just as bored as us. Then the side streets, the doubles with their shared porches and postage-stamp yards. The bumper-to-bumper parking where, come winter, lawn chairs and trash cans will guard shoveled spaces. The last street dead-ends in the old flour mill's lot. I kick a stone across the cracked macadam. The mill with its broken windows, and the dirty panes that remain catch the moonlight. At the lot's edge, we climb down an embankment. Before us, double tracks on a stone bed, and near the embankment's littered weeds, crude seats formed from planks and cinder blocks.

The beers are cheap but cold. My first sips came when I was five or six, a joke among the men in my mother's orbit. The bitter face I can now mask, a taste I've never liked. Jason hands out his pills, apologizing he didn't bring one for me and offering to split his.

"Half a fucking X?" Derrick scoffs. "Couldn't get a fly high on half a fucking X."

"I'm good," I say. "Thanks."

I sit apart, just enough to make it easier to wave off the bowl when I've had enough. I drink one beer to Derrick's two, two to his four. Jason talks about his Florida dreams, the warm winters and dirt bike racing, cooking ocean-caught fish over a beach fire. Andy laughs at everything. Derrick restless. His tapping toes, the clank of his wallet chain. He paces up and down the tracks, a shadow against the railbed stones. He's funny at first, but as he cracks another beer, his tone hardens. Snarling monologues. The old coach he'd love to punch. The girls he wants to fuck.

I shiver, saying less as the hours pass. I've spent my whole life around stoned people, and I fit us into our types. Jason desperate to be seen. Andy all grinning daze. Derrick hurtling toward a narrow-eyed oblivion. All of us lost, but some lost more than others. Our truths buried beneath stances and curses and the ever-itchier high that sparkles in our exhaled breath.

"You watching the news before?" Derrick's beer-holding hand points to us. "Those dudes getting snagged for that village shit? Doesn't seem right, asking them to be killers and then they get upset when they can't flip the switch and turn that shit off."

I feel the train first. A rumble in the stones. The engine's light a speck as it turns the bend, and in the moonlight, the long line of hopper cars.

Derrick stands. "They should be giving out medals for that shit. Not to the schmucks who did it, but to the DIs who trained them. The ones who made them killers. Those motherfuckers earned their money."

The train heading north. The Patch's crossings behind, and with it, the accumulation of speed. Derrick balances atop a rail. A long guzzle, the beer finished and the can tossed. In his hands, an imaginary machine gun, a shooting-from-the-hip pose. "You think we wouldn't have done the same thing if we were in their boots? Shit, I'm halfway there as is. I'd be their prize motherfucking killing machine."

The train closer and the engine's expanding light lifts him

from the dark. The horn's bleat an avalanche that buries our cries for him to get out of the way. We become refugees from a silent movie, wild gestures and gaping mouths and a train bearing down upon us, the scene's climax a blur, Derrick on the tracks, his gun abandoned for the raised hands of Jesus, the light so intense he glows. And with a bellow of grit and the wheels' spark, the light abandons us, the night rejoined. The locomotive's roar replaced by the hoppers' chug and clatter. Jason with his trembling hands, muttering "Fuck! No, man, no!" Andy and I stare at each other. Dumbstruck, unable to shake our silent movie roles, and for all that is certain, I might as well be toeing the quarry's ledge. The next step sure to send me toppling.

The train over a mile long. A blur of graffiti. The icy currents. We stoop and look between the rolling wheels but see nothing. Jason collapses, his ass on the stones, elbows on his knees and his head in his hands. The last car passes, and before the silence rushes back, there's Derrick. He laughs. Both hands flashing raised middle fingers. The stones shift beneath his boots as he descends the railbed.

"Jesus." Jason says. "Derrick, man. What the fuck!"

"Fuck you, man." Andy angry, then not. "The fuck, man."

"Come on, ladies, stop clutching those pearls." Derrick opens the last beer and chugs half of it in a long, sloppy gulp. He wipes his mouth on his coat sleeve. "You all needed to wake the fuck up. Night's getting fucking boring."

We walk back to town. We weave beneath streetlights then return to the dark. Sometimes I look up, imagining Derrick and the last-second rush of light, and I wonder if, put in that moment, I'd be able to move or if I'd be blinded, frozen like a roadside animal. Lost in the hurtling churn.

Rescued from the dead, Derrick becomes the night's

chosen one, and the rest of us straggle in his wake. We turn into an alley. Garages and back yards. Derrick grabs a picket fence's slat. He pulls, two hands, his shoulders hunched. His bulk sinks back, and the nails groan. The slat twisted until it breaks free, and with a heave, he sends it helicoptering over the fence.

Another block, and we stop outside a garage. The alley part of Derrick's after-school route. The door open during the day, his peeks inside, the puttering old man and his array of tools. Derrick tests a side door, and when it opens, he holds a finger to his lips.

"Enough, man," Andy says.

But Derrick's already inside, Jason on his heels. Andy shakes his head. I stand in the doorway. The garage black, its scents of grease and grass clippings. A spark, and Derrick's grin shines in a lighter's flame, and as he walks, the space comes into view. Toolboxes. Bicycles. A kayak hung from the rafters. A lawnmower and leaf blower. Derrick hands Jason the lighter, a dark moment, and when Jason flicks the wheel, there's Derrick, a chainsaw in hand, and in the flickering shine, he becomes another type I've come to know. Not the regular dopers of my mother's universe with their predictable orbits of scoring, getting high, jonesing, and scoring again, but the ones who fly across the sky like comets. Men reckless and fiery and always a breath away from disappearing forever or crashing into the earth, taking down themselves and everyone unlucky enough to be near.

The chainsaw's blade nearly as long as my arm, and I can't tell if the saw is new or just another of the garage's well-kept collection, everything around me clean and in its place. Derrick flips the toggle, presses the primer.

"Come on, man," Andy says. "You're already on probation. And what're you going to do with something like that anyhow?"

"What am I going to do?" He rips the cord. The engine spits, a *blat-blat-blat*, the stink of gas and oil, and when he hits the choke, the growl swallows Andy's pleas to *just put the fucking thing down*. Derrick's crazy grin in the lighter's shine. The saw held high. He guns the throttle, and the garage's hung tools and screw-filled coffee cans tremble. The saw's tip bites into the hanging kayak.

I'm backing out of the door when a hand clamps my shoulder. My yelp lost beneath the chainsaw's whine, and I turn only to be blinded by the flashlight inches from my face. I twist, my arm jerked free, and stagger into the alley. My veins jagged with adrenaline. My fear of the police. My greater fear of the system. Relief when I see the jacketless old man. A flashlight in one hand and, in the other, a leash strained by a growling pit bull.

The man pushes past me then stops at the door's threshold. The flashlight illuminates the garage's dirty windows, a jack-o-lantern's shine. The chainsaw snuffed, its throaty rev replaced by the dog's wild barks and the old man's orders for all to stay put because the cops are already on their way. I remain outside the door. The flashlight's beam passes from Derrick's face to Jason's, and somehow Andy manages to sneak out and join me in the alley. Then a scuffle, Derrick's linebacker's rush, and the old man staggers then tumbles. The flashlight drops, and its light spills over our sneakers. Derrick sprints past, Andy and I close behind, but the old man rights himself in time to wrap his arms around Jason, whose frightened voice fades as we run. "Hey, man, let go! Let go!"

A glance back. Two entwined shadows rise from the puddle of light, and between us and them, the charging pit bull. The jangle of its trailed leash. The clip of its nails and its muscled pant. "Dog!" I cry, and I pass Andy then Derrick. The dog on our heels, its bark replaced by the hard smack of teeth. We spill onto a

CURTIS SMITH

cross street, a birth into a blinding, hurtling light, and for a moment, I'm Derrick on the tracks, staring down death and the long, black corridor that follows, and in my darkness, I see not my mother nor Amy nor my father's faded pixilation but images of black and white. The Minotaur. The Lost Sheep. A heartbeat and we're returned to the alley. Behind us, the squeal of brakes, a soft thud. The barking gone. The old man's cry of "Daisy! Daisy!"

We keep running, and on the next block, a cruiser's strobe knifes between the houses. Another cruiser in its wake. We pause in a garage's shadow before crossing the next street. The disorientation of fear and escape eases, and I realize where we are. "Follow me," I say.

Moonlight spills over the dormant garden and the back-yard's slate path. Chief's spare key beneath a back-porch flower pot. I open the door. The house still. The streetlight through the living room windows, a moonscape inside. Cold, but not as cold as the night. The smell of primer. The tarp, white as moondust, ripples with our steps. We sit on the living room floor and catch our breath. Every so often, a car passes, and on the wall, a patch of light that stretches, condenses, then disappears.

I explain my work, the doctors who'll live here, the baby on the way. We shake our heads, relieved laughter, the train, the chainsaw, then fall silent when Andy brings up the dog. Derrick gets a text from Jason, his escape made when the old man ran off after his Daisy. Plans are made to rendezvous at the pizza shop, and we decide to leave one at a time in five-minute intervals. Andy goes first. The backyard surveyed before he returns to the alley, the promise to see us soon.

Derrick and I sit by the front window. He pulls a crumpled joint from his pocket and sticks it in his mouth. He pats his other pockets. "Shit, Jason's got the lighter."

"Just as well. Can't smoke here."

"Why's that?"

"My boss's rules."

He tucks the joint behind his ear. "Fair enough." He leans back and rests his head against the wall. "You should have seen your face when I revved that fucker."

I think of my father and how he feels near tonight. These hours of bad decisions. The paper-thin fortunes that can bring ruin just as easily as deliverance.

"You're fucking quiet." He taps the rubber mallet we use to seal paint cans in his palm.

"Not much to say."

"That chainsaw and the train and all that shit, I don't give a fuck about it." A car's headlights pass above us. "That's the trick of it all, right? Knowing when to give a fuck. We're drowning in it. In school. On our fucking phones. We're drowning, man, in a thousand fucking voices and a million fucking images. Everyone wanting a 'Like.' It doesn't mean shit." A siren in the distance. "And you know what's fucked? That somewhere in all that shit is that little fucking nugget of something that actually matters. And if you're not careful." He holds up the mallet. "If you're not motherfucking lucky as hell, you're going to miss it." He sets down the mallet. "Fuck, I'm sounding like a fool."

"Not really."

"That shit I was saying earlier, with the train? It scares me, man. Scares me because I can see myself doing it. Not wanting to, but doing it anyway. Losing myself, you know?" He stands, wipes his jeans. "Seen you talking to the recruiters. You signing up?"

"Maybe. Probably. You?"

"Was thinking about it at one time, but now, fuck no. Let

them come and get me." He walks to the back door. "Heard you're buying us all slices when we meet up."

Later, I do buy slices. Our shared story told from four perspectives. The fitting of jigsaw pieces. Bravado and disbelief. Fates tempted and avoided. Derrick stands, his empty hands holding the chainsaw. His eyes wild, and I laugh as much as the others.

* * *

The Tuesday before Thanksgiving, and a buzz passes through the cafeteria. Not a fight's eruption with the girls' screams and boys scrambling atop tables and chairs. This reaction subtle, a repeated name that breaks like a soft wave, and when the wave reaches my table, I, too, turn my gaze to the recruiters' station.

Ike Foreman was last year's quarterback. The basketball team's top rebounder. He wears a pressed khaki shirt, blue pants and a white hat. A Marine's buzzcut. He stands straight as a pole, chest out. He shakes hands with friends and teammates and teachers, and I wonder if he's come on his own or if this is a bit of theater. Lunch's captive audience and the hero's return. The recruiters smile at the periphery, chatting and handing out their wares.

I return my tray. A hello for the lunch ladies as I pocket my daily banana, and when no one's looking, I snag an apple. In Mr. Ford's class yesterday, we talked about the pressure parents put on their children, and while I usually try to help Mr. Ford out with a raised hand or two, I couldn't offer much. I never had anyone dream a dream for me, never had anyone create a bubble then invite me to inhabit it. I came up blank, without expectations. The future an abstraction, an indulgence in such an unsettled present, and in my daydreams of what might be, the military has long been my escape hatch. The ending I could write if all my other endings failed. The wars I grew up with simmering yet distant. Regimes propped up or torn down, dangerous, yes, but the lives of soldiers weren't much more dangerous than the men I'd grown up knowing, the ones who understood survival was a tightrope walk, who wouldn't dream of going out for a pack of smokes without tucking a pistol into their waistband. Soldiers, civilians. Heroes, criminals—it's all relative. The junkie gets locked up because we can hold their powders in our hands, the concreteness of their crime an easy fit into our black-and-white equations. But the crimes of scale go unpunished. The perpetrators who look like grandfathers. Like bankers. Like church-goers. Their thefts so deep and wide that we can no more comprehend them than we can take in the breadth of a starry sky. Overwhelmed, our perspective lost, we turn back upon the small-time crook, reassured by their ragged faces and handcuffs, our reward in the purr of a machine that offers us beer and football and sex while it does its real work of making the rich richer. A machine blind to a kid who has and comes from nothing until the day it decides to consume him.

The lunch monitors give the call to move out, and I join the flow. There's a break in the crowd, and Ike calls, "Mark! Mark Hayes!"

He extends a hand and smiles. He seems older than he was just a few months ago, a man to my boy, and although we didn't run in the same circles, we share a history. A year in the Patch, his family in a two-bedroom apartment across the hall. Our bus stop conversations. The building's thin walls and the mess of our parents' lives. The week I slept on his couch after my mother couldn't make bail on a paraphernalia charge. The Saturday morning I cracked our door to see the sheriff delivering their eviction notice. Ike always said "Hey," even though he became popular, and I, through my absences and uninvolvement, turned more and more invisible. Between us, the secrets kept by frightened children. The knowledge of hidden lives.

"How's it going?" he asks.

"Same old. I should be the one asking you."

"I'm good." He nods toward the recruiter who's handing a flier to a boy in a varsity jacket. "Heard you're thinking about it."

"We've been talking."

Ike passes a hand in front of his shirt. "Wearing this uniform is special. It's more than a piece of clothing."

"I can imagine." I spot Kate and begin to back away.

One of his basketball teammates steps forward, but as they shake, Ike continues to address me. "It's one of those special things no one can ever take from you, Mark. It's yours forever."

*　*　*

I rest my head against the bus's jostling window. Outside, glistening pastures. This morning after the first hard frost. The ridges of brown and gray. I think about Kitten, who I haven't seen for a few days. My backpack between my feet, and in it, my toothbrush, a change of clothes. Miles pass, and with them, the shedding of history. We stop in a half dozen towns. Each with its hardware stores and gas stations, its churches and bars. Each with its depot, some little more than a cinder-block hut. People get off and new ones board. A soldier with his duffle bag. College kids. A woman cradling a sleeping child. All of us part of the undertow. This anonymous current. Outside, the flow of pastures and orchards, and when I close my eyes, the molecules inside me strip their bonds, changing me from solid to mist, as light as the fields' icy haze. Another stop, and two girls I take for sisters get on. Their voices bright. They talk of the people awaiting their arrival, and I imagine what it would be like to feel the tug of return when I hear the word *home*.

The countryside fades. Industrial parks. Car dealerships. Traffic lights and shopping centers. Every so often, a glimpse of the city skyline. Another stop, this one shared with a rail station. I join the shuffling exit, pausing behind a mother gathering her baby's belongings. On the station's overhang, a name that matches my ticket, and among the macadam's small, shivering gathering, a woman in a blue scarf and matching hat. Her gaze upon the windows that shield me behind their tint and glare.

I step into the sun. The cold. The diesel's woozy stink. The woman in the blue hat locks me in a hug that knocks me back a step. I was the one who reached out to my Aunt Mary. A phone call last weekend, a check-in after not returning a dozen calls because what could I say? Mom's still a junkie? I'm going nowhere? I live hungry and in fear of the men my mother's crossed? I called to hear her voice—and to have my voice heard by someone who knew me. Someone who cared. My days with my aunt few, but our ties written on our faces. The eyes we share, the strangers who've assumed we were mother and son. She took the same script her sister was given and wrote another story. A woman who escaped and never looked back. A woman who put herself through college. Who paid her bills. Who turned to God instead of junk.

Our embrace lingers. This collision of memories. The two years since I've seen her an eyeblink and an eternity. She whispers. "I'm so glad you called." She steps back. "Look at you. A young man."

I stand a little taller, wanting her to see a man. Her life with its own troubles. The booze and violence of her childhood. The miscarriages that broke her heart. The cheating husband who broke it again.

Stopping at the mall is her idea. Tomorrow's Thanksgiving, but here it's Christmas. Skylights and their sunny columns. A pond where goldfish the size of ketchup bottles swim over polished rocks and pennies tossed for good luck. Christmas music and garland and window displays of cottony snow. We eat, a Chinese place, a sharing of dishes. Before we leave, a stop at a store, and I realize this was her plan all along. Our reflections in a three-way mirror. The trying on of winter coats, one after the other pulled off the racks and zipped up. The sales people helpful, an experience so different than the times I've shopped with my mother. No one looking to rush us along. No one spying on us in the ceiling's fisheye mirrors. We agree on a coat blue and warm, a pair of gloves thrown in at the register. We return to the sunlight, and I hold the sleeve to my nose, and what luxury, the wearing of clothes that come without the scents of other lives.

A stop before we return to her condo. Her college campus, her job as a counselor, and I think of the students lucky enough to know her. Her kindness. Her clarity. The wisdom that comes from walking the hard road. She retrieves files from her office, but again I realize she has other plans. The two of us alone on the wide sidewalks. Green stretches where I picture the flight of Frisbees and footballs. Ivy on brick. Lecture halls and dormitories. The still athletic fields and empty stands. Trees and hammocks and clusters of Adirondack chairs painted in the college's blue and white. The chapel bells ring the hour for no one but us.

"So how's my sister?"

"OK." I don't want to lie. "The same. You know."

"It wouldn't kill her to call me."

"You know how she gets."

"I do." Her smile short-lived. "She's always taken everything so hard."

We stop by a fountain. Its spray off, and in the water, brown leaves. She buries her hands in her coat pockets. "When we were little, she'd look out for me. If someone was looking to give me trouble, they had to go through her first."

"I can see that."

We sit on a bench, and I imagine the fountain on. Its splash. The sun's prisms in the spray. "Her heart, it's always been a complicated thing."

"I'd have liked to have known her then. Before."

"She had a fire."

I think of the knife she drove into a man's thigh. "Still does. At times."

"I'll bet." She turns to me. "Mark, I'm going to tell you a few things, and I want you to take them to heart."

"OK."

"Tell her she can always come to me. That my door is never shut."

"OK."

"And promise you'll never spend the holidays alone. Doesn't have to be with me, but never alone."

"Sure."

The chapel's bells silent now. Sunlight on the steeple and stained glass. "Sometimes I forget how pretty it is here. You work and keep your head down and get caught up in the day-to-day and forget." She turns to me. "Do you think about what's next?"

"Sometimes." A single cloud drifts across the blue. "More and more, I guess."

"You could come here, you know." Steam from her lips. "Maybe school's not your thing now, but I know you're smart. An education would open a lot of doors."

"Don't think we could ever afford that."

"Don't worry about that. Just think about it. I have money

set aside. And there's scholarships and loans. You'd be surprised. If you want, you could live with me." She smiles. "Or you could live in the dorms, but you'd have to stay out of trouble. Think you could manage that?"

"Maybe," I say, but only because saying it makes the moment easier. I haven't told her about Amy. Haven't told her her sister's been missing for weeks, lost in our town's dopesick undercurrent, holed up in a Patch shooting gallery or on the run. Perhaps locked up. Perhaps dead. My aunt and I might share blood, but I can't share the truth, at least not the truth that hurts the most.

A slow walk back to the car. I picture campus this time next week. The sidewalks filled. The first snow. I think of the teachers who've pulled me aside. Who've whispered encouragements. Who've offered hands and thrown ropes. For a moment, I picture myself here, but the only image that comes in clear is my inevitable stumble. My thoughts back home. The worry that's become my life's only sure thing. And I know my first missed step would soon become two. Then three, four, and on and on until the history I thought I could escape had come to claim me.

* * *

S moke rises from the old man's chimney. The morning frigid. The stillness rippled by a V of honking geese. This Monday after Thanksgiving, the first day of buck. Stillness again until Chief's truck bounces down the lane. "Dig the coat," he says, and I tell him about the bus ride and the kitchen smells I woke to on Thursday morning. I don't tell him about the hundred dollars and one-way bus ticket my aunt slipped into my pocket at the depot or about her invitation to come back any time, even to live, if that's what I wanted. The sun crests the ridges, shadows in the valleys, and I think of men in orange and rickety tree stands. Coffee in thermoses. Blood trails over fallen leaves. Quiet in town. The men in the hills and the children asleep, school closed for the day. A stop at Dunkin, Chief's treat. He says I shouldn't thank him because he's going to work my ass off today.

We eat in the Dunkin lot. The engine running. I open my

coffee and let the steam rise over my face. "Did your heater ever work?"

"Not since I've owned it. It gets a little warmer after a while." He unwraps his biscuit and takes a bite. "Or maybe that's just me getting used to the cold." He takes another bite. "What's your aunt's name again?"

"Mary." I unwrap my sandwich. "She didn't run with my mom, though."

"Guess not." He finishes his sandwich, wipes the grease from his fingers. "But she made good."

"She did." I blow into my coffee and take a sip. The warmth real and near, a grounding that makes the things my aunt and I talked about feel far away.

Today we're painting ceilings. Me with a long-handled roller. Chief on a stepladder, his hand steady along the molding. The house proves little warmer than the truck, but Chief's right—I get used to it. I give over to the day's rhythms. The roller's whispers. The pole raised. My strokes long and smooth. I lose myself in the task's simplicity and the blur of white on white. Lose myself in the smell that makes it hard to smell anything else. Lose myself in the music from Chief's radio, my ear now able to discern between adagios and allegros, between Bach and Beethoven, Mozart and Mahler. Every so often, I glance out the bay windows. The passing of sidewalk joggers. Mothers and their strollers. An old man whose dog sniffs the curbside lamppost, and as the old man waits, we exchange glances, and I think about dollhouses and empty campuses, and I wonder if it's normal, this habit of imagining other lives.

I pour more paint into the tray. "I met another kid who says his dad ran with mine. His name's Derrick. Derrick Beard."

"Beardsy." Chief dips his brush. "Guy was a hothead. Still see him around here and there. Guess he's settled some. What's his kid like?"

"Kind of like his dad, I guess."

"Apples and trees, right?" His brush feathers along a taped border. "Your old man wasn't like that, you know. If the universe were fair, it would be a guy like Beardsy locked up, not your dad." Another dip, the excess wiped against the can's top. "Your old man always did right by me. Not like some who only had to know my name or where I came from."

"I thought you were from here."

"Came up here, but I was born in Durango. That's Mexico, not Texas. In another life." He smiles. "A galaxy far, far away."

"What's your real name, Chief? If you don't mind me asking."

"Esteban. But when we landed here, my teachers changed it to Stephen. Then some kid called me Chief because he thought I looked like some TV Indian."

"I'll call you Esteban. If you'd like."

"Might not answer you." He repositions his ladder and climbs back up. "Never liked Stephen, but to be honest, I never minded Chief. I felt like it was a name I could lose myself behind, if that makes sense."

Morning passes. The sun's angle shifts, and the room grows lighter. The radio plays, and I think of the work of this life and what our labors amount to. The writing of music. The building of houses. The things that last after our hearts have stopped. I speak after a long silence. "Is it hard, staying straight?"

He looks down from the ladder. "Some days are better than others."

"So some days are harder."

He nods. "Many days are harder."

"But it gets easier?"

He runs the brush along the blue tape. "That's what they tell me."

A mid-morning break. Chief lights up on the back porch. I

clean the truck's cab, a gathering of coffee cups and sandwich wrappers. I think of Chief's saying about the Devil and idle hands, and while I'm blind to the Devil's plans for me, I do know he has less to say when I'm painting or chopping wood or walking alongside Kate. It's when I'm alone, in a house robbed of its voices, that he grabs my ear. His mockery. His impossible questions. His reminders of my birthright and destiny.

The yellow car stops, a squeal of brakes, then backs up. The driver and passenger-side doors fling open, and the thump of bass invades the morning hush. The car with its red pinstripes and ghost flames and tinted glass. The driver with his thin beard, his neck's ace-of-spades. High-top red Nikes, yellow laces the same color as the car. The passenger dull-eyed, as thick as the driver is wiry. Both in hoodies and baggy pants. Piercings in the skinny one's nose and the fat one's lip.

"Look who it is." The driver steps to me. The passenger drifts to the truck's front. I glance from one to the other and stumble over the curb. "Hope you delivered my message, cuz. Or perhaps I need you to deliver it with a little more urgency, you feel me?"

"Like with a busted-up face, punk," the friend says.

The driver grins. "That would get the whore's attention."

I back onto the lawn. The two of them five yards apart, the sidewalk crossed, and each pant-yanking stride limits my options. I ready myself to run. My fists balled in case I need to swing. Their curses lost in my skull's hum. My heel strikes the porch step, my thoughts a haywire flicker between fight or flight when a voice breaks over me.

"You boys need to go." Chief's boots heavy on the stairs. A slow descent, the rubber mallet in his right hand tapped into the palm of his left.

The driver steps back. "This don't concern you."

Chief stands in front of me. "Fuck it doesn't, son."

144

The two men with their eyes on Chief then me. They retreat, the slink of frightened dogs. The driver points to me. "We're not done. Tell that whore I'm getting what's mine, one way or the other."

Doors slam. A stomp on the gas and a swirl of leaves. The corner's stop sign ignored. Chief tucks the mallet under his arm then lights another cigarette. The flame cupped, his trembling hands. He exhales. I apologize and tell him the story about the chase. My damaged bike. "Don't know the particulars of his business with my mother, but I can guess."

A black BMW pulls to the curb. Chief stoops, grinds the cigarette against the sidewalk, and cups the butt in his hand. "The good doctor," he says.

The man who steps from the car is younger than I'd imagined. He's thin, but a healthy thin, the lanky type I know from the bike shop, the ones with the expensive gear and knotted calves. He's clean shaven. A tight haircut. A sports coat and bow tie. A hospital lanyard, and on it, a picture that echoes the smile he offers us. Chief does the talking. An update on our work. Estimates and predictions. The doctor nods, says "Great. That's great." Twice he presses Chief on the completion date— December 30th, his wish to give his visiting parents a tour of the house before they fly home. Every so often, his clear-eyed gaze drifts my way, an attempt to figure my role until Chief introduces me.

"A pleasure, Mark." We shake. His grip bony and strong. A smile of straight, white teeth. A different animal than the men who stood in this spot not two minutes ago, and I imagine the doctor's life, the books and manners and the house he grew up in—and I understand that in his eyes, I, too, am a different animal.

The doctor leaves, a toot of his horn. The wind picks up, and above, the sway of bare branches. I follow Chief up the stairs. My hand in my pockets and my shoulders hunched against the cold. "What kind of doctor is he?" I ask.

"A surgeon. Hearts and shit."

I follow Chief inside and shut the door. "He OK?"

"He hasn't screwed me yet, if that's what you mean." Chief smiles as he sets down the mallet. "But there's still plenty of time for that."

* * *

"Luke 2.8. Start there."

The old man's cane across his lap. Lunch made, the plates and counters cleared. Outside his window, the season's first flurries. Earlier, he waved off my rent money and told me to buy something for myself. When I protested, he smiled. "Only things I want now you can't find in stores."

The pages' rustle. My delicate touch. On the page opposite Luke 2.8, another etching. The manger and its star. The words familiar from a Charlie Brown cartoon. The story of angels and shepherds and glory to God—but hearing the words in my own voice is different. The vibration of skull and tongue. A shaking that cuts deeper than the rattle of Chief's truck.

I didn't believe before, and I don't believe now. The fault runs deep. A shoddy wiring. A foundation never laid. Yet I can't deny that sometimes these words—as confusing as they are—speak to me, and I've needed these months to figure out why. Oceans and continents and two thousand bloody years separate me from those dusty villages, yet little matters more than what lies at the heart of these stories. Do we care about the poor? Will we save the lost sheep? Do we judge a tree by its fruit? Do we forgive?

Yes, yes I find myself saying, yet I can't say yes to God. Or maybe I just can't say yes to miracles and answered prayers, and not because I haven't witnessed them but because I grew up yearning for them, my hands clenched and a thousand bargains offered to a God I wanted to come riding like the calvary into my upside-down life. A child's magical thinking, and perhaps I could have gone on believing—or at least harbored the comfort of hope—if my prayers had simply gone unanswered. Instead, my reward was most often the opposite. If I prayed for meat, I went hungry. If I prayed for money, the landlord kicked us to the street. If I prayed for my mother to stop making a scene, she was sure to ramp into a spitting, kicking rage.

I ask the old man if he needs anything then tell him I'll be back tomorrow. Outside, the flurries thicker, and on the sleeves of my new coat, individual crystals, each—I've been told—unique. Each perfect. My feet on the lane's gravel, and I think about our arrival. A day so cold, a year's cycle almost complete. A year of uncertainty. Of subtractions. I think of the strangers on the bus to see my aunt and the loved ones who awaited their arrivals. Closer now, and no smoke rises from my chimney, no lights shine in the windows. And I think of a manger and a belief rooted in a child's birth and the struggle to keep my feet upon the right path, and maybe I can't believe in God but I can believe in a light that shines beyond this darkness.

I start a fire in the stove. The crackle and heat. The metal's expanding sigh. I turn on the radio just to hear a voice. News of a new offensive, a push into the rebel strongholds, the prediction of swift victory. The President laying a wreath. Car bombs in Caraccas and Valencia. I pour milk in a saucer and set it on the porch, just in case Kitten returns. I lie on the couch, and at my feet, I see Amy, slumped and cold. Sometimes I talk to her, usually while I'm cleaning up. I tell her about school, about some silly thing I saw on TV that would have made her laugh. I tell her Grace is OK. Tell her I miss her and that I hope she's found peace.

I open my eyes, lost in the fringe of evaporating dreams and a winter's early dark. I hear the pop of gravel. Headlights on the windows, and the shine lifts to the ceiling as the car nears. I slide off the couch and crawl across the room. Boots on the porch. A knock that shakes the door's hinges. I picture the yellow car, veins straining beneath a tattoo. On hands and knees, I make my way to the kitchen entrance, calculating the seconds between the door being kicked in and my scramble to retrieve the gun from the silverware drawer. I make my way to a window and, with a hooked finger, pull aside the curtain. The car's headlights still on, and in their glow, a scrim of flurries and a collection of thin silhouettes.

An exhale, a breath I hadn't realized I'd been holding. Andy's car idles. The doors slam as he and Derrick and Jason settle back inside. Here are my night visitors. Here are the wisemen I deserve. Part of me wants to join them, to escape this hush, yet I remain still as the car backs up, not rising until the taillights are far up the lane.

* * *

Amy's plastic beads jangle from the rearview. A scrunchie in the shifter's console. The radio still tuned to the station that made my mother roll her eyes. The streets dark, this neighborhood of expensive houses and wide lawns. The night softened by Christmas displays. Lights strung along gutters and around doors, trees ablaze in an icy fire. I pause at corners, reading the signs, the names of flowers and trees and little girls. After a half dozen wrong turns, I find the street I'm looking for and park at the cul-de-sac's dead end.

I adjust the rearview. In the mirror, the warm houselights. A door with a wreath. The driveway's black SUV. I was hoping they'd be gone—the supermarket or some church function. Amy's heart-shaped jewelry box on the passenger seat, and I think of the bow-tied surgeon as I lift the box from the shadows. The lid sighs, and I retrieve Amy's crucifix. The cross twists. A touch of Christmas lights, and the silver rises from the dark. I return the necklace, careful not to twist its chain, a nesting beside the earrings and bracelets and photos I've gathered. Each with a memory as I hold them. Each with its own kind of death as I return them to the box. The contents topped with a note. A message I tore up four times. The awkward attempts at *I'm sorry* that would only bring more pain. The gesture of return—I hope—enough. The note nothing more than an invitation to come get her car, the keys I'll keep in the glove.

I cross the lawn. The box held before me. My offering set on the porch, a step back before I pause. The house's cold brick scrapes my coat as I fold into the shadows. The curtains pulled aside, this family with nothing to hide. A living room. A decorated tree. My exhaled breath passes through the light's spill, and I peek into another dollhouse. Amy's father, his khakis traded for sweatpants, Gracie in his arms. He paces, so slow and steady that I feel the brush of his socks against the carpet. His glasses perched atop his gray hair, his eyes closed. His lips near her ear. A comforting *hush now* that comes to me in the wind's stir. I should go yet I linger. This starry night. This manger. This child. The knowing that my goodbye, despite our history and the love I tried to share, is for the best.

Upstairs at the doctors' house, and Chief trusts me with the master bedroom's trim while he attends to the closets' nooks. Our work quicker now. My understanding of the process. Our sidestepping harmony. The smell of paint hangs in the chill. An afternoon of fading light and string quartets. Christmas just days away, and I think about next year and the lives that will fill these rooms, and even though I'll never step foot in here again, I feel good, like I'm helping them on their way. An old life stripped. These white walls. A clean start, that rarest of gifts.

Chief gives the word, and we gather our things. The cleaning of brushes and rollers. Cans sealed with the tap of the rubber mallet. The paint-splattered radio unplugged. Chief says he'll call after Christmas and that we look good to be done by the 30th. On the way out, he pauses in the nursery. He stands in the room's middle, a slow turn, and I imagine the calculations in his head, square footage and the paint needed to cover it. "Boss says he'll let us know soon about this."

"About what?"

"Pink or blue." He scratches his cheek. "Me, I'd keep it white, but what do I know?" I step over the threshold and look around. My hands filled with the things I'll return to the truck. Our reflections in the naked windows. "I have a kid, you know. Not much younger than you." He turns out the light, and I follow him into the hallway. "His mom and I split early on."

"Didn't know that. Does he go to my school?"

"Doesn't live around here. I was on and off the wagon. Off mostly. Did some time. I haven't seen him in ten years or so." He makes his rounds downstairs, shutting off lights, and I'm reminded of the night I sought shelter here, the cops outside. A dead dog. Derrick's talk of trying to find something that mattered. "Him and his mom moved west. She has people in New Mexico. She remarried, started a new family. It was all for the best, considering."

"What's your boy's name?"

"Oscar."

We step onto the porch. The cold breeze. A moment's push of smoke. We pile our things into the truck's bed. I imagine a boy my age. Imagine New Mexico, deserts and lizards and distant mountains, but I'm not sure if this picture is true or not. We climb into the cab. The first turn of the key yields a long grind. The second catches, and with it, the clamor of pistons and rusted bolts. "What's he like? Oscar?"

Chief shrugs. "Seems like a good kid. Seems like he's got his head on straight. At least straighter than me when I was his age, but that's a low bar." We pull from the curb. "Talked to him last month. Him and his mom. First time in a long time."

"So you don't talk much."

"Figured they were better off without me." A red light, and

the warmth of our bodies fogs the windshield. "Wasn't the easiest call. But it was good. There was a lot to forgive from their end."

"What did you say?"

"Not much. I didn't want to fuck with his head. Just wanted him to know I was thinking about him. That I'm here if he needs anything." The windshield's fog turns to green. "That I want to do right by him."

"You've done right by me. At least outside that first night."

He cracks his window and lights a cigarette. "That was some shit, wasn't it? You with that gun and me out of my head. I was in a bad fucking place." He twists his mouth, an exhale out the window. "And that poor kid."

I wonder if he's talking about Amy or Grace, and I guess it could be both. Chief fiddles with the radio and finds a station playing Christmas music. My knowledge of such songs scant, but this one I know. A tune Double D used to strum on the guitar he'd later trade for a teenth. *Next year all our troubles will be far away . . .*

"So what're your plans?" Chief asks. We leave the last of the lit streets and enter the country dark. "For Christmas and all."

"Not much. Probably check in with the old man. Make sure he's good."

"Doesn't he have kin for that?"

"Yeah, but I'll check on him later."

Chief begins to say something then stops. We turn onto the lane. The farmhouse's all-day lights. The kitchen light I leave on in my place, my uneasiness about returning to a dark house. We park and Chief pulls an envelope from his pocket."

"Better pay you today."

"Thanks."

"There's an extra twenty. Buy yourself something."

"OK. Sure." I shake the hand he offers. "Thanks."

The dome light shines when I open the door. "Hey," Chief says.

I stand outside. "What's that?"

He smiles. "Merry Christmas."

"You, too," I say. "Merry Christmas."

* * *

I pump gas at a mom-and-pop place outside town. An eye on the meter and memories all around. The stops I've made here, my mother's cigs and beer, the lot's handshake exchanges. I step inside. On the radio, the twang of countrified Christmas carols. A camera's red-eye stares, and I think of an old recording, the grainy pixilation of father and son. The white-haired man behind the counter glances from his magazine. The store small and cramped, a garage back in the days when gas stations fixed cars. Three aisles cater to the survival of travelers and transients. Band-aids and nail clippers. Aspirin and condoms and toothpaste. Quarts of Valvoline. Forties of Bud. At the register, a woman in a ratty coat scratches a string of lottery tickets. Silver flakes on the counter, the dime's *shh-shh*. She tosses the losers, hands over two cards, receives six more, and begins again. She clears the shavings with fingers red and chapped. Her nails chewed, the coat's cuffs stained. "Ten on one," I say. I tuck my gloves under my arm as I fish a ten from

156

my wallet. The old man takes my money and turns another page in his magazine. The woman's voice at my back. "Fuck. Fuck."

I drive into town. Ten bucks, not even half a tank, but half tank or full, it doesn't matter if there's nowhere to go. This morning, I cleaned up the car. Amy's receipts and coffee cups thrown out, Grace's bibs and nooks and rattles collected in a shopping bag and kept on the back seat. My desire to have everything in its place should Amy's parents come to claim what's theirs. I turn onto Main. I've seen pictures of this stretch from back when. The movie theaters. The department store. Their shells still standing, their guts picked over and sectioned off into thrift shops and liquor stores and pizza joints. I park in the potholed lot of a defunct supermarket chain. The store boarded up. The wood layered in graffiti and **No Trespassing** signs. The Patch a half mile away, but on this cold morning, I feel its creep.

I walk Main Street's shadowed side. The chill on my face but not beneath my coat, and I think of Aunt Mary and college, and again, I'm lost among the ghosts, this time not of what was but what might be. Yellow ribbons on the light poles, reminders of a distant war. Cigarette butts tumble on the wind, and above, the sway of town's Christmas decorations. Bells and stars and candy canes, the same grimed menagerie they've been hanging since I was a kid. An angel above me, and here are my childhood Christmas memories. Dollar Store toys wrapped in Sunday comics. My mother nodding out while the TV played movies about families discovering the holiday's true meaning. And most of all, my desire to speed the orbit of sun and stars until I woke on the 26th, free from the season's reminders of how different I was.

A bell announces my arrival in the dry goods store. This place one of the few remaining storefronts from those old photos. The business handed down through the generations. Simple displays. Worn wood aisles, and on the shelves, rubber boots and steel-toed shoes, overalls and waders and straw hats. I walk around, checking prices. A discount table, and from it, I pick a pair of women's gloves. The gloves not as nice as the ones my aunt bought me, imitation leather, but the insides warm. I check the prices, do some quick math, and in me, a softening. This giving in to hope. This match cupped against the wind.

I place the gloves on the counter. Behind the register, framed photos. The store through the years. Generations and hairstyles, and I wonder if a younger version of the woman who rings me up is staring down upon us. She smiles. "Not for you, I'm guessing."

"No ma'am."

"A Christmas gift?"

"Yes."

"Would you like it wrapped?"

I hesitate. "Is that extra?"

She smiles. "No. No charge."

"Then yes, please."

* * *

A pulled cord, and the crawl space's stepladder folds out. I climb until my eyes are level with the floor, wary of the mice who scratch their way into my dreams and the possibility of coming across something bigger. Another step, and I click the flashlight. Cobwebs hang from angled rafters, and from the roof, the radiating cold of last night's snow. I lower the light's beam. The wood floor unfinished and thick with dust. Near the ladder, a handful of boxes, and I take the one with Amy's magic-markered handwriting. **Christmas**, the "i" dotted with a star.

I lugged the box up last Super Bowl Sunday. Amy shrugging, an excuse she liked to stretch out the holiday. Inside the box, a tangle of lights, and beneath, nestled in crinkling tissue, her clay Nativity pieces, remnants from her childhood. I wrapped the figures during the game's halftime show. Amy drifting after her hit, her slur that it was important for Grace to grow up knowing such things. Grace asleep in the diaper I'd

159

just changed. Me wrapping the manger's animals, Mary and Joseph and the baby Jesus, her set missing one wise man.

I string the lights, remembering how they looked the day my mother and I staggered through the door, snow in our shoes and our stomachs empty. Balanced atop a chair, I secure the string from curtain rods, a doorway's molding. The TV on, the news, a video of the defendants being led into the court martial. Then still images. Bodies in a ditch. A village on fire. I unwrap the Nativity pieces and place them, one by one, on the coffee table. Last year, they shared the table with beer bottles and overflowing ashtrays. With spoons and candles. With unfurled plastic when there was tar and crumpled folds when there was powder. All that gone, replaced by the gloves I bought yesterday. The pretty wrapping I know won't be opened on Christmas morning yet which I set out anyway.

The pickup's rattle draws me to the window. The snow not deep enough to plow, yet Chief's truck fishtails on its way down the lane. He parks, and I meet him on the porch, the boards shaking as he stomps the snow from his boots. I assume he's come to fetch me to work, but he says that's not the case. I invite him in, and we sit at the kitchen table. He compliments the lights and declines my offer to brew some coffee.

His fingers drum the table. "I'll pick you up early on the twenty-eighth. We'll work straight through and make sure we're done by the 30th. That OK with you?"

"Sure."

"Didn't want to mess up any New Year's plans."

"No plans."

"OK." He holds his lighter, flipping it one way then another and tapping it on the table. "I'm leaving early tomorrow. Going to my brother's for Christmas. It's a long, fucking ride, but it beats spending Christmas alone."

"Where's he live?"

"Arkansas."

I imagine the map hanging in my social studies class, and I think of the truck, its misfirings and shakes. "That's pretty far."

"Thirteen hours. And that's without stops." He flicks the lighter then pockets it. "Listen, you can come if you'd like. Get you out of Dodge for a few days. Get a decent meal. My brother's woman is a hell of a cook. And they're cool. You'd have a room of your own to crash in. And you'd get to see some things." He smiles. "A lot of highway, to be honest, which isn't that exciting, but at least it'll be a different highway."

My reflex is to say no. To draw a border around my history and heart. To step away from anything that feels like charity. But then I see the deeper moment. The calls that have been made. The reaching out that's as uncomfortable for Chief as it is for me. I look into the living room where the lights soften the afternoon gray. The silent Nativity and a box that won't be opened anytime soon.

"Sure," I say.

* * *

I stamp the porch boards to keep warm. My gloved hands in my pockets. My lips chapped. The pre-dawn pearl of snow-buried fields, and in the east, dawn's blood-shine in the bare trees. Amy's gym bag by my feet. Underwear and socks, a fresh shirt. I see the headlights before the truck reaches the lane, and I think about Kitten, the untouched food I've left out now frozen in its bowl, my hopes she's found a home or at least a barn.

The headlights sweep over me, and when I climb in, Chief hands me a coffee and sandwich. "Thanks," I say.

"Welcome." He works the wheel. The crunch of snow. "It'll be good to have some company." The old man waves from his open door, and Chief honks. I wave too, knowing it means nothing. I told the old man about my plans last night. In the kitchen, the smell of onions and peppers and meat, the pot of chili made to ease my worries about him having something to eat. My visit ending with a reading from Matthew. Jesus in the desert. His time of temptation. The truth that man can't live on bread alone.

The lane's end, and we turn away from town. We pass the quarry. The sun behind us, and our shadow ripples over a road narrowed by snow. I finish my sandwich as we turn onto a numbered road. Sip my last bit of coffee as we loop onto the turnpike. The interchange's cloverleaf, and behind my seat, the slide of Chief's toolbox and his pile of wrapped presents. The classical station fades, and I fiddle with the tuner.

The turnpike's flow absorbs us. The truck's new speeds and new sounds. A heightened vibration, higher pitched, a frequency registered in my teeth and spine. We stick to the right lane, and when a tractor trailer passes, our cab trembles. Chief tells me about his brother, two years younger, and how they used to fight, usually with each other, sometimes against the boys who called them wetbacks and worse. Chief says his brother was the one born with better sense. The one who opened a savings account with his birthday money. The one who did his homework. After their parents split, Oscar returned to Mexico with their mother. For years, Chief lost touch with them. He pauses, swallows, and in his voice, the hesitation of regret. "Saw him for the first time after that about three years ago." He hits the wipers, a smearing of grit and salt. "But this time I'll be sober."

"So it will be different."

"It will."

"That's what Amy used to say. Not exactly, but kind of."

He readjusts his grip on the wheel. "Yeah." Then quieter, "Yeah, she was right."

We don't talk for long stretches. The silences we're comfortable with, our hushed hours in the doctor's house. Radio stations fade, and I tune in new ones. News from the war. Body counts. Updates from the massacre's court martial.

Protests and counterprotests. "Find something else," Chief says, and I do. The hills of western Pennsylvania. The snow deeper here. The miles and miles between exits. The forests of brown and green. The deep ravines, spans we cross as the wind whips around us.

"I could use the bathroom," Chief says. "How about you?"

"I could too."

A few more miles, and on the roadside, a small sign. **State-field Penitentiary Next Exit.** The truck's shamblings fade. A drift to a place my thoughts can't populate yet which I've long imagined. The face I know from the photos that have survived our upheavals. The videotape's thirty-seven words I've counted and committed to memory, a voice which must exist if not in my mind then in my bones and cells. We crest a ridge, and in the distance, lifted on poles a hundred feet high, the exit's welcoming signs. Gas and fast food. The highway's lifeblood, this road that stretches to the sea.

We exit. The ramp's slow turn. Trucks pull into a lot as wide as three football fields. Chief pays for gas, and I buy us the microwave burritos that will pass for lunch. We eat in the truck, and my first bite makes me wish I'd opted for the McDonald's at the lot's other end. Beyond the lot, a stretch of pines, and I think of my father and wonder how close I am, wonder if it's nerves or the truck's tattooed jostle or if I can actually feel him near. And I think perhaps this gut-churn has nothing to do with him and everything to do with the wilderness, a space so vast I'd never considered it until it spoke to me in his voice. Chief shifts into drive, and on the way out, we stop at the lot's exit. To my right, the road winds into the pines, and I imagine it passing the prison, and I think of the locals who drive by it without a thought, barely noticing its towers and barbwire. And I think of the turnpike's flow, this place just another exit in the blur. And I think of my father in a cell, lost in this great sea of not knowing and not caring, and I feel the way I did outside Amy's parents' house as I returned her silver cross to her jewelry box. The understanding there must be more than one kind of death.

We return to the turnpike. The hills of Pennsylvania level into Ohio's flatlands. Farms and pastures. Columbus and Cincinnati with their snarls and skylines, and with the sun reflected in a thousand windows, I imagine all the windows I've looked from, the beholding of the Patch's dirty sidewalks, the farm's wind-touched alfalfa, and I picture someone looking from one of these windows, seeing our truck and wondering, just for a moment, where we're headed. Kentucky next with its hills and valleys, its radio preachers and their beckoning of Jesus. As the sun fades, we stop to fill the tank.

I go inside after pumping our gas. The welcome warmth. Bright lights and narrow aisles. The char of coffee left too long on the burner. Chief at the counter. A glance, but he doesn't acknowledge me. A boy behind the counter. "What pump was that?"

"Three," Chief says.

"Do you mean tres, amigo?" The two men behind him heavyset. Beards, the ruddy cheeks of men who work outside. Their baseball caps and flannel coats. One on his phone, the other, the talker, with a twelve-pack of cheap beer.

The boy behind the counter pushes buttons and checks his display. "Sorry," he says. "It's my first day."

"No problem," Chief says. He places both hands on the counter, a steadying pose. The man with the beer keeps talking, words aimed at Chief. "We shouldn't be court martialing those boys. We should be putting them in charge. We're pussyfooting when we should be kicking ass. Go into a few more shithole villages and send a message to all of them. Kids, grandmas, it don't make a difference."

He squints me into focus, eyes beady and bloodshot, as I

join Chief at the counter. "You should wait in the truck," Chief says.

I look back. "No."

A manager joins the boy behind the counter. A push of buttons and an apology. Chief swipes his card. "It's OK."

The man behind us blusters on: "When we're done with those motherfuckers down there, we should take care of their compadres up North."

I turn, but Chief puts a hand on my shoulder. "Not worth it."

I follow him out. Chief's slow steps. A steady look from the one with the beer. "Got something to say, amigo?"

"I'll leave the talking to you, amigo. Seems to be your strong suit."

Back in the truck, Chief lights a cigarette. The other men exit the store. "What would you have said?" he asks. "Think there's any words that would get through to someone like that?"

Their truck jerks from its spot. A deliberate circle of the pumps, a slowing down as the driver points, his finger a gun, a shot squeezed off. A flash of red brake lights at the lot's exit before they speed off. "Some people just need to shut up," I say.

"Amen, but life's not a movie, man." He rolls down his window and exhales. "You don't often think of the right thing to say, and even if you do, no one's listening." Another drag. "Did you want to fight them? You don't think they've got a gun or two in that redneck limo? You can make the first step, but once you do, you've invited them into your life, and there're no guarantees how it ends." We pull out, our headlights on, and turn back to the highway. "Thanks for stepping in when you did."

"You had this look. Like you couldn't hear one more word."

"I was praying."

I think of Amy's funeral, the bowed heads and folded

hands. The words everyone knew but us. "What were you praying?"

"To not turn around and punch his fat face."

"What happened to 'Life's not a movie'?"

"It's easy to forget good advice when you feel like killing someone." The truck veers over the shoulder's white line when he slides out his cigarette and cranks the window shut. "If God works in crazy ways perhaps I know him better than I thought."

We hit Nashville. The lights smeared by drizzle then smeared again by Chief's wipers. My voice dry, the dust of miles. My eyes glazed with all they've seen. I'm solid and whole, but when I close my eyes, I dissolve, a decomposition into molecules and vapors. I find our first classical station since Cincinnati. The rain steadier. Ahead, glowing signs. Denny's and McDonald's and Exxon, and here are the night's guiding stars. Traffic builds as we near Memphis, and Chief sings a song about a telephone operator and a lost number. "You don't know that one, do you?"

"No."

He rubs the bridge of his nose. "Feeling a little loopy."

"I know what you mean."

"So you're the co-pilot, and here's the co-pilot's job—you've got to slug me if you see me nodding off or if we start to drift. You got that?"

"Yep."

"I'm not shitting you. You keep me awake, OK? Think you can do that?"

"I think."

"I'm a heavy sleeper." He pats his arm, high up, near the shoulder. "Go ahead. Hard as you can."

I hit him.

"That's not going to do the trick. Again."

I punch him, harder.

He rubs his arm. "OK. That might work."

Chief rolls down his window and invites me to do the same. The city lights give way to black, and the road lifts us, a hump of macadam and steel, four lanes then six. For a moment, we're alone. The wind swirls, a current cold and damp, and beneath the girders, the echo of our troubled engine. Halfway across, a sign. **WELCOME TO ARKANSAS**. I can't see the river, but I can smell it, a wetness different than rain, a scent earthy and thick, and perhaps Chief's loopiness has worked its way into my head, but I swear I can feel the tide, the churn that demands its return to the sea. The water's push below, and in my chest, its echo joins the pull of planets and stars and all the broken histories I've been left to piece together.

The girders' flicker ceases. We angle down into a sister city, smaller, and on its outskirts, we leave the highway. A numbered route north. A deeper night here. The wilderness. "The last hour's the longest," Chief says. I no longer tune the radio, and we move in silence.

We reach a little town. Gas stations. Churches. Windows ringed with Christmas lights. I compare the street signs to the map on Chief's phone, but I get turned around, north-south, east-west. Curtains pull aside as we make U-turns in dead ends and driveways. House numbers hidden beneath wreaths. We stop, park. A porch light on. A plastic snowman, his insides lit. Chief holds the phone to his ear. An exchange in Spanish and a weary smile.

The house's door opens. A man in short sleeves and jeans, broad shoulders, visible for a moment before he descends the stoop and becomes a shadow. Chief gets out, and at the light's fringe, the brothers embrace. A slap of backs. Whispered greetings that aren't mine to hear.

* * *

I wake in a baby's room. The end of a narrow hallway. A stuffed bear on the floor, wooden blocks. A changing table. A mobile above a crib. Shelves of brightly colored books. Plastic on the window. The bathroom on the wall's other side, my dreams underpinned by the push of water, a flushed toilet. The bed small, but I'm warm. A night of deep sleep and startled awakenings, my heart calmed with muttered truths. A reflex rooted in a lifetime of opening my eyes in strange places. *I'm OK. I'm safe. I'm OK.*

Last night, I found myself sneaking glimpses of my hosts, wondering what stories they'd been told. Wondering if they were expecting a boy half-wild. Chief's brother Oscar as thick as Chief is wiry, but their noses the same. Their laughs. Oscar's girlfriend Louisa, her black hair in a bun, still wearing the scrubs from her nursing-home shift. Their conversations subdued, the sleeping baby, the stretches where they lapsed into Spanish, words I didn't understand, their welcome unmistakable. The tapas I devoured and Louisa's smile as she brought me more. I didn't say much, but after coming so many miles, it felt good to rest in a house clean and bright.

In the bathroom, I splash water onto my face. The mirror's reunion. A grounding. *Arkansas*, the name repeated, and the knowing I'll be leaving tomorrow makes the word feel like it might not be a word at all. Like it might be a bird's song. The rush of wind in the trees.

The others sit around the breakfast table. Sun on the window. The smell of coffee. Smiles all around. Their Spanish abandoned, and I appreciate the gesture. Chief holds the baby. Esteban, a namesake, a story Oscar told last night about naming his first-born after the brother who always had his back. Luisa hands me a cup of coffee. "Merry Christmas."

"Thank you." I raise the cup to her and the others. "Merry Christmas."

We eat. Sweetbread. The cinnamon churros Oscar invites me to dip into my coffee. Oscar and Chief joke about old times. Their daredevil stupidity. Their brushes with the powers-that-be. The worries they gave their mother. The times they had little and the times they had less. Louisa and I listen, laughing as we imagine the men we know as boys, crazy and reckless, yet, at their cores, little different in the most important ways. I consider the baby's fat cheeks, his shock of black hair. Louisa offers a bottle, and I get the feeling Chief is lost in his past as he holds the nipple to the baby's mouth. The baby latches, and Chief turns silent, mesmerized by the baby's mechanics of face and throat. The rest of us join the quiet. All of us witnesses, this simplest of acts. All of us thinking our own thoughts, Chief perhaps with his own boy, so far away, me with Grace. And I think of Amy's parents and what they must feel this morning. A child they have and a child they've lost and a future so unsure.

The bottle finished, and Chief jokes about the appetite the boy's inherited and the pounds Oscar's put on. Louisa takes the baby, burping him as she leads us into the living room. A small tree in the corner, glass ornaments and tinsel. A star on top. A handful of wrapped presents beneath. Louisa holds the baby, and her other hand reaches for Oscar's. A prayer, at first in Spanish then in English. A thanks for this world's blessings. I bow my head too, and as I listen, I vow to keep my heart open, an admitting that the person I am now isn't the one I will always be.

The presents modest. Warm socks. A shirt. Most for the baby, and Louisa sets him down to crawl through the shred wrappings. There's even a gift for me, a scarf Louisa knitted, a joke that Chief didn't give her much of a heads-up. I thank her, and she smiles in a way that reminds me of Amy when I tell her I've never owned one before. I wrap the scarf around my neck. The wool soft against my skin.

Oscar hands Chief his phone and asks him to shoot a video. A final present, small and hidden, a box with a lid, and he kneels before Louisa. She covers her mouth, nods, and when Oscar stands, he hugs her, her socked feet lifted from the floor. She's crying, the happy kind of tears I rarely see, and she waves Chief over, an embrace for their family's lost sheep, and then a wave for me. "You too, hijo."

I join them. Oscar's strong arm pulls me close. I am a stranger, a boy whose name they'll one day struggle to recall. A boy delivered then washed away upon the tide. But this morning, I am with them, planted in the moment by the picture Chief snaps. His arm extended. The five of us smiling, crowded into a tiny frame, captured in this joyful moment.

* * *

Breakfast the next morning. The sweetbread and churros a day old but still good. Oscar's forgotten lunch pail next to the coffee maker. Louisa with the day off, and as I help her put the dishes away, I catch her admiring her ring. Her hand outstretched, as if questioning its connection to her body. Chief jostles the baby on his knee, and I hold a dishtowel in front of my face. A game Grace loved. The laughter that brought tears to daughter and mother. *Peek a boo.*

Louisa refills our coffees, and Chief tells her stories about Oscar. A filling in of history. The boy he was. Chief describes their poverty as a kind of gift, a stripping down that made it easier to understand what was important. He says he didn't cry when Oscar drove off with their mother, but he's cried a hundred times since. And for all his first memories—of fear and love, want and joy—his brother was near, his presence like a color Chief could never erase.

172

He hands back the baby. He's never talked about his mother and the decision to split their family, and while I might not know the details, I understand the greater story. The upheaval. The stillness that waits after the fire has burned to ash.

Plans are made. Chief insists on fixing the kitchen's leaky faucet, and after we go to the hardware store, we'll swing by the chicken plant and drop off Oscar's lunch. The morning cool but not cold, but I still wear my scarf. The roads quiet. Last night's wilderness lost beneath the sun. A call from the doctor, and Chief reassures him we'll be done and out by the 30th if the doctor has the nursery's paint waiting for our return.

In the hardware store lot, Chief texts his brother for directions. Our last mile behind a trio of loaded grain trucks, a wake of golden dust. Our windshield coated, and when Chief hits the wipers, he says to remind him to stop for new blades before we leave. The plant comes into view. A long fence. Lots crammed with cars. A water tower with the company logo. Storage tanks three stories tall. The plant long and low, flat roofs topped with steam-spewing vents. The wind shifts, and I pull the scarf over my nose.

The trucks roll through the main gate, but the security guard stops us. He says Chief can go in, but if his truck doesn't have a tag, it's got to stay outside. Chief texts Oscar, a plan made, a drop off Chief says will only take a minute. He backs up and parks on the shoulder. "Guard the castle," he says.

He waves to the guard then disappears amid the lot's sheen, the sun fractured upon the sea of windshields and mirrors. I think of our ride home and how the cities and hills will look in reverse—everything backward, east for west, night for day. An unwinding of these past two days until I'm spun back to the old man's farm.

A black SUV rolls up to the gate. The sun a dark star in the windows' tint. The passenger window rolls down, an exchange with the guard. The gate's arm lifts. A man in sunglasses and a black windbreaker exits the SUV. He holds a walkie-talkie to his mouth then waves down the road. In me, the sensation of motion, a trick because I'm not moving yet all else is, the service road a speeding parade, a convoy that, once beyond the gate, fans across the lot. More black SUVs. State troopers. Sheriffs. Then the busses—long and white, the windows reduced to slivers by metal slats, a construction little different than the highway's livestock trucks. The man at the gate turns, and on the back of his windbreaker, the lettering I see multiplied beyond the fence. **Police—ICE**. He's halfway in his SUV when he spots me. He walks over, his stride efficient, crisp. I roll down my window. He leans close, my reflection in his sunglasses.

"What're you doing?"

"We're dropping off a lunch—"

Chatter over his walkie-talkie. "You need to move this truck."

"He'll be out in—"

"I don't care, kid. You need to move it. Now."

Men and women in rubber boots and head-to-toe white coveralls exit the plant, their hands atop their heads. Cruisers with flashing lights block the lot's exits. Overhead, a helicopter, its whir echoing in the cab. The sun lost for a moment in its shadow.

"Do I need to give you a ticket, kid? Do I need to get a goddamn tow truck?"

I slide into the driver's seat. The key in the ignition. The engine catches on the first try, and the silver skull nods. The agent walks off, the walkie-talkie held to his mouth. I cut the wheel but pause when I see Chief. He's the only one not in white. His hands, like all the rest, atop his head. The helicopter makes another pass. I wrestle the wheel, shift into reverse on the opposite shoulder. A final look back. On the service road, I'm a fish against the current. The opposite lane streaming with cruisers. TV vans. Prison busses. My rearview choked with their rush.

* * *

A three-lane stretch. The main drag's traffic lights and gas stations. The questioning of memory as I grope my way back. The bad news that's mine to deliver. My thoughts a carousel of muddled faces and shooting sparks. I find the street, then the house. Louisa's car. A plastic snowman.

I knock. Louisa opens the door, the baby in her arms, and my words melt her smile. I tell her about the cops and the busses and helicopters. Tell her how Chief was herded to the busses, his hands raised, but I can't say for sure about Oscar, everyone else in white. An army of surrendering snowmen.

I hold the baby as Louisa makes ever-more frantic phone calls. To the plant. To Oscar's coworkers. The baby cries, and I try to soothe him, rocking, whispering, but nothing works until Louisa hands me his bottle. As the baby sucks, I consider Louisa. Her paleness. The eyes that can't rest. The voice that grows more and more drained. I've only known her two days, yet I recognize her as my sister. A kinship of dashed hopes. The unbalanced math of poverty—our strong backs and the fragility of our lives—the weariness of living every day so close to the bone.

Hours pass. We don't eat. Phone calls upon phone calls. Other lives, houses like this one where the day started like any other. Truths in short supply, but there are plenty of rumors. The busses taken to a detention center an hour west. Others insisting they've headed south, Louisiana, Mississippi. There's talk of families gathering at the plant to demand answers. Dusk brings the evening news, and we sit by the TV. Shots through the plant's fence. The white parade into waiting busses. An interview with the square-jawed man who barked at me to move the truck. Louisa holds the baby, and then, the day's first tears. What if the raids continue tomorrow. What if she drops her boy at daycare and there's no one to pick him up that evening. What then. What then. I rub her arm, but say nothing. All of my assurances hollow.

Louisa warms up soup, but she can't eat. Dark now, and outside, the return of the wilderness, its crouch outside the door. Her phone buzzes, and even though I don't understand, I know it's Oscar. Her smile. The tears she wipes. She writes on a notepad and glances at me. "Sí. Sí." She places the phone on the table and switches it to speaker. "He wants to talk to both of us. Go ahead, Oscar."

"Mark?"

"I'm here."

"I can't talk long. My brother—they've taken him. The company didn't claim him, so there's no bond. They ran his name and found a warrant back your way. Word is they're taking anyone they have paper on to Jackson, but we're not sure. We only had a minute to talk, but he wants you to take the truck back if you're OK with that. He said there's an envelope with cash in his toolbox, and the registration and pink slip are in the glove. He says you need to get back home and finish the job you've been doing. Once he's straightened all this out, he'll be in touch."

Voices behind him. A man telling him to wrap it up. "Louisa? Louisa? Te amo. No te preocupes. No te—"

The silence sudden. Louisa cries. Her fingers on the black screen.

* * *

My sleep fitful. This child's room. The knowing I have to go. That I'm a stranger who's overstayed his welcome. The baby cries, and yes, Esteban, I feel it too. The uncertainty. The hurt beyond words. Outside my door, the padding of Louisa's feet. The assurances she whispers. My waking thoughts divide the world into two halves. The tears we cry. The words we shape to ease the pain.

Louisa greets me in the kitchen. She wears her work scrubs but says a friend is covering the first half of her shift. There's no further word from Oscar, but the plant has directed families to a bail bondsman, and Louisa hopes they'll be reunited tomorrow or the next day. I have coffee and toast and cereal, and back in my room, I gather my things. I think of the coming hours. Of the city snarls and empty miles. Of the preachers flitting through the radio static and the eye-glaze of a thousand highway miles. I'll be swallowed by the day, as it should be. My problems just a drop in this sorrowful ocean.

Louisa waits in the living room. A bag in her hand, bottles of Gatorade and water, five peanut butter sandwiches, the last of the churros and the apology there isn't more.

"You be safe," she says.

"Thanks. Thanks for everything." I cinch the bag, a crinkle of brown paper. I think of her fears and the life she's trying to carve from this hard rock. "I'm sorry. About everything."

The baby in one hand, and her other reaches out for mine. A squeeze as she closes her eyes and prays for the day's end to find us all in a better place.

"Amen," she says.

"Amen," I echo.

A hug, her hand on my shoulder. "God bless, hijo."

* * *

I feel my way out of town. The wheel's shimmy. South on a numbered state road. Everything backwards. Everything fucked, and I drive into the teeth of it all. Any speed over sixty brings a deeper vibration than the one I'm used to—or perhaps it's just closer now with my hands on the wheel—the rattle a daring of collapse, of thrown rods and busted axles, and I keep to the right lane. Another realization—the skewed alignment, the pull that knots my shoulder before I reach I-40. Then the Mississippi, and I roll down my window. My lungs filled. A taste of the river and the cold, and I think of Chief and wonder if I'll ever see him again.

A traffic jam just east of Memphis. An overturned flatbed. A spill of pipes, and as I inch forward, I add another hour to my trip and try not to think about the night that cuts deeper and deeper into my journey. A trooper waves me by. His hat's low brim, the strap tight to his chin. I keep my eyes forward. The wish for invisibility. The knowing that I've done nothing dishonest—yet the fact of being here and alive makes me a criminal.

Nashville, and in time, Kentucky. A clear stretch, and I eat another sandwich. Steep hills where even the semis pass me, then my shambling descents, my weight poured into my foot, the brakes I hope will see me home. Twenty minutes outside Louisville, I stop for gas. A moment of rest, but the highway's motion stays with me. A sky of ash and static and coming snow. At the pumps, license plates from Michigan, Nebraska, Ontario. Inside, faces I'll never see again, and I think of the way the alfalfa rippled in the summer breeze and how so much of this life comes to us with goodbye stamped upon its hello. I pour myself a cup of coffee. Say "Have a good one" at the checkout. As I cross the lot, the lights high above flick on. The winter dusk, a gray breath before the night.

I return to the interstate. I calculate how far I've traveled and how far remains. I envision the road's straight-line simplicity. I think of the thick night I drove Amy and Grace home from Kmart, the daydream of simply keeping my foot on the gas, of exchanging our troubles for a blank page. And here I am, the same boy with deeper troubles, only now I'm surrounded by anonymous interchanges, each an entrance to a maze of backroads and sleepy towns. I imagine an exit picked at random. Imagine driving until my gut tells me to stop, my only possessions the most important things. A blank page with nothing but my name. My body. My memories and hauntings.

Outside Columbus, the first snowflakes. Traces in the headlights' shine, and soon, the road shifts with powdery swirls. I hit the wipers and remember Chief's plans to buy new ones. I flex my fingers. The numbness of the cold and the wheel's tremors. The jangle of too much coffee and last night's troubled sleep. The snow heavier as I cross into Pennsylvania. Windblown sheets, and I blink, unsure where to focus, then, in a breath, I'm lost. The road gone. The night reduced to the truck's throttle and my wild heart and this tunnel of smothering white. I fishtail, skid, a frantic pawing of the wheel as I come up too fast on a pair of blinking hazards. I put my own hazards on, slow down and follow, yet even at this crawl, I sometimes lose track of the car in front of me. I can't pull over, the shoulder's painted line and guardrails lost. My fear I'll fall into a ravine or be slammed by a tractor trailer. The greater fear that I wouldn't be missed, just erased. Gone.

An exit sign. A name buried beneath the slanting snow, a crawling mile until I veer onto the off-ramp. In my heart, the weariness of a hope stretched thin. I slip my way up the ramp. The plows unable to keep pace, and on the overpass, I fight to align my tires with the snowy ruts. The truck stop an oasis, and beneath the lot's tall lights, funneling dances. A McDonald's at one end, and across the stretching lot, a restaurant and general store and rows of pumps. In the shadows in between, a lineup of trucks, travelers parked for the night.

I duck my chin and walk into the wind. The flakes still find my eyes, my shoes lost in the snow. Behind me, a pickup trundles back and forth. My shadow cast in its orange strobe, its plow's scrape a current in my bones. Inside the McDonald's, the warm thaw. I stomp my boots on the mat, wipe my nose. A few take a moment to consider me. The counter workers in their uniforms and headsets. The dazed customers who've joined me in this refuge. My order taken by a girl my age, and I'm neither hungry nor un, just buzzing. Thankful. The high that comes after fear. I think of watching TV in the Patch, a screen of blues and greens, a cartoon, a talking zebra running for his life, the background a repeating loop of trees and rocks and staring animals. I take my tray and claim a table, the restaurant's insides reflected in the window glass, and in the moment's rest, I'm both the zebra and a ghost of the endless loop. Outside, the snow falls in slanting sheets. The light poles tremble, and beneath, the scurrying plow, its strobe's heartbeat flicker. And I think of the days that brought me here and the days to come. I think of the greater blizzard that will swallow me just as it swallows this life's politicians and millionaires and movie stars, its junkies and convicts. All of us born naked and bloody. All of us with our goodbyes written in our hellos.

An ad hangs on a nearby wall. A pretty girl. This meal she craves. The burger lifted to her beaming smile, the moment between anticipation and fulfillment. I take another bite. The mechanics of chewing. The taste of salt and grease and fat. I'm mesmerized by the girl's teeth. Whiter than snow. Whiter than the sky's brightest star.

The plow's lights pulse in the fogged window. I could crawl up in this booth and sleep until sunrise, and the thought fills me with weight. I bus my tray, zip my jacket. The girl who took my order waits by the door, and as I leave, she answers my question about the name of this town, and with it, the cartoon's loop snaps.

My footsteps muffled. The only sounds the wind and the plow. The truck already lost beneath the snow, and I let the engine run as I clear the windows. When I'm done, I pull to the lot's edge and park. Shadows here, and the gusts funnel between the semis on either side of me.

I dig through my bag, take off my boots and put on an extra pair of socks and lace back up. The sweatshirt Chief stashes behind the seat stinks of grease and cigarettes when I pull it over my head. Louisa's scarf wrapped tight before I secure the hood. Then my coat, my gloves, and deep beneath, me.

Snow piles on the windshield. Pretty at first, but in minutes, all disappears. The cab hums with the plow's ebb and tide. I think of my twin and the life he never lived, think of his imperfect heart, and I move my numb lips and whisper his name, "Jason." My drift sudden, this day that's felt like three. The miles I've come. The cold heavy but not unpleasant. A darkness that feels like a womb one moment, a coffin the next. I close my eyes, assuring myself the storm can't last forever.

* * *

I blink. The cab brought into focus, but I don't move. I've woken into the cold before—busted pipes, cut-off utilities—but this cold cuts deeper. Stiffness in my joints, my fingers and toes numb, but in my head, a begging inertia for this body to stay at rest. The call to remain still and let the blizzard finish its burial. Snow on the windows, and I can't be sure if it's day or night. The cab vibrates, the rumble of engines. Diesel fumes mix with my breath's steam. My door stubborn, the ice's grip, and I lean in, a push from my shoulder until the door swings open. The morning's gray deeper in the semis' shadows. The snow's ended, and to the west, the promise of a lighter sky. The semis idle, the exhausts' light-headed stink. The pickup starts on the fourth try. Twice I drop the scraper, my gloves taken off so I can breathe into my cupped hands. I imagine a map, a dropped pin for home, other pins for where I've been and where I am now, and in me, the wobble of a lost satellite. My abandoned orbit. The pull of space. I brush off the snow and more slides into its place, and there are moments the labor feels hopeless, and what choice do I have but to keep going. I try to think of the day, and I believe it's Saturday, but I can't be sure.

I return to the McDonald's. A stop in the bathroom to run warm water over my fingers. The girl who took my order last night hustles at the drive-through window. I wait behind a pair of bowhunters, eavesdropping, my Saturday beliefs confirmed. I eat, the same booth, watched by the poster of the pretty girl, and I think of Chief, a silent thanks for the mornings he brought me breakfast. I order a second cup of coffee and scan a left-behind newspaper. The war, the justifications of those in power, the dying of the powerless, and the words fade into the morning's white noise. People leave and new ones come. Behind the counter, the workday rush. The calling of orders, steam from griddles and friers.

In the bathroom, I splash water over my face. I consider my reflection, and I think of the truth beneath the lies I've offered the world. I return to the pickup and let the engine idle. I think of the ride home and whether the snow made it over the mountains, and if so, has the old man's nephew been out to plow his lane. I think of the day my mother and I arrived at the farmhouse. Our car stuck in the drifts and our trudge as we lugged our scant belongings and the deafening shot my mother fired into the frigid blue, and I now understand that shot was a starter's pistol, a race I'm still running, only now I'm alone, the others lost along the way.

I pause at the lot's exit. Left back to the interstate. Right to the two-lane that twists into the hills. I adjust the rearview. Behind me, a glimpse of the pickup plow, its work almost done. I pull onto the road. The engine clatters. The slip of my wheels.

* * *

Signs point the way to the penitentiary. A service road, then more signs. No hunting. No trespassing. No unauthorized weapons beyond this point. Above, a glimmer of sun. I take this as a sign, and I think of Derrick and our conversation in a dark room, and I wonder if my life is empty of signs or if they're all around, and I'm just another blind man. The pines break, and there's the prison. A sister to Oscar's chicken plant. An industrial efficiency. A central hub and radiating wings. Steam from rooftop vents. Guard towers and a double-circling of razor-wire fence. The guard at the main gate eyeballs me from behind his booth's glass. A sip from his thermos, a nod when I tell him I'm here for a visit. He waves me through, and inside, I follow the red arrows to the visitors' lot.

I dig through my bag until I unearth my school ID. Others hurry through the cold. A woman pauses by the door, keeping it open for another woman with a child in her arms. I follow,

188

THE LOST AND THE BLIND

and I shiver as the wind hits the building and turns back upon me.

A holding room. Concrete and cinder block. Rows of plastic chairs bolted to the floor. I count eight adults and five children. Whispers. Jackets unzipped. Admonishments to sit still and the wiping of tears. The woman holding the infant waits at the check-in window. I stand behind her, a little to the side, watching. The woman signs a form, and the child held to her shoulder looks back at me. The child's eyes brown and wet. The snot I have the urge to wipe.

The woman steps aside. The guard behind the glass doesn't look up. His focus on his shuffled papers. "Name?" His voice distorted by the glass's embedded speaker.

"My name's—"

"Inmate. Inmate's name." Another flip through his papers. The light's shine on his bald spot. "Who're you here to see?"

"My father. William Hayes."

He checks his computer. Meaty fingers and a keyboard's clack. "And your name?"

"Mark Hayes."

"What time's your visit?"

"I don't have a particular time. Anytime that works is good."

For the first time, he looks up. He reminds me of my shop teacher. A man who's endured too much noise, a countdown to retirement. The door opens. A push of cold air. Another woman with a child. Assurances whispered in Spanish, and I think of Louisa and a little home and the prayers that started my journey. "You don't have a scheduled time?"

"No, sir. I just—"

A guard steps through a heavy door at the room's other end. "Ten o'clock. Ten o'clock visitors, line up." The others stand. The woman with the brown-eyed baby the last in line. One guard checks bags. Another waves a metal detector. A mother swats her son's hand as he tries to pet a German shepherd tethered on a short leash.

The guard behind the glass addresses the woman who's just arrived. "You a ten o'clock?"

"I'm late. Sorry."

The guard waves. "Step aside, kid."

I take a seat. The woman speaking Spanish puts on her visitor's pass as she hurries to join the line's end, and when the door shuts behind her, I'm alone. The room still. The voices gone and the chairs unclaimed. A clock on one wall, and on the other, a poster listing visitors' rules. I return to the check-in. The guard busy with his papers. "Sir?"

He lifts his gaze. "You can't just pop in here, kid. It's not that kind of place. There are rules."

I open my mouth, but I'm frozen. Frozen from the night sleeping in an icy truck. Frozen by the momentum of my days and their crash against this rock. Frozen by the emptiness that waits at the end of a thousand unanswered prayers. And when the spell breaks, I break too, and my words, usually so guarded, pour forth. How I drove through a blizzard and how I woke, numb and buried, in a truck stop. How all I have are pictures and I live over three hours away and it's a miracle my truck's made it this far and I don't know if I'll ever be back. I slide my school ID beneath the glass and apologize for not having a license but he can see this is me, can't he? And I don't realize I'm crying until I feel the tears' warmth, and I say I'm so close here. So goddamn close. Closer than I've ever been before.

He looks at me, his expression unchanged. "Visitors need to call a day ahead. Minimum." The door opens. Another woman, a child who breaks away, a solo race through the waiting room's aisles. The squeak of rubber boots and cries of "Mama, mama!"

I step aside and slump into a chair. The child continues to

run, a blur at the edge of my vision. Stupid, my belief that fate
was holding my hand. My hope that the stars might deliver me,
perhaps not to resolution but at least to a place where I could
give voice to a ghost.

I get up. The guard behind the glass gone. I step outside.
The cold. The wind's bite. I think of the ride ahead, and I'm
thankful at least for clear skies.

"Kid! Hey, kid!"

The guard in the opened doorway. Shirtsleeves. His cheeks
red. He waves me over, and inside, he takes my ID to photo-
copy, gives me a clipboard and a pen. The first pages full of
rules. No exchanges of gifts or money. No bad behavior. No
inappropriate dress. No physical contact outside the visit's
beginning and end. More visitors straggle in. Women with and
without children. An older couple. A preacher. Whispers. The
corralling of children. The clank and buzz of secured doors.
And beneath, another frequency, perhaps one I alone hear. A
seashell hum. The churn of the world lurking beyond these
walls. I take off my gloves, and with pen in hand, I answer the
form's questions. Relationship to the inmate. Length of time
I've known the inmate. Have I been convicted of a misde-
meanor? A felony? Do I associate with known criminals? I sign,
and when I return the clipboard, the guard gives me my school
ID and a visitor's tag. "Call ahead next time, kid."

"I will." A reflex, the desire to shake his hand. The stifling
of block and glass. "Thank you."

The waiting area. My elbows on my knees, and in my
hands, the visitor's pass, and only now, when there's just one
more hill to climb, does the situation's gravity find me. The
years of wondering. The moment's living, breathing reality. I
study the others. An infant, her eyes wide. The preacher with
his hands clasped atop his Bible. The older couple opposite me,
the woman who sighs as she rests her head upon the man's

shoulder. A buzzer and the door at the room's far end opens. The ten o'clock group exits. The snot-nosed baby asleep in her mother's arms. I try to read their faces. Longing. Regret. Acceptance. Each different yet each with a shared expression I recognize. A drawing from a book. A cold room in the Patch. A man who pushed a boulder up a hill. The weariness of labor without end.

Another buzzer, and a guard steps into the room. "Eleven o'clock visitors."

I take my place at the line's end. My name tag read, a check on the guard's clipboard. My arms lifted as another guard waves his metal detector. A march to a new room. The same sterile gray. The same echoes. Small tables bolted to the floor, and bolted to each table, four seats. A row of vending machines against one wall. High above, caged windows, and from them, a dust-dancing light that cuts the room in half. I follow the others' lead and claim a table. I think of church or a movie, all of us facing the same direction, waiting for the show to begin. Another buzz, and then a procession behind the partition of reinforced glass. A guard in front, and behind, men in tan jumpsuits.

I spot my father. The moment blank, the gasp of quarry divers who, for a flicker, wonder if they're falling or flying. His hair shorter than I'd imagined. Ashy skin. His face a shattered mirror, and in the shards, bits of myself. Then the deeper current as he shakes his head and smiles. I stand to greet him. His hug hard, wordless, a slap of my back then another. An embrace held until a passing guard says, "Enough now."

We sit facing each other. Our hands on the tabletop, close but not touching. He smiles. "So."

"So I was on the road and found myself nearby."

"On the road? Like how?"

"I was with a friend for Christmas. I'm on my way home

192

now." I haven't been with him a minute, yet I feel our time slipping away with each pause, each search for the right word. "Figured I was this close."

"Christ. Christ almighty." He turns his palm up, an invitation, a squeeze quick and hard when I place my hand in his. A wetness in his eyes despite his smile. "Don't know what to say. Sometimes you think about something forever, and when it happens, you can't find your tongue."

"I know."

"Your mom? How's she?"

"OK. The same."

"Yeah, I figured. I sent letters you know. Years of them. For her and you."

"We've moved a lot. I still have a few letters. And some old movies."

"That camera. Shit. Forgot about that."

"I didn't plan well. Should've brought you something."

"What do I need?" Another squeeze for my hand, and the guard behind me says, "Back off there."

My father pulls back and rests his hands on his lap. A toddler runs by, and from my father, a smile as the boy pushes buttons on the vending machines. "Tell me everything," my father says.

I tell him about the farmhouse, but not about Amy. Tell him about chopping the old man's wood and reading his Bible. Tell him about Thanksgiving with Aunt Mary and the recruiters I've been talking to. Tell him about Chief, who he remembers with a smile, and our work at the doctors' house, but not about his lockup with ICE. Tell him I'll be better about writing even though I can't say how long I'll stay at the old man's house. The room's voices fall away. Whenever I pause, he smiles and urges me to tell him more. I talk to stall the clock, talk more than I've ever talked before. Talk until my throat goes dry. Talk until I barely know what I'm saying. Talk to fill his image of me, to give him the colors that might rescue me from the fog.

A buzzer, and the others gather their things. Hugs and prayers. A child cries. My father stands. "Don't be a stranger."

"I'll write. Promise."

"I'll look forward to it." He opens his arms, and I go to him. He holds me close, a whisper. "Sorry, bud. I didn't make it easy for you."

"It's OK."

He steps back, hands on my shoulders. "Keep your head on straight."

"I will."

The buzzer sounds again. The door opens, and I join the exiting line. I look back, a final glimpse, but he's already on his way out, lost among the other tan jumpsuits.

* * *

The pickup bucks its way up the state's western hills, and on the brake-pumping descents, the valleys open up. The slate rivers. The pen strokes of naked trees against the white. I squint. The sun, the windshield's salt. The radio off, but there's music in the engine's shudder. Cars pass then disappear, and for long stretches, I'm alone. I'd imagined my reunion with my father a thousand times. Backdrops borrowed from TV shows and movies. Our exchanges dependent upon my moods, tearful or angry or ripe with prison-Zen. What I hadn't imagined was finding a heart gouged as deep as mine. What I hadn't imagined was that the pain I've carried wouldn't be doubled in his eyes but halved. My shoulders lighter. This burden shared.

Road signs count down the miles to familiar cities. At times, I struggle to focus. Weariness, the glare of endless snow. My eyes fixed not on the road but the passing forest, a wilderness less wild without my father's ghost. I take the next exit. A

195

truck stop, cars at the pumps. Bundled travelers filing in and out of the diner. I fill the tank, but when I do, I realize my gloves are missing. I check my pockets, the cab, and the last place I can remember having them is in the prison waiting room, and I hope they've been found by someone who needs them. My hands in my pockets, my feet shuffling. I picture the distance to home and the sun's place in the sky.

Inside, I claim a counter seat, order coffee and cherry pie. I listen to the room's conversations. Listen to the music from the kitchen radio. The waitress tops off my coffee and calls me "Sweetie." My fork scrapes the plate even after the last crumbs are gone, and I think not about my life's hunger and upheaval, its blood and beatings and death, but about its tide of small kindnesses. A tide that hasn't delivered me to shore but which has at least kept me afloat. Chief and the old man. My aunt and Louisa. Mrs. Pike and Mr. Ford and a prison guard who hustled into the cold to help a kid too ignorant to know the rules. A refilled coffee cup and a caring word. A second chance and another chance after that. I may be down to my last dollars, but I'm coming to understand another kind of currency. One that has nothing to do with my wallet.

I finish my cup, leave what I can for a tip. A turn of the key, and I smile, a memory of my first ride. The thermos I considered using as a weapon. The wondering if the truck would survive the five miles to the farmhouse. I return to the highway. Daylight's last hour, and the truck's shadow stretches ahead, longer and evermore distorted until it crumbles into dusk. I think of Theseus, and I'm happy not to be returning beneath black sails. Happy to be surrounded by moonshine as white as spilled milk.

Chief's voice with me as I exit the highway. *The last hour is the longest.* My only desire to stop moving. To step across the threshold and spark the fire that will burn long into the night and then sleep until I run out of dreams. Home, I've never felt the pull as much as I do now. *Home*, I think. *Home*, and I say it out loud, say it over and over in a delirium of mind and body. I pass the quarry. A final turn onto the farmhouse lane. The lane plowed, the snow here half of what I woke to this morning. The tires' muffled crunch. The back end's sway.

I park by the farmhouse porch. The engine kept running so the old man knows it's Chief's truck. My feet the first through the snow. I see him inside, the naked windows and bright lights. A smile as he feels his way to the door.

"Mark?"

"Yes, sir." I take his groping hand, a grasp joined by his other hand then mine. "Merry Christmas."

"Merry Christmas, son." Another beat, a final pat of my hand before he lets go. "It's good to have you back."

"It's good to be back. I'll come by tomorrow morning and shovel. Is there anything you need tonight? I can run into town if you'd like."

"No, no. I'll see you tomorrow." He waves toward the truck. "Tell your friend I said Merry Christmas." I'm halfway to the truck when he says, "I gathered up a bunch of old blankets. Walked them down before the snow. Set them on your porch."

I thank him then continue down the lane. The headlights reach ahead. Amy's car gone, and I'm glad her parents came for it. Glad they've cut their ties to this place and are now free to remember her as they please. I roll to a stop but don't get out. The house dark, and beyond the plowed path, a pair of tracks through the snow. I pull closer, and the headlights sweep over the porch. The windows unbroken. The door still on its hinges.

The old man's pile of blankets bigger than what I'd expected. The blankets not folded but heaped in a sloppy mound, and I imagine him, blankets in hand, his tapping cane, a journey that must have felt like its own kind of wilderness. I kill the engine, but when the pile stirs, I leave the headlights on. I think of squirrels, raccoons, the animals that keep me up at night with their scurryings. The pile lifts, and beneath a blanket's halo, a face. Eyes that reflect my headlights' shine.

* * *

I turn off the headlights and get out. In the snow, my footsteps beside hers. I picture her back-road trudge. The headlights that lifted then returned her to the night. A porch board groans as I kneel before her. I lift the blanket, and in this faintest of lights, she blinks, with me but not. A face half-drowned in polluted waters. I coax away the blanket she's clutched to her throat. Her body lost beneath a sweatshirt two sizes too big. A stain on the sleeve I hope isn't blood.

"Mama?" I whisper.

I ease her to her feet, and I'm taken back, wondering if she's lost weight or just so dopesick she can't put one foot in front of the other. Her body reduced to whispers and ash and the night's faint breeze.

Inside, and we squint beneath the sudden light. She slumps onto a kitchen chair. I adjust the thermostat and hope there's enough oil *to see* me to the next delivery. I spark a fire in the stove. The flame slow to catch, but then its crackle. I pause, crouching, studying the flame through the grate. Not wanting to face her until I know what to say.

The stove's heat on my cheeks. "Are you in trouble?"

A voice like smoke. "Water."

I fill a glass and her hands tremble as she brings it to her mouth. A sip, then another before she retches. A thin string from her lips. I dab a paper towel over her face then the floor.

"Where's your car?"

"Don't have it anymore."

"You in trouble?"

She lifts her head, and for the first time, she looks at me. "Where have you been?"

"Wouldn't believe me if I told you."

She raises the glass. "Try me." A sip and a wince, but she keeps it down.

"I saw Dad."

Her eyes return to mine. "Fuck you did."

"He's OK. Considering. We had a good talk."

"I'll bet." The glass slips from her hand. It hits the floor but doesn't break.

"You're sick." I pick up the glass.

She shakes beneath the blanket. A quivering in her shoulders and arms, and I'm reminded of a bird I found last summer in the barn. Its wing broken. The shadows' tail-twitching cats.

"When did you last fix?"

"Yesterday." A pause. "I'm kicking."

"Kicking or just out of money?"

"I can't do it anymore." She coughs, the sound dry, painful. "I've got nothing left."

I guide her to the bathroom and turn on the shower. The room cold, and the steam builds. I help her strip to her bra and panties. The butterfly tattoo that matches Amy's. The tracks across her veins. Her bruises and scars. The roadmap of a hard life. I turn away as she takes off the rest and steps into the shower, but I stay near. A seat on the toilet and a towel on my lap.

I listen to the water. My toe nudges her sweatshirt and dirt-crusted jeans. I've seen enough to know what waits. The sickness. The wishing for death. When the shower ends, I hand her the towel then gather sweatpants and a T-shirt from the clothes she's left behind. She collapses back into her old bed, and then the long night. The bucket I hold as she retches up bile and then the retches that bring up nothing. Double D, who'd kicked twice in jail, described the pain as the clutch of a giant fist, his bones breaking beneath his skin. When she's not groaning or disoriented, my mother curses, not at me, although I'm the only one to hear. Her hate aimed at something bigger, something vast, something you'd never think of until it fell from the sky and smothered you. "Fuck," she mutters. "Fuck you," and I wonder if she's surrendering or throwing up her fists in a final, snarling defiance.

Her molars grind. Her arms clutch her gut, a doubling like she's trying to fold herself into a period that could end this story. The room's sourness—sweat, vomit. I dab a washcloth over her face. I don't tell her everything will be OK; I just remind her that I'm near. This night longer than any I've known, yet dawn still comes, not with the sun but with a stubborn easing of black, and it's in this grizzled light that my mother finally sleeps. The silence heavy, and I arrange the old man's blankets on the floor, and when I close my eyes, I think of a stone tossed into the quarry. Falling, falling, until I disappear.

I stay with her all the next day. The snarls. The murmurs to just leave her the fuck alone. Her face as bloodless as Amy's the afternoon I found her slumped on the couch, but at least Amy escaped her pain. I help my mother to the toilet, and in the bedroom, she collapses back into the fever that consumes us both. Chief and my father no more real than a dream. My world reduced to this dank room. This wilderness. This monster.

Evening. Sunset after a day of clouds. As my mother sleeps, I count my money and imagine its dwindle. I haven't eaten since a truck stop's cherry pie, and in me, the imbalance of emptiness and weight. The inward consumption, the cannibalization of cells and tissue.

I sit on the bed's edge. The washcloth gentle on her brow. "I'm going into town. Get us some food, OK?"

She squints me into focus and manages a nod.

"I'll be back soon." A dab for her chapped lips. "Promise."

I stop at the mailbox at the lane's end, and amid the old man's seed catalogues and assisted-living fliers, an envelope for Amy. I read the return address then slide out the card, and I remember the hot afternoon I helped Amy activate her first SNAP card, her so high she couldn't keep from nodding, but it all comes back to me now. The Greeks had their gods, and I have the system's bureaucracy. Each brutal, each careless. The footsteps of giants. The scurry of mortals. Yet each with their strange gifts, the breadcrumbs that fall from the feast. I close my hand around the card. A thanks to the dead who still have something to give.

I choose the supermarket nearest the Patch. A place where food stamps don't raise eyebrows and no one will care that the name on the card isn't mine. I fill my cart. Fruit and meat. The items canned and boxed that will see us through this week and next. The aisles bright. The speakers' music. A final thought— crackers, an extra loaf of bread to toast, ginger ale—the foods my mother will be able to keep down when she comes through the other side. The checkout made without a hitch, and as I carry the bags across the lot, I feel justified, buoyant, my finger —for a moment—tipping a scale that's so long been set against us.

I stop at the doctors' house. My plan to return tomorrow. To finish our work and clean up and, if the doctor comes by, explain. The key beneath the back-porch planter. The lights turned on—kitchen, dining room, living room. Spaces clean and white, and in the corners and along the walls, the items I'll gather. Trays and tarps and tape. The rubber mallet. A radio. In the foyer, a gallon of blue paint. A post-it on the can, the hospital logo I've seen printed on bills stamped *Past due* and *Final notice*. A message scribbled in ink.

It's a boy!

* * *

I set my roller in the tray and step back. The nursery's first coat done, the blue overwhelming after these weeks of white. Bach on the radio, a violin concerto, and between songs, the prediction of tonight's single digits. I've listened to this station at home, but it's not the same. I prefer my Mozart in empty rooms. A space where the notes can swell then sink into themselves. I circle the room, my eyes on the borders and corners and trim. I feel Chief near, and I want to do right by him.

The front door opens. The doctor calls up the stairwell. "Mark?"

I step into the hallway. "Up here."

He bounds, two steps at a time. The bicycler's spring. His suitcoat and bowtie. The swinging lanyard. He reaches the top, offers his hand, but withdraws it when he considers the paint on mine. I follow him into the nursery. "It looks different on the walls, doesn't it? The color I mean."

"I think that happens sometimes." I step out of his way as he circles the room. "I'll be back tomorrow to give it a second coat." I unplug the radio. "And I'll clean everything up and be out of your hair. Should I leave the key on the back porch?"

In his gaze, the look of a future that doesn't include me. "Yes, that would be fine." He turns to me. "Big plans tonight?"

"Plans?"

"New Years. Do you have any plans?"

The date lost in the week's haze. "Yes," I lie.

"Here." He reaches into his vest pocket. "Your boss got in touch with me. Said he got delayed in his out-of-state job, but he was happy that you're finishing things. Guess you already knew that."

I imagine a prison phone. The impatient murmur. A snarling guard. The doctor produces an envelope. "He asked me to give you the second half, but he said it had to be cash, which is a bit of a pain."

He opens the envelope, and inside, a fanning of green, but before he hands it over, he removes two fifty-dollar bills. "The work was promised to be done by the 30th. That was our agreement." He pockets the bills and hands me the envelope.

I hold the envelope. I think about the bills inside—and the ones he made a show of removing. His phone rings, and he turns to me. "Got to take this. I'll stop by tomorrow." He hurries down the stairs. "Yes, yes. I'm on my way." The door slams behind him.

Midnight, and I step onto the porch. The cold steals my breath. My mother asleep. Still sick, yet in a different way. Pale, wrung out, but there's no more groaning, no more cursing. There was even a smile when I told her what day it was. "Well happy fucking New Year to us." Words that sounded like they were whispered from the bottom of a well.

Snow on the fields. The stars above. The cheers and music from town lost in the miles between us, and though part of me is lonely, I'm content to be left to my thoughts. I've never cared much for New Year's. The clamor over a turned calendar page. Another excuse to get high—but tonight, I soften. I pull Louisa's scarf tight to my neck and consider the value of pause. A breath to remind myself of what's important. The chance to contemplate the empty rooms that will be mine to fill.

* * *

The old man's kitchen. A boiling pot, and in it, the remains of last night's chicken. The water browned, fat and skin and marrow, the floating chunks of celery. A squeeze of tongs, and when I lift, the bones fall away, and what remains on a bird most would throw out is enough for two meals, maybe three.

The old man sits at the table. His nose lifted, an inhale before he tells me about his mother's soup. Her belief that using every part of an animal was the deepest kind of respect. An honoring of life and the gift of sustenance. I pick and shred, careful not to burn my fingers, and by the time I'm done, the piles of bone and meat are more or less equal. I return the meat to the broth and stir in the rice that's been cooking on another burner. I set the pot aside to cool and join the old man at the table.

I gather myself, the truth I need to share. "My mom's home. Maybe you already knew that."

He nods. "Knew something was different. The rhythm of things at least."

"I've been taking care of her."

"She's sick?"

"She's getting better. Slowly."

"Is it drugs?"

"It is. Or was. She hasn't used since she came back."

"The sheriff's been stopping out. Usually when you're at school. My daughter worries, you know. I don't want anything like what happened to Amy happening again."

"I don't either." I rest my elbows on my knees, my hands squeezed and rubbed until I conjure the right words. "You've been good to us. I don't want to overstay our welcome. I don't want you to feel that way. You never agreed to rent to us in the first place. I don't even know if Amy asked if we could move in."

His gaze just over my shoulder. "You stay as long as you like. No need for a good house to go unused when there's people who need it."

I stand and busy myself. The counter cleaned, the dishes rinsed. A moment to breathe. The kindnesses that rock me harder than any punch. The swooning gap between the world I know and expect and the one that ambushes me with its goodness. I don't need to say anything—the old man sees and understands. I keep my back to him.

"How's the soup look?"

"Got a lot here."

"Good. You take some. Enough for the two of you. What am I going to do with so much?"

* * *

I make my mother toast, brew the last bag of Amy's herbal tea. The toast my mother's first solid food. Crumbs on her plate and shirt. The tea sipped, her hands wrapped around the mug. Her chewed nails and scarred knuckles. "So it's a school day?"

"I don't have to go."

"Alarm. Shower. Sure looks like you're going."

"I wanted to be ready just in case."

"You head in. Be nice to see your friends again." She pushes back her hair. "So how's school going?"

"OK. No worries."

"You've never been a troublemaker, have you?"

"Not my style."

"Had enough trouble at home." She brings the cup to her mouth and blows back the steam. "More a lover than a fighter."

"What about you? What will you do all day?"

"I'm not going anywhere but back to bed." She dabs the

crumbs off the plate and brings her finger to her mouth. "Maybe I'll make us some dinner. Maybe I'll go for a walk, just out to the road and back."

"It's cold. I'll leave my coat."

"Don't do that."

"I've got my old jacket. And my sweatshirt. School's plenty warm."

Her fingers drum the mug's side. "It's a nice jacket. Where'd you get it?"

I'd lie to the stoned her. A truth better kept to myself. Her temper. The baptism incident. The bonds the sisters had forged through mere survival worn out by my mother's broken promises. The things she's stolen. Her betrayals. But in the morning light, her eyes are clear, and she deserves the truth. "Aunt Mary bought it for me. I spent Thanksgiving with her."

She nods, sucks her lip. "How is she?"

"She's good. She asked about you. She said if you ever needed—"

She closes her eyes, an expression not of avoidance but of pain. "I know. I know."

"I have something for you." I leave then return with the wrapped box that's been sitting on the coffee table amid the Nativity pieces. "If you go out on that walk."

She gives the box a shake. "Really?"

"I wanted to be ready. Just in case."

"You said the same thing about school today."

"Maybe I had a feeling."

She turns the box one way then another. "Look how pretty."

"They wrapped it for me."

She peels back the paper and lifts the lid. "Will you look at that?" She brings the gloves to her nose then slides them on. "I'll be ready for that fucking walk now, won't I?"

She stands, and we embrace. "My little man." She steps back. "Better get going. Don't want to be late and fuck up your perfect attendance."

Perfect attendance—an old joke, a truant officer's scolding before my mother told him to fuck off. "Go, go," she says, a wave of her gloved hand. A dismissal and the promise to call if she needs anything. The truck stubborn in the cold. The key's third turn comes with a prayer and a curse, and when the engine catches, I keep my foot on the gas. The exhaust coughs, and every bolt rattles. Soon, the morning will come when no coaxing will get her to turn, a scenario I've been anticipating since my first ride. A storm and a funeral and a man I feared. The miracle of surviving the hills of Pennsylvania and Kentucky. The luxury of living on borrowed time.

I retrieve the doctor's envelope from the glove and lift the flap. I fear my mother finding the envelope. Her fragility. Her weakness. Even more, I fear the cops. The straight arrows who'd hear my last name and scoff at the contention that I'd earned it. The crooked ones who'd pocket the stack and leave me with a black eye and the threat of worse. The engine idles as I take the envelope to the barn. The junk heap coated in frost. A cat scurries between my legs. I think of the barn's mice, the things they'll eat, and I pick through the junk until I find the old man's toolbox. His initials etched into the grimy lid. The box dented but intact, and the latches' rust powders my fingers as I snap them into place. Then the groan of an oven's hinges, the toolbox placed inside and the door shut. A burial. Another secret.

* * *

I wait for Kate after lunch. Above me, a sky-blue banner. *Winter Dance*, white paint, snowflakes and stars. Faces stream by, and I think of the highway, the cars and cities and lonely farms, and I think how we're all mysteries to each other. The surfaces we offer, the stories we tell. The balancing act of what to keep buried and what to set beneath the sun.

Andy appears, shakes my hand. "Happy New Year, brother." Derrick and Jason pause, and we offer each other fist bumps. "We stopped out," Andy says. "You're a hard man to track down."

"Was out of town for a while."

Andy brushes his bangs from his eyes. "Dig it. I got to jet. Can't be late for math again."

Jason follows him, but Derrick lingers. "Out of town, huh."

"Took a little trip." I look over his shoulder, not wanting to miss Kate.

"Good for you. I can't wait to shake off this shithole." He

212

rubs a finger beneath his nose. "Been thinking about that house where we hid. The place you were working."

"Yeah?"

"The key." He steps closer. His voice low and his pupils wide. "I'm thinking we make a copy and wait for the doctors to move in. No doubt they'll have some good shit. We wait for the right moment and make a few things ours. Reappropriate. Steal from the rich and all that."

Birth and fate are strands of the same rope. Teachers and cops and preachers—they love the fairy tale that we're all equal. The good ones even believe it. In their fairy tale, the space between *Once upon a time* and *happily ever after* is filled with a childhood of new clothes and music lessons and dentist visits. Their stories don't have room for people like Derrick and me. We scare them, our origins, our wildness. Our poverty reminds them of how far they could fall and that their fairy tale is bullshit. I have no allegiance to the doctors, and my gut knots when I think of the surgeon's manicured nails plucking those bills. Derrick is more my people than the doctors will ever be, and my *no*, despite the understanding it's right, feels like a betrayal.

"Can't do that, man." I spot Kate, but when I step toward her, Derrick slaps his hand against my chest.

"Don't let a good thing pass us by, man." There's nothing good in his tone or the increasing pressure of his palm.

I grab his wrist. "Back the fuck off." The stream slows. Heads turn. Derrick's reputation. The anticipation of spectacle.

"Hey there," Kate says. Her smile fades as she glances to Derrick then me. I let go of his hand, a shove to match his, an exchange of stares before he walks off.

Her hand on my shoulder stops me from looking back. "What was that all about?"

"Nothing." We join the hallway flow. The corridor's echoes and shuffling pace. My heart eases.

"You guys friends?"

"Not really. Same circles, I guess."

She adjusts her backpack. "He can be a dick."

"I know."

Her hip bumps mine. A game we play, trying to knock the other off balance. "So did you miss our after-lunch chats?"

"I did. Truly."

"How was your break?"

"OK. Went some places. Kind of a spur of the moment road trip."

"Yeah? Where to?"

"Arkansas. And everywhere between."

"Well, that wouldn't have been in my top five guesses. How was it?"

"OK. A lot of driving. How about you?"

"How do you expect me to top a road trip to Arkansas?"

A turn down the science wing, and we pause outside her class. "I'll fill you in on the details if you let me drive you home after school."

She raises an eyebrow. "You traded in your slick bike for a car? Do tell."

"A pickup. An old one. It's not mine. It's a work thing. It's a little rough and rusty, but I'm pretty certain it'll get you home."

"Now I'm intrigued." She smiles. "Meet me at my locker, OK?"

I end the day in Mr. Ford's class. My mind on Kate, what it will be like to sit beside her, just the two of us. My window seat, and Mr. Ford's talk about a red wheelbarrow thins. The playing fields covered in white. The flurries that trace another cloudy afternoon. I think of my mother, marooned by miles of farm-land, no phone, no money, no car, and the knowing I won't come home to find her with a needle in her arm, that the next time my phone rings it won't be the hospital or the police, makes me feel gutted, but only in the best of ways. This life of worry, at least for today, eased, and in the place where I'd buried those fears now waits a void, clean, full of light and air.

"Mark?"

I look away from the window. Mr. Ford stands at the aisle's end. The girl in front of me turns in her seat, a mirror of Mr. Ford's gaze.

"Are you with us, son?"

I sit up. "Sorry, Mr. Ford. I was just looking outside."

He offers a put-upon look. "You'll hurt my feelings if you tell me this overcast afternoon is more interesting than Mr. William Carlos Williams."

"I was just thinking."

"About what?"

"About how sometimes the world is a kind of beautiful place."

Mr. Ford smiles. The girl in front of me cocks her head, an expression like I'm speaking a different language.

I park in front of the doctors' house. The driveway empty. The windows still naked, and in the glass, a dull reflection that reminds me of the old man's eyes. I think about Kate. A joke as I dropped her off, a handshake that lingered into my awkward goodbye.

My boots in the yard's snow. The porch. A hand held above my eyes, a peek through the window. The view that stretches into the dining room shadows. I lift the planter and place the key beneath, making sure I'm returning the original and not the copy I just had cut at Home Depot. A final look before I return to the truck.

* * *

Later that week, I return from school. The lane's snow packed and icy. The days' slow melt. The shivering nights and my thanks for the old man's blankets. Clear today. Blue skies and a frigid sun, and from the fields, a glare so bright I don't notice the black pickup until I reach the barn. A man stands on the porch. He's thick in the shoulders and gut. A bushy beard and a blue skull cap. Jeans and boots and a corduroy jacket. I peg him for a bail bondsman or repo man, a business just north of legal but as dirty as any corner hustle in the Patch. I grope beneath the seat and pull out the rubber mallet. I get out but leave the door open. The man nods. "Well look at you." His breath steams, his face, for a moment, lost. "All grown up."

"What's your business?"

"Your mom called, Mark, and I came out." He hits his fob. The black truck starts, a thick rumble, even and steady. He

217

takes the porch steps one at a time. I inch closer to the cab but then realize his focus isn't on me but the ground. The slick snowpack and a boot that drags behind the other.

"Do you think you can drop your mom off in town tonight? I'd fetch her, but my girl has dance class." He shakes his head. "Dance class, if that's not a racket."

"I'll give her a ride anywhere she needs, but I have to hear it from her."

He climbs into his truck. The raised cab. The practiced hoist of a leg that appears to be formed of a matter denser than the rest of his body. "I think she's willing. You know where the Methodist church is, on the north side?"

I shut my truck's door. I know the church. Amy's casket. Grace's blabber. "I do."

"Great. See you there around seven. And Mark?"

"Yeah?"

"Your mom needs you now. You've helped her through this —and I know what that takes." He shuts his door. The sun glints on the bed's silver toolbox. A goodbye beep halfway down the lane.

Inside, my mother sips coffee at the kitchen table. Another mug, half-filled, across from hers. "There's some brewed in the pot. Decaf though."

"Who was that?"

"You didn't recognize him?"

"No, but he knows me. What's he want with us?"

A wrinkle of her pale lips. "No need to worry. If anyone's scared of the other, it's him."

I open the grate and add another split to the stove. "Enlighten me."

She lights a cigarette. "You seen me stab him."

Still crouched, I turn to her. I see a dirty kitchen. Summer hot and buzzing flies. A flicked cigarette. A steak knife driven deep into a thigh. His ungodly cries and blood-soaked jeans. His glassy stare gone but a limp that's followed him through the years. "Shit. What was his name?"

"Roger." A shift of her jaw, a side exhale. "Good old Roger-dodger."

"And he wants you at church?"

A lazy flourish of her cigarette-holding hand. Above her head, a smoky halo. "Maybe they'll hose me down in holy water."

"You're not answering my question."

She takes a puff. Her sober smoking different. Slower. Deeper. Each inhale held for an extra beat. "I saw him around Thanksgiving. I wasn't in a good way. He said he'd been straight nearly nine years. Said to call him if I ever needed a hand."

"And you said yes?"

"I said fuck off. Said I'd stab his other fucking leg so he'd have a fucking pair. He says I spit on him. That I don't recall, but it could be true. He gave me a business card, which I tossed, but I remembered enough to find him in the book."

"I didn't think they made phone books anymore."

"The old man has one. Used it and his phone." She pantomimes the rotary dial, another smoky halo.

"So the church thing is a meeting. AA or whatever."

"Roger goes every week. More if he's feeling the need. He wanted to take me, but he has some kid thing. That's why he was waiting on you." A final exhale before she grinds her cig into the ashtray, and even this is languid. The ashes stirred. The butt crumpled. "Who would've guessed old Roger-dodger would pull up again, all front and center?"

She returns to bed. I bundle up and visit the old man. I make him eggs and bacon and clean the kitchen. I bring wood from the porch and tend to his stove. We talk about my mother, and he tells me about a brother who drank himself to death. For years, he says his heart was broken, but now he's free to remember the person he loved before the demons took hold. Before he stopped loving himself and the world. "I believe," the old man says, "if there's a next life, that's the brother waiting for me."

Back home and another dinner made. A plate set before my mother, and when she compliments me, I tell her a boy can learn anything on YouTube. She says the most cooking I'd seen her do was with a spoon. She laughs, then she doesn't.

She's quiet on the ride to town. The countryside's early dark. Town's snow-piled curbs. Main Street's Christmas decorations packed up but the yellow ribbons remain, their brightness faded. A handful of cars in the church lot. I turn off the engine but neither of us get out. Spotlights on the steeple and stained glass. Another building radiates from the church, a wing of brick and dark windows, and I imagine the Sunday school classes Amy once told me about. Veggie Tales and Jesus loves me, this I know. A floodlight above the entrance.

"I should have gone to her funeral." She's wearing her new gloves, and her knuckle taps the window glass. "I was scared. Again. Like always. I'm just seeing that now, how scared I've been."

"I went."

She turns, and I imagine myself rendered in the same shadows.

"I went for both of us. It was sad. I didn't want to make her folks feel any worse, so I sat in the back. That's where I met up with Chief."

She rests a hand on my shoulder then lets it fall away. Her smile has little to do with happiness, but it's a smile all the same. "I'm scared now. To go in. To say it out loud."

"Never thought of you as scared. Not after some of the folks I've seen you take on."

"I was. I've always been—but I'd rather die than let anyone see it."

"How do you feel now?"

She studies the lit door. "Like I want to fight. Or run. Or get high as fuck."

"I'll come in with you. If you want."

She turns to me. There are no smiles now. "We've seen each other through some shit, haven't we?"

"We have."

"I know part of this is making amends." She nods. "Don't know if there's enough breath in my body to say all the sorrys I owe you."

"I don't need any sorrys. Not now."

A car door shuts, and a man crosses the lot. A pause at the light's fringe, a cigarette's final inhale. My mother opens her door. I follow, careful to let her take the lead. The light over the entrance harsh, and my mother shields her eyes. Inside, a dry heat. The long corridor dimly lit, and before us, a white board. An arrow pointing toward a stairwell, a note in blue marker. *Recovery Group Downstairs.*

"Guess recovery group sounds better than junkies' meeting."

The steps taken slowly, with thought, her hand on the railing. The stairwell empties into an open basement, a sweep of red and black tile. At the near end, a tiny stage. An upright piano. Along the walls, bins of children's toys. God-themed posters. At the room's far end, a table with a pair of coffee makers and a stack of Styrofoam cups. Beside the table, a circle of folding chairs. About half the chairs claimed. Men and women who sit in silence. Their coats draped across their laps. Some on their phones. Others staring at the floor. A few stand

by the table. Quiet conversations. The sipping of coffee. Shuffling feet.

We pause inside the entrance. We shared an embrace from
the beginning, the womb and the life I found there, the world
that nurtured my brother and me, and ever since, it's been like
that. The moment so often lost on her, and the roles I assumed
—conduit, buffer, interpreter. Tonight, she's present, and her
apprehension becomes my apprehension. Her fear mine. My
hand on her elbow. Her body rigid. An encasing in ice and the
threat of crashing into a thousand irretrievable pieces.

"Jill." Roger exits the stairwell behind us. His limp agitated
by his hurry. He puts an arm over her shoulder, a gentle
guiding to the chairs. A glance back at me. A nod.

We sit. The chairs scrape the tile. The last stragglers join
the circle, and around me, the smell of bad coffee. Some say hi
to Roger, but their gazes linger on my mother. Recognition, if
not in person then in spirit. A mirror of themselves and where
they've been. A different kind of recognition for me because I
know these people, too. Our place along the margins. The
things we've done and the things we do without. Our ripped
coats and worn shoes. The stories written on our faces.

A man with glasses and salt-and-pepper hair calls everyone
together. He takes off his glasses, rubs the lenses with his shirt
tail and thanks us for the opportunity to share the next hour or
two. He puts his glasses back on and retrieves his clipboard.
Updates on the foodbank's hours. The helpline numbers for
unemployment now that Amazon has made their seasonal
layoffs. The church's clothing drive.

He sets the clipboard beneath his chair and folds his arms
across his chest. "So remember we're all here for each other.
And we're all on the same voyage. So let's be good to one
another."

Some in the circle nod. The man next to me, the one with

222

the tattooed knuckles, mutters "Amen" as he stares into his coffee cup.

The man with the glasses stands, a single clap. A period. A summoning of strength. "So I'm Bob."

The circle's low response. "Hi, Bob."

"And I'm an addict."

He speaks, and it's hard to tell where his confession ends and his sermon begins. A reflection on the New Year's Eves of his past. Some hazy, some lost. Some outright criminal. One with a wrecked car. Another where the woman he loved walked out of his life. The holiday a reminder that every night is a temptation and that every dawn brings a chance to get things right. His admission that the struggle never gets easier, but it does get familiar, and perhaps that is enough.

Heads nod. "Amen," repeats the man with the tattooed knuckles.

A pause, and I feel something tangible, the circle a living thing, its single purpose, the rhythm of focus and breath. Roger stands. An explanation of his nickname. Roger-dodger. A laugh then the sting of the truth. The years he sidestepped and shirked. The lies he told and the lies he told to cover those lies and on and on. The trusts he undermined. The tears his family cried. For nine years, he's been trying to erase the past, and while others have forgiven him, he can't forgive himself. The fuckup. The man who saved his worst for those who loved him most. But here's the twist—he's thankful for the Dodger. His roadmap of bad decisions. The knowing of who he doesn't want to be the first step in discovering who he is.

He sits. "Amen," says the man with the tattooed knuckles.

My mother reaches for my hand. A squeeze and I squeeze back. She stands, holding on for a moment before letting go. Her eyes closed, and I see her at the quarry's edge. The room still and then the thin ribbon of her voice. "I'm Jill, and I'm clean for what—a week?"

The circle speaks. "Hi, Jill."

A breath. A lift in her chest. She opens her eyes and looks back at me then to the others. "And I'm a mother-fucking addict."

* * *

Upon learning my work at the doctors' house was done, the old man had me buy a few gallons of white and repaint his downstairs. Saturday morning. The taping and trim completed this week after school. Chief's radio, Satie and Mendelssohn and Liszt. Updates from the war. Firebombs. Kidnappings. Curtainless windows and a dull sky. The furniture and floor buried beneath drop cloths. The feeling of being lost in a cloud.

The old man in the kitchen. He's spread newspaper over the table, and in his wrinkled hands, a knife and block of basswood. A pastime from his youth, and he's shown me the creations rescued from the attic. Bears and dogs. A soldier at attention. A chess set. I keep an eye on him, worrying, the blade, the hands that struggle to open jars and bottles. The knife set aside as he turns the block one way then another, and after a minute or two, he marks a spot with his thumb and retrieves the knife. A different kind of vision as the blade bites into the wood.

A break between songs, and the announcer talks of snow, a few inches tonight. Maybe more later in the week. I glide the roller over the wall and think again of Kate. I've given her a few more rides. Our talks as we're parked outside her house. The tension I once felt replaced by a kind of ease, but beneath, a new worry. The fear of doing the wrong thing. The greater fear of doing nothing.

Mozart's Requiem, and I think of those long dead and the good that can remain. And I think of the war, and I feel its pull. I have no idea what the next year will bring, but the only future I can fully imagine is carrying a gun through a strange land for a cause I don't understand. Somewhere in the world, a symphony is practicing Mozart. Somewhere in town, there's a family who cares about the old man and respects the life he's lived. The death that awaits me a hundred times deeper. A thrown rock that casts no ripples. A boy who's never been in love. Never had the chance to make good.

The old man pauses his whitling. Outside, Roger's pickup eases down the lane. He parks, and my mother steps from our house. She wears my coat, her Christmas gloves. Today is her first shift at one of the warehouses along the highway inter-change. A trial, a favor, Roger's network of recovering addicts, and in me, the feeling of those left ashore as a boat pulls away. The knowing my hopes and wishes mean little upon the wide sea.

The truck turns and heads back up the lane. I'll pick her up later. We'll talk, go to the supermarket, and I'll buy her what-ever she wants. I dip my roller in the tray and apply another swath. White on white, the wash of new snow upon old. She's been different these past few nights. Her AA confession gushing and tearful and profane. The high of breaking down, of giving over—but since, a kind of hangover. The silent hours. The chair she's pulled to the window. The long pulls from the cigarettes she's rationed to one an hour. Her bundled walks up and down the lane and her returns to our kitchen, red-cheeked, her nose running, the cold upon her. Over coffee this morning, she said she felt like she's woken into a new country, the scenery identical but all sense of meaning unmoored. Everything slippery. Everything a breath away from crumbling.

His fingers upon the twine, the old man enters the living room. "How's it going?"

I set the roller down. The wall behind me done. "Getting there."

"I like the smell. It's clean, you know?" He reaches out, pointing. "Stay right there. The new white's brighter, isn't it?"

"Some, yeah."

"I can see you better. Just a bit."

He waves. I wave back. He smiles.

* * *

I pull up to Kate's house. Snow along the curbs but no longer on the roofs. Sunday, and across the street, a family returning from church. Dresses and sport coats and polished shoes. The mother with a hand on a little girl's shoulder. The girl blowing a pinwheel, glitter on the spinning blades. A glance from the father as he locks the car. A sizing up. The territorial urge. I stay in the truck, Kate's directions to just park and wait, the engine's rattle better than a knock. On the curb, two girls stop and tie a wide yellow ribbon on a light pole. The ribbons all over town now, a push to have one on every street since last week's news that Ike Foreman's gone missing. Perhaps captured. Perhaps dead.

Kate steps out. A wave from the driveway, and behind her, the red garage where her father shot himself. Town's rumors of the work ledgers that didn't add up. Money owed to the wrong people, and the police closing in. Then the newer troubles Kate's hinted at. Her mother's drinking. The eggshell weekends of tiptoeing and lowered voices. Each of us with our masks.

She bunches her hair into a ponytail. Yoga pants and a sweatshirt beneath her down vest—and I feel less self-conscious about my sweats. She shuts the cab door, and I breathe in her watermelon gum. She blows a bubble, and when it pops, she asks, "Ready?"

I pull from the curb. "Yes, ma'am."

"Where's your spiffy new coat?" Her sneakered toes tap the floorboard.

"Came right from painting. Didn't want to get it dirty." I turn onto Main Street and head out of town.

She tussles the hair that's grown shaggy without Amy to cut it. "Got some up here though. Looks like you're going gray. Very distinguished."

I tilt my head, an invitation for her touch to linger. "I guess that's a good thing."

"No wonder those recruiters love you." She gives a final fluff. "Get you in that barber chair and there's one less hippie in the world."

News on the radio. Another Army helicopter crash. A mortar strike on a Marine barracks. I turn it off, and as we near the highway, we pass the warehouse where my mother works. The trucks and loading docks and barbwire that could just as well belong to a chicken plant in Arkansas or a prison in the Alleghenies. Then the highway, a new speed, the cab's whine and rattle. Our voices raised above the rumble.

My last visit to the mall years before, an afternoon with Double D. The food court. The purchase of guitar strings and, no doubt, a score of one kind or another. The full lot I remember from that day whittled back. The cars clumped around the entrances, and beyond, a run of unclaimed macadam. The Sears that anchored one end closed, and inside, a quarter of the stores gated and dark. Their signs taken down, the imprints of letters outlined in grime and faded paint. Above us, a vaulted ceiling. Skylights and shafts of dust-swirling sun. We aren't alone, yet after being used to school's after-lunch maw, it sometimes feels that way.

A stop at the Cinnabon. A shared treat and the collision of plastic forks. We talk about her nursing school acceptances. The maze of scholarships and financial aid. The debt that already presses upon her. Her middle-of-the-night panics. The fear of not being smart enough. The fear of going and the fear of staying. She says once she gets her degree, she'd come back for the right opportunity, because it's not the escape she needs but the knowing it's possible. A soldier and a girl claim the table beside ours. The sandy browns of the last war traded for the greens of this one. I watch him and wonder what he knows. What he's seen. In my head, the mall speakers' cheery pop and the roar of all the oceans I've never seen.

Our mission—the sporting goods store. The sales staff dressed like referees. The baseball aisle's leathery scent. Two weeks have passed since my off-hand comment about maybe trying out for track. Not a give-me-liberty-or-give-me-death declaration, although this is the way Kate remembers it in her teasings. It was just an utterance to fill an awkward moment. Words I hadn't thought through and which I now can't walk back. Kate's sneakers bought here last week, and in her hand, the coupon that will ease the price tag's sting. She helps me— the attributes of different brands, the kinds she's worn. I try on a few pairs. The feel different than my no-name basketball sneakers. The raised heel, the slight forward angle. The light- ness. I stand before the mirror and do some quick math, her coupon then sales tax. Kate nods when I pay with one of the doctor's crisp hundreds. "Way to roll, G."

We walk around for a bit, and I keep looking down, these

sneakers the color of ice cream and soft as pillows. We check out the movie theater's posters, and Kate says maybe another time. Monday's bio test, she explains. Tuesday's English paper. The group project in government she's going to have to rescue now that her partner's come down with mono.

I park in front of her house. The sky fragmented by bare trees. A woman walks her dog. A man balanced atop a ladder, rubber gloves and gunk pulled from his gutter. This street, the mall—and there are unclaimed moments in which I forget about the wars in the Patch and the wars in the jungle and the wars at home, and I don't want to be blind, but every once in a while, I need to stop seeing. Need a rest before I push on. The moment can be empty, the lull of a quiet street's dog walkers and ladder-balanced husbands. And I look at Kate and think the moment can be so full that I feel like a child again, one who believed in prayer and hadn't given up on wonder.

Kate opens the door but doesn't get out. "I still need to do my run. You up for that? We're both dressed, more or less. Can break in your spiffy new kicks."

I don't have a lab report or a test to study for. Don't have anything calling me but the farm's fields and our house's stillness and the hollow spaces my mother and I have been struggling to fill. "Haven't been working out much. My bike's been out of commission for a while."

"Then it's a good time to start. Only five weeks to the first day of practice."

"Take it easy on me."

"Maybe." She climbs out. "Maybe not."

I thank her for the pace she sets. The first blocks easy, then the spike in my heart, and I focus on the breeze, the sun's gleam on glass and chrome—anything but my body's complaints. Three miles, she says. Streets I barely know, others I've passed a hundred times. The doctors' house. The driveway's BMWs, one black, one blue. Drapes in the windows. A new life.

We talk. Movies we like. Our favorite seasons. Why she wants to be a nurse. The places we want to see. The traps we fear. I begin to struggle, but try not to show it. My words timed between my breaths. Overhead, a V of wing-beating geese, and I think of nature's calendar, the cycles that make me feel like a radar's blip. A honk from a passing car, and I realize it's Andy. A passenger's-side view of Derrick, a smirk and a raised middle finger.

Our route returns us to her block, and we stop at the corner. The flush on our cheeks. "Not bad for a starting point."

I hold my hands atop my head, then lower them when I think of my last glimpse of Chief. "I've got some serious work to do."

"Bring your stuff to school this week. We can go after."

The trees overhead, a striping of skeleton shadows. The chill on my face and my body's warmth, and in my ears, Amy's seashell hum. My hand brushes Kate's, an asking of permission. We stop, a cushion between us and her front door. When we kiss, it's soft. A moment's linger before I pull back and open my eyes.

A smile and she says, "I've been waiting for that, you know." She clasps her hands behind my neck and draws me near.

* * *

I wait in the truck. Mist and drizzle, and in the old man's fields, the last patches of white. Soon the tillers, the stink of manure. Soon the birds and the crystalline sunshine impossible to conjure in winter's last, dragging weeks.

My mother steps onto the porch and zips the coat that's now more hers than mine. The cab door slams. Her hair pulled back beneath one of Amy's sun-faded headscarves.

"Didn't have time for coffee," she says.

"Need to get up earlier." The lane's ruts, and we jostle in our seats.

"I'm going to be an hour early as is."

"I can't be late for school again."

"You and that perfect attendance award." She vents her window and lights a cigarette. "Boss better not give me shit today." She aims her exhale toward the window. My hope—that she finds peace as she toe-dips into the straight life. The everyday absurdities. The offhand slights that pierce her heart.

When the road is clear, I sneak a glance. The search for cracks. This brittle sobriety.

"Boss's job is to give folks shit sometimes."

"Someone can give you shit without being shitty about it."

"So there's no chance you're moving from the floor to the phones?"

She sucks a drag. "He says I'm not a people person. Which is probably true, but I don't like hearing it from him." She exhales. The smoke not drawn out the window curls against the windshield. "He's so fucking judgmental."

I hit the wipers. The old ones finally replaced. "Don't know if I'm a people person either." The truck shakes as I pick up speed. "You've got to roll with it. Can't let the little stuff get under your skin."

"You sound like a fucking motivational poster." Her voice raised above the engine's spat. "And letting little things go, at least when I'm not high, has never been my thing." Another drag. "And speaking of judging, when am I going to meet this girl?"

"I don't know."

"You ashamed of your mother?" She exhales. "Sorry. That's a shitty thing to ask."

"It's OK."

"So will I get to meet her? One day at least?"

"It's nothing serious. And it's not like I'm hiding her or anything. I'm just not bringing her around for Sunday dinner."

She takes a final drag, slides her cigarette through the window's opening, and turns the crank. "We're not people persons. And we're not the Sunday-dinner type, are we?"

I smile. "Nope."

Her knuckle taps the window. "Know what I was thinking about last night? Your birthday. Big eighteen."

"I always think of my birthday as warm. The beginning of summer. That feels a long way off today."

"We'll make it special. I'll do something motherly, like bake a cake." She laughs, and so do I. She delivers a soft punch to my arm. "You said someone could teach themselves about that kind of shit on YouTube. Give me a chance. This new life ain't easy."

"I'll look forward to it."

I park in the warehouse lot. A long, curved roof beneath a leaden sky and not a window to be seen. My mother scratches her neck, and I, too, feel the itch. The knowing of our place. The knowing our best scenario is the chance to work an honest job until the day we fall over dead. I tell her to be in touch if her ride bails. Remind her that we have leftovers in the fridge. She gets out, but before she shuts the door, I say, "Your boss is going to judge you. That's what he does."

The door a frame, and how small she looks. A sigh. "This fucking life. How about it?"

* * *

Saturday afternoon. The morning rain stopped, and in its place, a fog so thick it warps the light from the old man's windows. I set out, choppy strides to avoid the lane's puddles. Five weeks, Kate said, and I've been hitting the road, at first every other day and now two days on, one off. The first half mile with its hitches. The pain waiting in my last mile. And sometimes, between the two, an emptiness. A whittling to the rhythm of my sneakers and not a thought in my head. Running out here is different than my jogs with Kate. The smells. The hush. The wide fields. The sky that stretches from horizon to horizon, but which today has fallen all around me. I hear an approaching car long before its headlights pierce the fog, and I step onto the shoulder. The grass wet around my sneakers. My hand in my sweatshirt pocket, the buck knife I carry in case I cross paths with the man in the yellow car. The pickup a ghost, a notion in the mist, then real—a passing swift and violent—before it disappears.

I press on. The buck knife slaps my belly. The fog thicker, and down long lanes, the barns and farmhouses I know exist but which today I can only imagine. I think of the old man, his rooms of shadows and dark. And I think of a distant jungle and laying a rifle's sights on another man's heart and wonder if I'll be able to pull the trigger.

The fog. The road. This bubble carved by my pulse in these fallen clouds. Then, not far off the shoulder, barbs in the mist, and it's only when I draw closer that I recognize the clutch of trees surrounding a rusty fence. I've come too far. The spot where I'd planned to turn lost a mile back.

I stop, catch my breath. I go to the fence. The ground wet. This dreamy vision, the fence's hole. The path less clear. I pause by the last tree. The sky open but I can't tell where it begins and ends. The quarry right before me but lost. I grab the tree, then step back. The fear of what my next step could bring.

* * *

The Marine recruiter sets up his display outside the cafeteria. The hallway empty. The security cameras above, and I imagine myself passing through the checkerboard of the office's video display. A hall pass in my hand. My locker at the building's other end, an excuse to stretch my legs, to have a moment to myself. Sun streams through the cafeteria's windows, white shafts on tables awaiting the lunchtime rush. From the kitchen, voices and clatter and the scent of grilled meat.

The recruiter straightens his table's piles. Not a wrinkle in his dress blues. Gold buttons and red trim. The pins and medals above his heart. His table draped with a cloth that matches his uniform, and on it, his neat arrays. Pamphlets and bumper stickers and glossy booklets. A trifold adorned with photos, the center panel a sun-backed silhouette. A soldier with a rifle in his hands. Beneath, *Earned. Never given.* At the table's edge, a clipboard and a chained pen.

The recruiter shakes my hand. His grip strong. "Heard you signed up for track."

We've been talking since last spring. Passing exchanges, sometimes more—the meaning the Corps brought to his life. What it can offer me. The hints I drop and the pictures he fills in. I appreciate that he doesn't pry. I imagine his life as one filled with order and the understanding of priorities—and this picture sets me at ease. "I'm getting myself ready. Or trying to."

"What event?"

"Coach thinks the two-mile."

"Coach Ford's a good man."

"He is."

"Two-miler. It's a tough event. I was an 800 man. I was a little leaner then." He stands with his hands behind his back, his chest out, a rigidness softened by his smile. "What made you join?"

"A girl, to be honest." I take one of the pens from a coffee cup. Everything branded with the Marine logo. "But there were other reasons, too."

He nods. "Sometimes our hearts lead us. Sometimes we're led by forces we don't quite understand."

Beside him, a patch of sun. Glare on the tiles, a reflection off his mirror-polished shoes, and I think of Ike Foreman standing in this very spot a few months ago. "I've got to get back to class." I wave the pen. "Thanks for this."

"Take this too." He hands me a card even though I already have a few. "Good luck with track. I'll look forward to hearing about it."

I back up. "Thanks. I'll see you around."

"I'll be here. Don't worry about that."

* * *

Kate and I stretch on my back porch. A cat prowls the edge of the barn, and I think of Kitten, of Amy speeding and full of light. Another Saturday, my mother already dropped off at the warehouse, and in two days, season's first practice. This week of rain. The creek out of its banks and the river high. Yet today, the sun. The breeze cool but beneath, a hint of warmth. The snow a memory.

I've told Kate about my country runs, and today, she's driven out to join me. She holds a quad stretch. A balancing grip on one of the porch columns, and I can't stop staring because I've never seen her nails painted. I imagine her in her room. Her concentration, her brush's dip and stroke, and the picture touches me. The ways we try to understand ourselves. Our clumsy attempts to reach out. And I think of her parents and mine. Think of their trajectories and the paths, once traveled, that are easier for us to follow. I think of the doctors' son, the things he'll be given and what will be expected of him. At

240

my mother's first AA meeting, the man with the tattooed hands spoke about choosing to walk in the light or the dark, but a child can't choose the direction their feet point, and all they know is how tiny their hands are. All they can see are the giants of their world, the broad shoulders that eclipse the sun.

Above, blue skies and white clouds. Mourning doves on the sagging electric line. I turn to Kate. "You know about my mom, right?" I pull up my other foot and grip the porch column just above her painted nails. "She's trying to live right, but it's not easy. It's never been easy, and it probably never will be."

Kate says nothing, a look not blank—in fact, quite the opposite.

"And my dad," I say. "You know about him, right?"

She sets her foot down and shields her eyes. A mask of shadows. "And you know about my dad."

"Some, but that's just people talking, and I don't care what they say. I just care about what you think. And if there's anything you want to know, just ask, and I'll tell you." The barn's weather vane creaks. The goat's slow-motion graze. "And if there's ever anything you want to tell me, you can."

She squints. "We're alone here, right?"

I nod up the lane. "No one but the old man."

She takes my hand and spreads my fingers over her open palm. "Can we go inside? Just for a bit?"

* * *

The school bathroom. My hands cupped beneath a faucet that offers only cold. My reflection in a cracked mirror. Over one shoulder, a recruiting poster, its backwards print, a soldier's face painted green and black, his eyes shining white. Over my other shoulder, a gathering in the last doorless stall. A low voice, one I know. My name called as I dry my hands.

"Marcus," Andy says. Andy and Derrick huddle in the stall. Andy holds his history text, and on the cover's image of the founding fathers, Derrick chops lines of crank with his school ID. He leans forward, a rolled bill held to his nose. A snort and a grimace. He hands the bill to Andy and holds the book. Andy snorts. "Fuck, fuck, fuck," and Andy pinches his nose, his eyes watering as he asks, "Hey, man, how's track going?"

"First week's OK."

He smiles. "You were a fucking streak that night with the

chainsaw. Just pretend that old guy and his dog are on your ass."

"Yeah, maybe so."

Derrick licks the edge of his ID. "Saw you running with that chick. What's her name?"

"Kate."

"Kate, yeah." He leans over the sink, runs a fluffing hand through his hair. "She's kind of hot in her own way."

"We've got to bounce, man," Andy says.

I say nothing.

Derrick continues to play with his hair as he steps back from the mirror. "Chicks with issues can be interesting, you know."

I should leave, but I don't. "I don't think I understand what you're saying."

"Her daddy." He cocks his thumb and presses an extended index finger to his temple. "You know why he did it, don't you? He was a fucking perv. Sick shit on his computer. The kind who tiptoed into his kids' rooms after the lights—"

I grab two fistfuls of his sweatshirt, a bum rush that bends him against the sink. My fists slide up to his chin. My face in the mirror, an expression remade in my mother's anger. Derrick twists, but I don't let go. His first punch misses but not the second. I think of Chief's words and how I've now invited Derrick deeper into my life. I'm too close for him to unleash, yet the knuckled jolt floods me with heat, and for every punch he throws, I throw one back. He catches me flush on the cheek, and I buckle, but only for a second before I clamp a hand under his chin. My other fist a blur, a piston, a jackhammer, and he's not punching now, his hands covering his face. And I punch him again for the hate-machine the Marines will make of me. And again for the nowhere life of this town. And again for my blood's fucked-up tide of addicts and outlaws.

Andy lassoes my middle and yanks me back. He steps between Derrick and me. "Come on, man," Andy says. He turns me around, pushing me toward the door. "It's over."

I glance back. The bell rings. Derrick says nothing, and in his eyes, not fear or shock or pain, but a slow hardening, and I know I have one more reason to watch my back.

I stagger into the empty hallway. My breath ragged. Sparks across my eyes. My class door open. The health teacher in her blue track suit, a lifting of her gaze from her clipboard, but when she sees me, her scolding stops short. The story I can't hide. My flushed face. The numbness around my eye. My shirt twisted and bunched. My teacher's stare joined by others as I make my way to my seat. The girl in front of me hands back some papers, and I pass them on. The teacher rejoins her lecture. The danger of drugs. I fish the Marine pen from my pocket. My hand's throb. The tremble that makes it impossible to write my name.

* * *

I drive Kate home after practice. I'm sore, but less so than the first week, and with each day, Mr. Ford's running vocabulary sheds some of its mystery. Ladders and Fartleks. Intervals and stride-outs. His encouragements as I cross the finish line. My slow climb from the pack's rear.

In the hallways, I hear whispers behind my back. I've said nothing about the fight beyond an incomplete explanation to Kate. Derrick, with his eye blacker than mine, has no doubt said less, and into this void, the school's breathed its rumors, the most common narrative centering on a drug deal gone bad and the lack of honor among thieves. Our wounds heal, and by week's end, the buzz fades beneath newer dramas.

I park in front of Kate's house. Over her shoulder, the driveway, and at its end, the red garage she refuses to enter even though it wasn't her who found her father with half his head blown off. We kiss, then a little more, and I think of our hearts as a series of locked boxes. Our haunted rooms. The names we no longer say. Sometimes when I hold her, I feel her already slipping away. The moment eroding before I can exhale. Then times like today where I lose myself in the dark and where all that matters are the places where our bodies meet.

She opens the door, but then turns back and reaches for my hand. A last goodbye. Behind her, the garage, the wood in need of a new coat of paint, a backboard and a hoop without a net. And I'm sorry, Kate, that you have to see that door every day. And I'm sorry that sometimes when we kiss, I think of Amy—not the physical her but the lost her. The woman who'll never get to kiss again or feel the sun after a long winter. Each day I live adding to the ones she's missed, a burial a thousand times sadder than the dirt upon her coffin.

I ease down our lane. The clocks turned ahead last weekend, and in these afternoons, a new light. The crows atop the barn's peak. The old man's porch with its stack of cardboard and junk mail I'll later haul to the burn bin. Roger's truck in front of our house. He leans against the door, and in the nearby grass, a little girl. White leggings and an unzipped purple coat. A streamer in her hand, a fluttering pink banner.

I park, and he waves as I approach. "Hey."

In my head, the imagining of possibilities, none of them good. "Everything OK?"

He checks out my eye. "Maybe I should be asking you that."

"It's nothing."

"I should see the other guy, right?" The little girl spins in dizzying circles, the baton above her head. The banner corkscrews as she turns and turns. "I brought your mother home. Thought I'd wait for you before we left." He lowers his voice. "Spotted her walking along the road. There was a little dustup at work."

I look toward the house. "Thanks."

"I called her boss when we got here. Put your mom on, too. She apologized. He understands. He's been there. She's going back tomorrow."

The girl stops. Her steps unsteady, her eyes seeking balance, and I imagine the horizon's tilt. The banner curled upon the grass until she notices the goat. Then a sprint across the lane's gravel.

"Mind your distance, sweetie," Roger says.

The girl stops. "I am."

He turns to me. "Told your mom I'd pray for her."

"Thank you."

"I'm lucky." We walk around the truck. His gimp, my shortened stride. "Lucky to be where I am after where I was. Lucky to have found God." He leans against the truck's gate. His daughter squats, her knees as high as her face, a closer look as the goat nibbles the grass. "But it doesn't have to be God. It can be love. Or duty. Or playing the piano. Or whatever it is that gets us out of bed in the morning. Whatever it is that makes us a little less lonely or a little more connected. We just need to give up one thing and pick up another." The goat lifts its head and bleats, and the girl turns, a charge and a leap into her father's arms. He rests his lips near her forehead and offers me a smile. "Sometimes it's the surrendering that saves us."

I check the mailbox at the lane's end. Junk for the old man. Another SNAP card for a dead woman. Perhaps I'll take my mother to town later. A slice of pizza, and I wonder how she sees such moments, wonder if they're torture or bliss or horribly awkward. This new landscape. New customs. New ways.

The day thick, and earlier on my run, a summer's sweat. Flowering trees. A building wind. Clouds in the west and a charge on my skin. I park. Off in the field, a tractor pulls a tiller. The thickness of turned earth. The porch boards sag, and when I slide my key into the lock, the door swings back. A glance behind me, a check for the yellow car. I cross the threshold and ease my bag onto the floor. I hold my breath and listen. The living room dark, then the ransacking commotion from the bedrooms beyond. The haste of careless thieves, the roustings of those one step ahead of trouble. I'm frozen, split between claiming the gun from its new hiding place atop the cabinet or turning tail, when I hear my mother's cursing.

"Mom?"

The cursing stops, and we meet in the living room. Behind her, the bedrooms' shotgun hallway. In one hand, the silver and gold dangle of the necklaces that escaped my gathering of Amy's things. In her other hand, Amy's prized lamp. The tortoise-shell patchwork of stained glass. She only sees me for a second, a pale glance that considers then erases me. A truth that doesn't have to be spoken.

"I'm getting my shit." She half-trips on the lamp's dangling cord. "Fuck."

"Nothing you got there belongs to you." I don't ask about her job. About how she got here. None of that matters.

"I'm going to need a ride into town." She sifts through the cardboard boxes by the TV. The first, a box of Amy's clothes, which she kicks over. She retrieves a DVD player from the second box and tucks it under her arm, and another dangling cord traces the mess she's made.

"I'm not driving you anywhere to score."

I step forward when she pulls out the camcorder. We wrestle for a moment before I twist it from her grip. I eject the tape then hand back the camcorder. "Won't get twenty bucks for that. No one uses that shit anymore."

She upturns a box, shaking out the last of Amy's clothes, then fills it with her take. "I know someone who'll pay for all of this." She considers me. Her eyes hollow. "I need that ride."

I block the way to the kitchen, my hand on her shoulder. "You slipped up. It happens. We can make it right. Let me call Roger. I'll drive you to see him."

She stares. Says nothing.

"What's his number?"

She lowers her head. "His card. It's in the bedroom somewhere."

I step past her. "You're doing the right thing."

"I don't know what the right thing is anymore."

The bedroom, and what order I'd imposed is lost now. Drawers upturned. The mattress flipped. The closet's spill. I'm bent double, picking through the mess when I hear the pickup's sputter. I run onto the porch to see her speeding down the lane. The truck's buck and kick. A cloud of dust. Thunder, closer now. A vein of lightning over the open fields.

* * *

I pick through the barn's junkheap. Grime on my hands. The fear of a clattering avalanche. Gaps between the barn's slats, ribbons of light. Mildew and rust. Swallows dart from the sun to dark and back again. I clear away a bedframe. A kerosene heater. Wooden skids and paint cans. Mice scurry with the stove door's creak. The dented toolbox, the envelope. I slide a hundred into my pocket and count what remains, and in my head, calculations of the days ahead. Subtractions. Compromises.

The pop of gravel, and I return the toolbox to the stove and step outside. Roger alone behind the wheel. I think of Theseus's black sails and brace myself. Three days she's been gone. That first night, Roger and I cruised the Patch. The thunderstorm clearing the hot corners, but when the rain stopped, we watched ghosts rise from the mist. Chief's pickup found in a riverside lot. The macadam cratered with potholes, weeds

straining between the cracks. The keys dangled from the ignition, and I thought of Chief's joke that the best security system
was having a ride too shitty to steal. The lot staked out until
midnight. Roger and I talked and then didn't. Our understanding growing with each silent minute.

Roger climbs from the cab. Dirt on his knees, and today, a
deeper hitch in his limp. He brings rumors, and I imagine
myself as the last link in a game of telephone. The word passed
from lips to ears and over again, and who knows if Roger's
reports are true. The narrative unsurprising. The relief she's
escaped the morgue for another day. I don't tell him I've done
my own looking. The railroad tracks crossed after I drop off
Kate. A slow cruise through the Patch, and in my head, a
remembering of all the places where I'd bled and fought and
cried, and I might not know the prayers of church-going folks,
but I know the prayers of a junkie's child. A hope against hope.

"I'm down at the foodbank on Tuesday nights." Roger
removes his cap and mops his brow with a blue bandanna.
"That's where I do most of my asking up on her." He reaches
into the bed. The box he hands me heavier than I expect. "I do
some deliveries too. Nothing fancy, but it'll keep you going."

"Thanks."

He hoists himself into the cab. "I'm doing some masonry
and landscape at the house you and Chief painted. The
doctors' place."

"They have their kid yet?"

"Yep." He starts the engine. "They OK?"

I shrug.

"They're gone for the week. Some seminar in Pittsburgh.
The kid and the nanny, too." He puts on his sunglasses. "He's
pretty fired up that I start after they've gone and finish before
they get back."

"Sounds like him."

Roger shakes his head. "Think a guy that smart would know I don't control the weather." He starts the engine. "Take care of yourself, kid."

***

The alley. My face shadowed by my sweatshirt hood. The truck parked a block away. Clouds, this moonless night. A light of chalk and ash. Cars and garages, gardens and play-sets. Everything but me still and in its place.

A final glance before I slip into the yard. Darker here. The shadows of trees. The grass's dew. In the yard, Roger's concrete mixer. Wheelbarrows. A coiled hose. Stakes and twine. Careful steps, then my key's easy fit, the locks unchanged, and as I step inside, I walk beside my father. The moment's blindness and the precipice so close. A tripped alarm. A nosy neighbor. The doctors' unexpected return. A cop with his finger on the trigger. All of it in play.

My heart hurls itself against the stillness. I've come because I can't shake the image of the doctor pinching those bills. Because he made a show of the subtraction, wanting me to see who had the power. I'm here to claim the kind of justice that means more than his whole envelope of bills. I stoop and pick up an infant's knit cap, and in a breath my vision changes. The work Chief and I did lost beneath bookshelves and hung pictures. The rooms' open spaces claimed by carpets and chairs and tables. I set down the cap and pick up an end table's statue, a foot-tall piece of silver. There's nothing here that means anything to me, and even if there was, I wouldn't want it. Not if it had once been the doctor's.

I lock the back door behind me. The key heaved, a silent landing in a neighbor's hedge. I pull up my hood and return to the alley. Empty-handed yet richer than before.

* * *

M r. Ford's class, and the nerves I'd expected before my first meet wilt beneath the day's news. Outside, the flowering cherry trees and a view that stretches to the foothills. Inside, a hush, even the jokers quiet. The TV on, Mr. Ford's lesson abandoned, just like last period and the period before. A dirty bomb, a trawler outside Tampa Bay. Reporters in head-to-toe radiation suits. Maps with a bullseye and rippling circles, doctors explaining how death will come to each zone. The President to address the nation in the coming hour. Rumors of martial law.

Silence then whispers then silence again. All of us watching. Some texting. This war we're poised to inherit. Our brothers and sisters, our mothers and fathers. Our kind who built the pyramids and laid the railroads. Our kind who always do the lion's share of the sweating and fighting and dying.

The bell rings, and I stop by Mr. Ford's desk. "The meet's still on?"

"I guess." He's barely spoken all period. His cheeks pale, a soldier's sad knowing. He shoulders his workout bag. "I'll see you out there."

My track uniform skimpy, and my first lesson is to mind my legs' spread when I stretch. The second lesson—there's a lot of waiting in a track meet. The sprints' repeated heats. The setting up and taking down of hurdles. The other events in the periphery—the jumpers and throwers, the pole vaulters' rise and cushioned fall. The field sectioned into camps. Our team beneath the north-end goalpost, the visitors at the south. The goalpost's shadows over us, and what small talk there is rings hollow, and how strange, the day's beauty, the puffed clouds and blooming forsythias. The mile among the early events, and I wish Kate good luck then give her some space. Her confession of pre-race jitters. The focus that shuts out the voice that says she's not good enough. When the race starts, I take my place at the high-jump pit. I cheer even though I know her ears are flooded with her pulse and the smack of her sneakers. Her thoughts narrowed to body and will and the task at hand. By the second lap, the pack thins, and Kate stakes her place in the middle, holding off some, closing in on others. I'm mesmerized. The stream of faces, the chuffing breath. This reduction to pursuit and escape.

After her race, I bring her water. Her flush and calming breath, her smile after Mr. Ford tells her her time. She leaves to help rake the long-jump pit, a quick kiss with the promise she'll be cheering me on. The other events tick off, and when I'm not stretching or warming up, I lie on the infield grass. The earth vibrating, footsteps, the hum of passing traffic, and in these tremors, a lifting into the stained-glass sky. All of it beautiful. All of it out of sync, this peace, a bullseye on a map. I flinch with the starter's next shot.

The call goes up, "Two mile. Boys' two mile to the start."

We line up, four from each team. Our number one then theirs. I take my place near the line's end. On either side of me, a boy in a different uniform, and no one says a word. The starter stands back. His gun raised, and for a moment, all is still.

A trigger's squeeze, and in my gut, a kick. This shot meant for me. The first turn's jostle, elbows, the claiming of space. A near-sprint before we fall in along the backstretch. The pace quicker than practice, and a hundred miles away, the President is talking, and a thousand miles away, an invisible fire burns skin and lungs, and in the Patch, my mother is sticking a needle in her arm, and I was wrong about living against a cartoon loop background because I now understand I'm part of the loop, and I lose myself in the swirl. Lose myself in a haze more complete than a foggy country run. Halfway through, and I'm alone with a pair of runners from the other team. None of us bound to place, but when one pulls away, I go with him. The other runner falls back, and we become two. The gun lap a surprise, my count off, and in the backstretch, I pass him. His breath in my ear then not. I don't care about beating him. I just want a clear view. I just want to see the finish line before I stumble across it. The homestretch, and all my hinged parts numb and unruly. The cartoon loop sputters, a haywire projection. Bodies in a ditch. Amy's head between her knees. Kate's face so close. A map's red bullseye.

* * *

The truck's windows down, and in the fields, the first green sprouts. The last days of April, and behind me, a month of track meets. Sometimes I finish third on our team, sometimes second. The line toed, and I brace for the gun, more nervous than that first day because I know what waits. The questioning of self. The bargains I make to justify another stride. In the background, the war's drumbeat. The bombings. A deserted city surrendered to men in hazmat suits. The deployment of the largest US force in fifty years.

When I park in front of his house, the old man's daughter steps onto his porch. At first, I'm worried, but her easing of the door tells me he's resting. She wears her bank clothes, a blazer, black slacks. A yellow ribbon on her lapel. A pair of sunglasses she pushes atop the hair that's grayer than the last time we talked.

"How is he?" Last night, the old man and I talked about today's appointments. Another drive to the VA. Last week's shivers in a skimpy gown. His stillness as their machines whirred and clicked. A vision somewhere between the sight of man and the sight of God.

She opens her mouth, stops, then says, "There're spots on his liver. And lungs. I don't know how much longer he can stay out here."

"I'm sorry to hear that. For you and him." I wish I knew the right thing to say. "I'll do whatever he needs."

"I appreciate—we all appreciate—what you've done for him."

"Whatever I've done for him, he's done double for me."

We walk to her car. "He thinks moving into town would be the beginning of the end." A button push and her door unlocks. "Maybe he's right. There'll be a nurse stopping by from now on. Maybe you can pop in sometime and see how they're getting along."

"I will."

She opens the door. The silver tips of her hair lift on the breeze. "When this works itself out, I won't be able to keep this place. You won't have to leave right away, but I can't say—"

"I understand."

* * *

A kiss, and I open my eyes. This bed that was once my mother and Amy's. Kate and I naked, a pillow shared as we lie on our sides. Her face as big as a movie closeup. Sometimes smiling. Sometimes staring, thinking her own thoughts. Anchored in this moment and adrift in a thousand more. The window open, and the breeze on our skin. Our clothes tangled on the floor, and between us, a deeper nakedness, the offering up of the imperfections and scars we've hidden from the world. She touches my nose and asks what I'm thinking. I tell her three months ago I couldn't have imagined today. Being with her, touching her. Couldn't have imagined last week's prom. The suit I borrowed from the old man. The boutonniere drying atop the dresser, and beside it, a varsity letter. Kate plays along, suddenly serious. "Yeah, who are you, anyway?"

"I don't know." And I tell her I wish I could stay here forever, just like this, happy and at rest.

"A guy deserves to be happy on his birthday."

"Happy birthday to me."

"Eighteen."

"Eighteen," I say.

She turns. Her back nestled against my chest and my arms around her. I close my eyes and think of the dollhouse. How my favorite thing wasn't marching the dolls around or voicing their interactions—it was posing them just so then sitting back. Watching them do nothing. The hush of a world at peace.

We dress. Her post-season job at a pizza parlor. Every penny saved from now through August. The books she'll need. The clothes. Her meal plan. I admire her vision, her gift of seeing how today leads to tomorrow and the tomorrow after that. But tonight after her shift, another plan. A birthday slice of pie at the all-night diner. A chance to hold her hand and kiss her goodnight.

She leans against her mother's car. "You know my school's only an hour away." She nods toward the truck. "If that thing can make it to Arkansas—"

"And back."

"Then there's no reason it can't—"

I place my hands on her waist and bring myself close. "No reason at all."

I hold her like that, and over her shoulder, I see the barn, the fields and sky, and I think about the old man. How when he learned he was going blind, he'd stand out here and just look. His hopes of remembering it all.

She leaves. Her car blurred by the lane's dust. The mourning doves resettle atop the power line. In the barn, I rummage until I find the weed whacker. A worn wood handle and rusted shaft, a double-edged blade. A stop on my way up the lane to peek in the old man's window. He sleeps on the couch. His mixed-up notions of day and night. The sickness that confesses itself in his trembling hands. The deepening lull between his words.

The ditch runs fifty-some yards along the road. A scar shallow yet too steep to be mowed. In summer downpours, the ditch churns with runoff, but today, it's dry. I take my first swing. The weeds shin-high, and in a few weeks, my work will be lost beneath new growth. The blade whispers, a pendulum's back and forth, and around me, plumes of dust and pollen, the scatter of felled weeds. The stalks fall back to earth and lie in crisscross patterns around my shuffling feet. I think of a ditch along another road. The bodies of women and babies. I cough, the scratch in my throat, and I take off my shirt and tie it over my nose and mouth. My progress slow, and I switch hands. Grass and dust cling to my sweat. The sun on my neck. Ahead, a fleeing groundhog, the stir of grass, and with my next swing, a flash of white. I crouch, push aside the fallen stalks. The bones bleached by the elements. Skull and ribs, and even though a dead stray means nothing in the country, I can't help but think of the day we adopted Kitten. The car ride with Amy and Grace and my mother. My life of ghosts. And I think of the joke the Pirate used to tell about the Patch—and perhaps I'm a ghost, too—I just haven't realized it yet.

A shower when I'm done. Dirt circles the drain. The water's sting on my sunburn. Our house's cool shadows. I stretch out, smelling Kate on the sheets. The curtain stirs on the breeze, and I smile, imagining myself staring in, a spying giant, this still room. This peace I've tried so hard to imagine.

* * *

I blink the clock's blue digits into focus. 9:16. A sleep longer than I'd planned. In my head, the frayed ends of a dream in which I was lost—or perhaps it was my mother who was lost—a giant hallway where everyone stood with their backs turned, and around me, her echoing voice. Moonlight on my pillow, and I think of Kate and how good it will be to see her. I hear my name again. I roll over, and there's my mother, a doorway silhouette.

I'm paralyzed. Lost in the knowing of what's real and what isn't. The bed's slight sag as she sits. She smells of cigarettes. Her words tentative, as if she, herself, is unsure if this is a dream. "Did you hear me calling?"

"I did."

She brushes hair from my forehead. "Are you happy to see me?"

"I'm happy you're not dead."

"And?"

264

THE LOST AND THE BLIND

"And I'm guessing you're here because you want something. Something you couldn't carry away last time." I sit on the other side of the bed. My back to her as I slide on a shirt. "Take what you want. Take anything."

"I need a ride to town, baby."

I stand. I pick the boutonniere from the dresser. The petals dry and stiff. "How did you get out here?"

"Bummed a ride part of the way. Walked the rest."

"If you came from town, how come you need to go back?"

"I'm coming back. Back here. I need the truck to get some things."

I sit on the other side of the bed and pull on my socks. "You mean the truck you stole."

"I just need a ride and a strong back to help me get my things."

I tie my sneakers then sit, elbows on my knees. I've just woken, yet I'm so tired. This life of running, of trouble. I want to tell her I'm done with cleaning up her messes. With slipping cigarettes and needles from her limp fingers. With making excuses for her absences or making excuses after she's shown up. I want to remind her that it's my birthday and that the day she's always claimed was her life's happiest is lost in the haze that's swallowed everything good we've ever known.

I take the truck keys from atop the dresser. My mother follows. We pass the couch, and in me a shudder, Amy with us then not. The dark lit by my phone as I text Kate. An apology. A confession, the truth I've hid for so long. A pause, the desire to tell her I love her, but instead I type *Will call when things settle.*

A jostle in the cab, the lane taken faster than I should. My mother's hand braced on the dash. A spit of gravel as we turn toward town. The moonlit fields. The earth no longer bare. Alfalfa. Corn. I haven't spoken since my room. The struggle to control my anger, to not push her into another corner. On the radio, news of riots. Tear gas and overturned cars, Memphis and Houston and Los Angeles. Pacifists beaten. Immigrants murdered. The world on fire. I turn down the volume. "So we went through all that shit just to get back here?"

She rubs a sleeve under her nose. "This is different. I've got it under control."

"So you're clean."

"I've got it under control."

"Bullshit."

"Don't lecture me."

We pass the first gas station. Twenty-four pumps. An oasis of light. "Calling bullshit isn't a lecture." In the station's lot, a police cruiser, and I ease up on the gas. "You wanted a ride. I'm giving you a ride."

"You're more like me than you know." She places a hand on my shoulder. "In a good way. In a stubborn, calling-bullshit way."

A red light, and after I stop, I turn to her. "Let me call Roger."

Her hand pulls back. "If I want that life, I can do it without that scene."

In town, she gives directions. Past the doctors' tree-lined street. Past Kate's neighborhood. Down to the river and the outskirts of the Patch. A block of abandoned houses. A narrow alley. Garages with broken windows. A dog's wild barks and a fence's rattle. The alley dead-ends into a gravel lot, but I stop short when I see the yellow car with the pinstripes and ghost flames. The car parked outside a white clapboard shack. Peeling paint and clinging vines. The windows black. "What're we doing here?"

"I need to get something."

I readjust my grip on the wheel. "What about the guy? The one with the neck tattoo?"

"You know Dale?"

"I know he's looking for you."

"Not anymore." She turns to me. "He's in there. I told him to take it easy. Told him this batch was strong and that I'd fix him, but he wouldn't listen."

There's a bigger story here, a truth she isn't sharing. One I don't want to know. "We need to go."

"Didn't come all this way to turn back." She opens the door. "I need your help."

"I'm not helping with shit."

"Fuck it then. Just wait."

She passes through the headlights. The door unlocked then left open. A silent mouth. From down the alley, the barking dog, the fence I pray will hold, this crumbling landscape. She appears carrying what I believe at first to be a microwave. Her arms hung low, a bowlegged struggle, an echo of her pregnant waddle eighteen years ago. She crosses the threshold but loses her grip, a quick sidestep to avoid smashed toes. She curses and calls me to help.

Do you know what a monkey rope is? The old man, his fingers upon the twine, told me once of the whalers' gear. The lashings and harnesses that bound one man to another, and if, during the hunt on a heaving sea, one man fell overboard, they were both lost. And so I find myself in the headlight shine, pulled again into the current. My sole hope not to drown. To steer us back to a safe harbor. It's only when I join her on the porch that I realize what she's dropped isn't a microwave but a safe. "What the fuck?"

"You think he needs it? You want the cops to get it? What do you think they'll do with it?"

The headlights reach inside, a shine on the dirty kitchen

linoleum, and in the light, a body's lower half. A scene out of *The Wizard of Oz*, the witch's ruby slippers replaced by red sneakers and bright yellow laces.

The safe solid, heavy and hard to grip. Its rounded corners, its smooth sides. A strained, gravel-kicking shuffle to the truck, and I think of the bodies I've walked away from. The ones I've feared. The ones I've loved—and perhaps I've always been at war. My mother lowers the gate. I hoist the safe into the bed and cover it with a tarp.

I keep to the side streets. The Patch left behind, and nearer to school, the routes I've run and biked. The gardens with their planted flowers. A strip mall, and in it, the lit windows of Kate's pizza parlor, and I think of our broken date. Think of the spiral of our lives and how fate has given us not a monkey rope but two boats upon a tossing sea, and already, the drift. The knowing she's bound for a different shore. The knowing that the pillow-talk that filled my heart will fade beneath the wind and the water's splash and the boat's creak.

The ride silent. My mother drawing on her cigarette or biting her nails. I don't care what's in the safe. My brain tangles with a dozen monkey ropes, a hundred pulling directions, none of them good. I park in front of our house. The trash can toppled again, and in the spill, a racoon, its eyes alight. I turn off the engine. My mother climbs out, but I linger. The gate slams. "Come on," she says.

I tell her I don't need her help. I get a good grip and lift. My steps labored, a shuffle over dirt and gravel. The strain in my shoulders, and in the weight, the memory of the slurry nights I kept her moving, fearful of a sleep from which she'd never wake. The steps taken one at a time, and when I reach the porch, I let go. The safe strikes the boards with a thud.

She crouches beside the safe. "Tools?" She looks up. In her,

THE LOST AND THE BLIND

the itch, the junkie's singular focus. "A hammer? Chisel? The old man's got to have that shit."

I leave, saying nothing. I open the barn door, and my phone's flashlight passes over the clutter. I clear a hasty path to the stove. Cobwebs, the crash of glass and metal. Along the way, I snatch a sledgehammer. Above, the rustle of nesting birds. I'm crying. My tears a surprise but then welcome, and I think of TV preachers and a sinner's realized grace. This breaking. This sad halleluiah. This is how it ends. My prayers and bargainings and all my magical thinking—and if I can't say what's to come, at least I can say what no longer is. The oven door creaks, and I pocket the envelope.

The sledge's head scrapes across the yard's dirt. My stretching shadow in the headlights as I hand her the sledge then step back. She lifts the hammer. A two-handed grip. Her ropy muscles, her scarred arms. She brings the hammer down three times, four. The blows amplified beneath the porch's overhang, and I imagine the din radiating over the fields, running and running until each thud dies in the stillness. Her next blow glances off the dial and cracks a porch board.

"Fuck." She catches her breath and extends the sledge. "Here. I've got the shakes."

A whisper, although this isn't my intention. "No, mama."

Her expression ebbs—anger, confusion, and finally, a kind of tenderness. "OK then."

"I can't. I can't anymore."

Her fingers flex around the handle. "You staying?"

"No."

"Where're you going?"

"I don't know."

She nods. "You're a man now. You can do as you like."

"I'm sorry."

"You have no need to be sorry. None. Remember that."

269

The lights burn in the old man's house. "I can still take you back to town. We'll find Roger—"

"You'd better be on your way." She rubs her forearm across her brow, pushes back her hair. "I won't worry because you've been taking care of business half your life, haven't you?"

We meet each other on the steps. Our hug long. Her hand rubs my shoulders, and here is our love—one written in our miseries, in the blood we share and the blood we've shed. "Be safe, mama."

A final pat. A whisper in my ear. "Love you. Now go."

I start the engine. I want to tell her I love her too, but I'm afraid saying the words will make leaving impossible. I back up. The headlights upon her as she brings down the sledge. I shift into drive and cut the wheel. A final sweep before she's returned to the dark. The clanging receding as I speed up the lane.

***

I stand at attention, my back to the wall. A space half the size of Mr. Ford's classroom, only there are no windows. No views of green playing fields or distant hills. No blue skies or falling snow. Lining the perimeter, twenty echoes of myself. Our green T-shirts. Our shaved heads and polished boots.

The DI gives the command and we don our masks. On the day we arrived, he paraded before our ragged line and promised that for the next twelve weeks, he would become our mother and father, our way and light, and I now understand that truth. The voice that leaps straight into my spine. The actions of my feet and hands a reflex of his will.

I secure my mask and test the seal. The smell of rubber. The goggled view. A table sits in the room's center, and on it, three cannisters. The DI steps forward and opens the first cannister.

The gas billows, a sickly yellow. The DI's mask muffles his voice, but we understand every word. He circles the room, asking questions. We shake our heads, no and yes, and beneath my mask, I can't help answering. *Sir, no, sir. Sir, yes, sir.*

"Jumping jacks!" he shouts, and we count off, trying not to smack each other in this cramped space. The first coughs, and I can't tell who's now doubled over, the last shreds of our identities lost beneath our masks. The next command to run in place. "Pick up those knees!" the DI snaps, and the room vibrates with the smack of boots.

He opens the second canister. A snake's hiss. The gas so thick I can't see across the room. From the fog, retchings and gasps, and the first man is led out, a shadow in the mist. I keep running, and here's another truth the boy who stepped off that bus on day one didn't understand—the freedom that comes with the separation of body and mind, and released from the moment, I reel back, thinking of what I've left behind. The graduation I didn't attend. The diploma Mr. Ford's promised to hold onto until I come back. The truck I sold for three hundred dollars, and the check I mailed to Oscar and Louisa. I think of Chief, the two of us consumed by different parts of the same machine. I think of the old man and hope he's not in pain. I think of the twin whose name I carry. And I think of Kate's letters, the ones I've read over and over, the words I've committed to memory and hear in her voice when I'm at my loneliest.

The recruit on my left doubles over and vomits into his mask. The DI barks for us to take three deep breaths, and he counts out, "One . . . two . . ." and in my mind, I'm with the quarry divers, the gathering of will before the leap, and as the DI's about to count three, I think of Amy and a kiss long ago and the last breath that separates this world from the next.

"Break your seal!"

I take off my mask. My eyes closed. Sweat on my brow. The struggle against reflex. This submersion in a world that can't sustain me, and when I fear I'm about to burst, the command comes to don our masks.

I've been practicing. These days of drills upon drills, but in the only moment that matters, I turn clumsy. My nerves. My wild heart, and a single gasp triggers the burn, my lungs, my eyes. My chest squeezes, a drowning panic, the spittle and bile I cough out and am then forced to breathe back in. The order comes to exit, but I barely hear above the swirl. The DI grabs my shoulders and shoves me toward the door. Another recruit with his hand on my back and my hand on the shoulder of the man before me. A blind march through a holding chamber before we stumble into the sun.

I rip off my mask. My hands on my knees and the coughing I can't stop. The stab in my throat. A hand lifts my chin, and the DI's voice cuts through the haze. "Do not rub your eyes." He sprays water into my face. "Do you understand me?"

I gasp. My voice whittled. "Sir, yes, sir."

I stagger off. The wetness in my eyes and the green blur of late summer. Yesterday, I thrust my bayonet into a hanging stack of tires. The tires swayed, a clank of chains. A different fire in my throat, the scream that drowned all the notions of goodness I'd been taught. Another scream from my DI, and his vision became mine. The tires no longer tires but another man. His face as clear as my own. A man I'm meant to kill.

Mama, I feel you near. The two of us stumbling. The two of us poisoned, struggling for focus. And mama, I think of all the people, well-intentioned and not, who told me you were sick. And it's not that those folks were wrong—they were just short-sighted, their failure to understand the whole fucking world is sick, and what more proof do I need than the gutting and rewiring of your son to go off to another country and kill another boy just as poor, just as lost as me.

Mama, I don't blame you. I never did. The world can have

my body, but inside, I've arranged my rooms and posed my memories, and here I can live in the light of the goodness I've known. The kindness of those who owed me nothing. The love of a girl as we held each other's damaged hearts.

I don't blame you, mama. Never did. Never will.

The DI steps before me. The sun behind him. His face lost in the shadows. He lifts my chin and splashes more water into my eyes. "Are you seeing better, recruit? Can you see what's in front of you now?"

I pull myself straight. A breath to steady my heaving. My reply delivered in the strongest voice I can muster. "Sir, yes, sir."

ABOUT THE AUTHOR

Curtis Smith's award-winning stories and essays have appeared in over 150 literary journals, and his work has been cited by or included in *The Best American Short Stories, The Best American Mystery Stories, The Best American Spiritual Writing, The Best Small Fictions, The Best Microfictions,* and the WW Norton anthology *New Micro.* He is the author of six novels, five story collections, two essay collections, and a book of creative nonfiction. His last novel, *The Magpie's Return,* was cited by *Kirkus Reviews* as one of the 2020 Best Indie Books of the Year.

ACKNOWLEDGMENTS

I'd like to thank Lisa Kastner and Peter Wright and all the good folks in the Running Wild family for their support of and belief in this book.

And, as always, my deepest gratitude for my family, without whom I'd be both lost and blind.

Running Wild Press publishes stories that cross genres with great stories and writing. RIZE publishes great genre stories written by people of color and by authors who identify with other marginalized groups. Our team consists of:

Lisa Diane Kastner, Founder and Executive Editor
Mona Bethke, Acquisitions Editor, RIZE
Benjamin White, Acquisition Editor, Running Wild
Peter A. Wright, Acquisition Editor, Running Wild
Resa Alboher, Editor
Rebecca Dimyan, Editor
Andrew DiPrinzio, Editor
Abigail Efird, Editor
Henry L. Herz, Editor
Laura Huie, Editor
Cecilia Kennedy, Editor
Barbara Lockwood, Editor
Kelly Powers, Reader
Cody Sisco, Editor
Chih Wang, Editor
Pulp Art Studios, Cover Design
Standout Books, Interior Design
Polgarus Studios, Interior Design

Learn more about us and our stories at www.runningwildpress.com

Loved this story and want more? Follow us at www.runningwildpress.com, www.facebook.com/runningwildpress, on Twitter @lisadkastner @RunWildBooks

RUNNING
Wild
PRESS